Crossing

Sabrin Hasbun was born in Palestine, spent her childhood in Palestine and Italy, and now lives in the UK. She holds a PHD in Creative Writing from Bath Spa University and lectures in Creative Writing at Cardiff Metropolitan University where she teaches and researches decolonial strategies through collective creation and action.

Crossing

A love story between Italy and Palestine

Sabrin Hasbun

FOOTNOTE

First published in the UK in 2025 by Footnote Press

www.footnotepress.com

An imprint of Bonnier Books UK
5th Floor, HYLO, 105 Bunhill Row,
London, EC1Y 8LZ

All rights reserved.
No part of this publication may be reproduced, stored or transmitted in any form or by any means, electronic, mechanical, photocopying or otherwise, without the prior written permission of the publisher.

Copyright © Sabrin Hasbun, 2025
Winner of the Footnote x Counterpoints Writing Prize 2023–24.

The right of Sabrin Hasbun to be identified as Author of this work has been asserted by her in accordance with the Copyright, Designs and Patents Act, 1988.

Lines from the poem 'Dedication', from Fady Joudah's collection *[...]*, is reproduced with permission from Out-Spoken Press.

Map designed by Sergio Korchoff.

A CIP catalogue record for this book is available from the British Library.

Hardback ISBN: 9781804441527
Trade Paperback ISBN: 9781804441824
Ebook ISBN: 9781804441534
Audio ISBN: 9781804442180

1 3 5 7 9 10 8 6 4 2

Design and Typeset by Envy Design Ltd
Printed and bound in Great Britain by Clays Ltd, Elcograf S.p.A.

MIX
Paper | Supporting responsible forestry
FSC® C018072

Every reasonable effort has been made to trace copyright holders of material reproduced in this book, but if any have been inadvertently overlooked the publishers would be glad to hear from them.

This book is a work of Non-Fiction. Some names have been changed to respect the privacy of those mentioned.

The authorised representative in the EEA is
Bonnier Books UK (Ireland) Limited.
Registered office address: Floor 3, Block 3, Miesian Plaza,
Dublin 2, D02 Y754, Ireland
compliance@bonnierbooks.ie

To my mother

To my father

To those whose memory, imagination, and bodies, are my memory, imagination, and body. From the collective to the one under the same assault, no matter our location on Earth.

Fady Joudah, 'Dedication'

AUTHOR'S NOTE

This is where I'm going to say that even the truest stories are nonetheless stories, and therefore fictions. What became clear to me in the writing of my family story is that we make our memories and our stories as much as our memories and our stories make us, in a constant process of remembering, telling and retelling, writing and rewriting. I tried to stay true to this.

I was able to write these stories with the help of generations of my family from both sides, members of all my communities (in Palestine, in Italy and in the UK), diaries and letters of various people covering various periods of time, interviews and conversations, gatherings and confessions. To this polyphony and proliferation I wanted to stay true as well.

This book has been written over almost ten years and has been shaped by events – past and ongoing – that kept changing the perspective on the life my family lived for the last hundred years. In Palestine the wound of history never closes. It is an ongoing story that we have to keep writing into if we do not want to be written out of it. To this as well I have to stay true.

So this story is written in the way it came to me: with many narrative voices and in at least three different languages – sometimes, words and full sentences enter the narrative without translation, as it would happen and did happen in real life. I kept those moments untranslated to share the beauty of misunderstandings before a deeper understanding.

Finally I wrote this book following an emotional, rather than simply chronological, timeline: when I started to write about my mother the only way I could cope with the grief was to make my mother and myself into characters; I created Anna and Sabrin on the page and let my mother and (the) I be soothed by their story.

I have provided a glossary, a timeline of historical events, a map of Palestine and a family tree to help going through this story without feeling lost. But to feel – to really feel – what it means to live as I do, as my family does, as my people do, as many people around the world who are displaced, or have been migrating or mixing, or crossing for generations, then to let yourself feel lost could be the best way to read this book.

FAMILY TREE

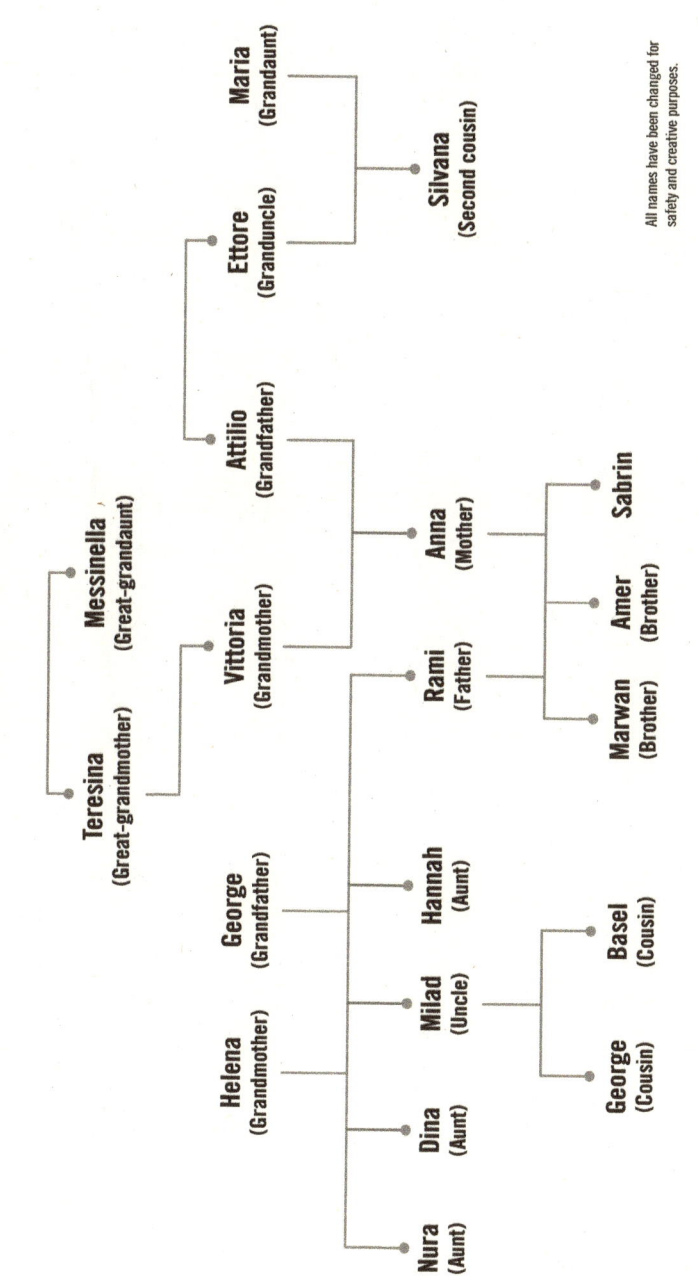

- **Teresina** (Great-grandmother) — **Messinella** (Great-grandaunt)
- **Vittoria** (Grandmother) — **Attilio** (Grandfather) — **Ettore** (Granduncle) — **Maria** (Grandaunt)
  - **Silvana** (Second cousin)

- **Helena** (Grandmother) — **George** (Grandfather)
  - **Nura** (Aunt)
  - **Dina** (Aunt)
  - **Milad** (Uncle)
    - **George** (Cousin)
    - **Basel** (Cousin)
  - **Hannah** (Aunt)
  - **Rami** (Father) — **Anna** (Mother)
    - **Marwan** (Brother)
    - **Amer** (Brother)
    - **Sabrin**

All names have been changed for safety and creative purposes.

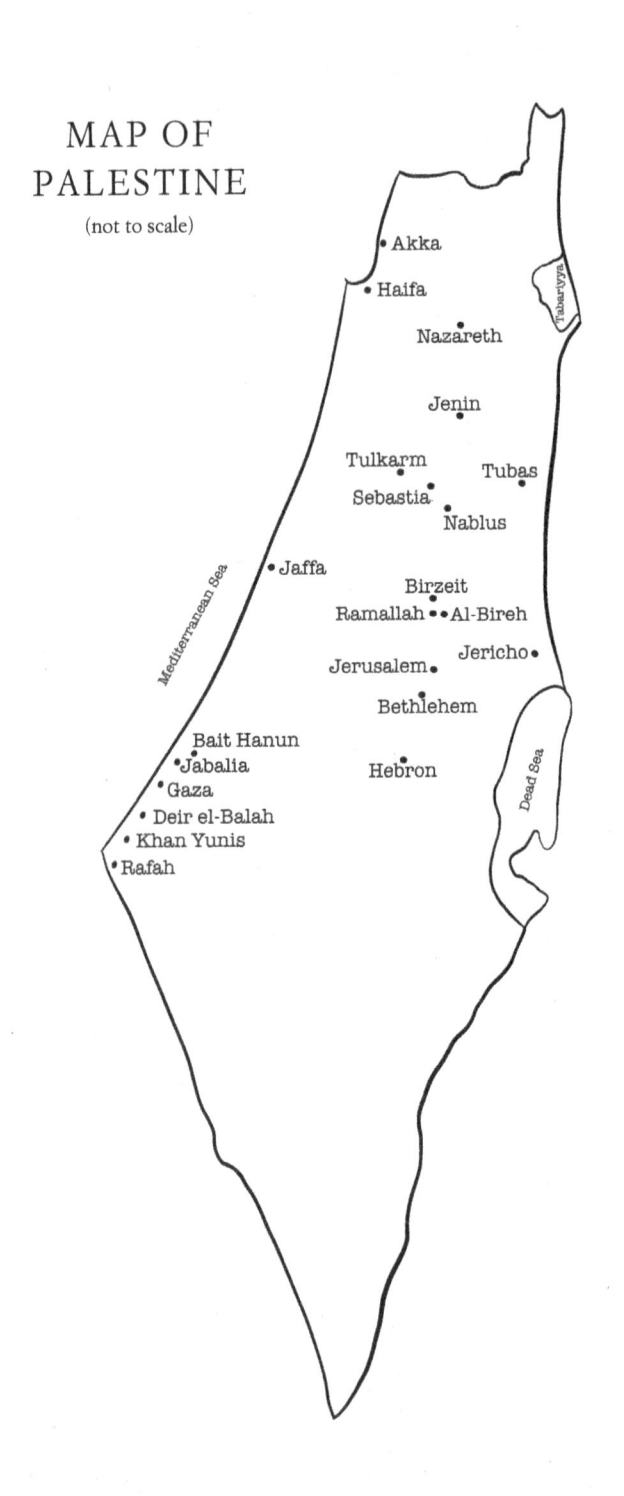

MAP OF PALESTINE

(not to scale)

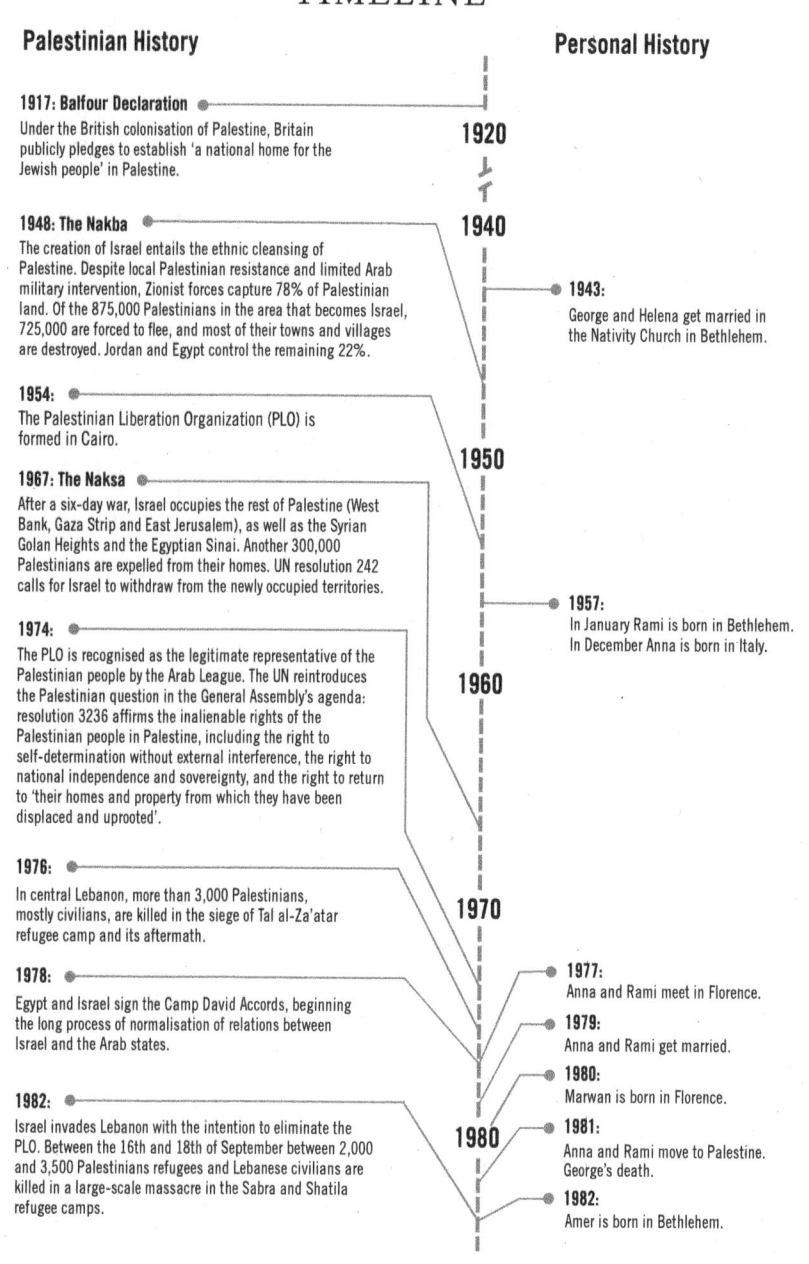

TIMELINE

Palestinian History

1917: Balfour Declaration
Under the British colonisation of Palestine, Britain publicly pledges to establish 'a national home for the Jewish people' in Palestine.

1948: The Nakba
The creation of Israel entails the ethnic cleansing of Palestine. Despite local Palestinian resistance and limited Arab military intervention, Zionist forces capture 78% of Palestinian land. Of the 875,000 Palestinians in the area that becomes Israel, 725,000 are forced to flee, and most of their towns and villages are destroyed. Jordan and Egypt control the remaining 22%.

1954:
The Palestinian Liberation Organization (PLO) is formed in Cairo.

1967: The Naksa
After a six-day war, Israel occupies the rest of Palestine (West Bank, Gaza Strip and East Jerusalem), as well as the Syrian Golan Heights and the Egyptian Sinai. Another 300,000 Palestinians are expelled from their homes. UN resolution 242 calls for Israel to withdraw from the newly occupied territories.

1974:
The PLO is recognised as the legitimate representative of the Palestinian people by the Arab League. The UN reintroduces the Palestinian question in the General Assembly's agenda: resolution 3236 affirms the inalienable rights of the Palestinian people in Palestine, including the right to self-determination without external interference, the right to national independence and sovereignty, and the right to return to 'their homes and property from which they have been displaced and uprooted'.

1976:
In central Lebanon, more than 3,000 Palestinians, mostly civilians, are killed in the siege of Tal al-Za'atar refugee camp and its aftermath.

1978:
Egypt and Israel sign the Camp David Accords, beginning the long process of normalisation of relations between Israel and the Arab states.

1982:
Israel invades Lebanon with the intention to eliminate the PLO. Between the 16th and 18th of September between 2,000 and 3,500 Palestinians refugees and Lebanese civilians are killed in a large-scale massacre in the Sabra and Shatila refugee camps.

Personal History

1920

1940

1943:
George and Helena get married in the Nativity Church in Bethlehem.

1950

1957:
In January Rami is born in Bethlehem. In December Anna is born in Italy.

1960

1970

1977:
Anna and Rami meet in Florence.

1979:
Anna and Rami get married.

1980:
Marwan is born in Florence.

1981:
Anna and Rami move to Palestine. George's death.

1980

1982:
Amer is born in Bethlehem.

TIMELINE

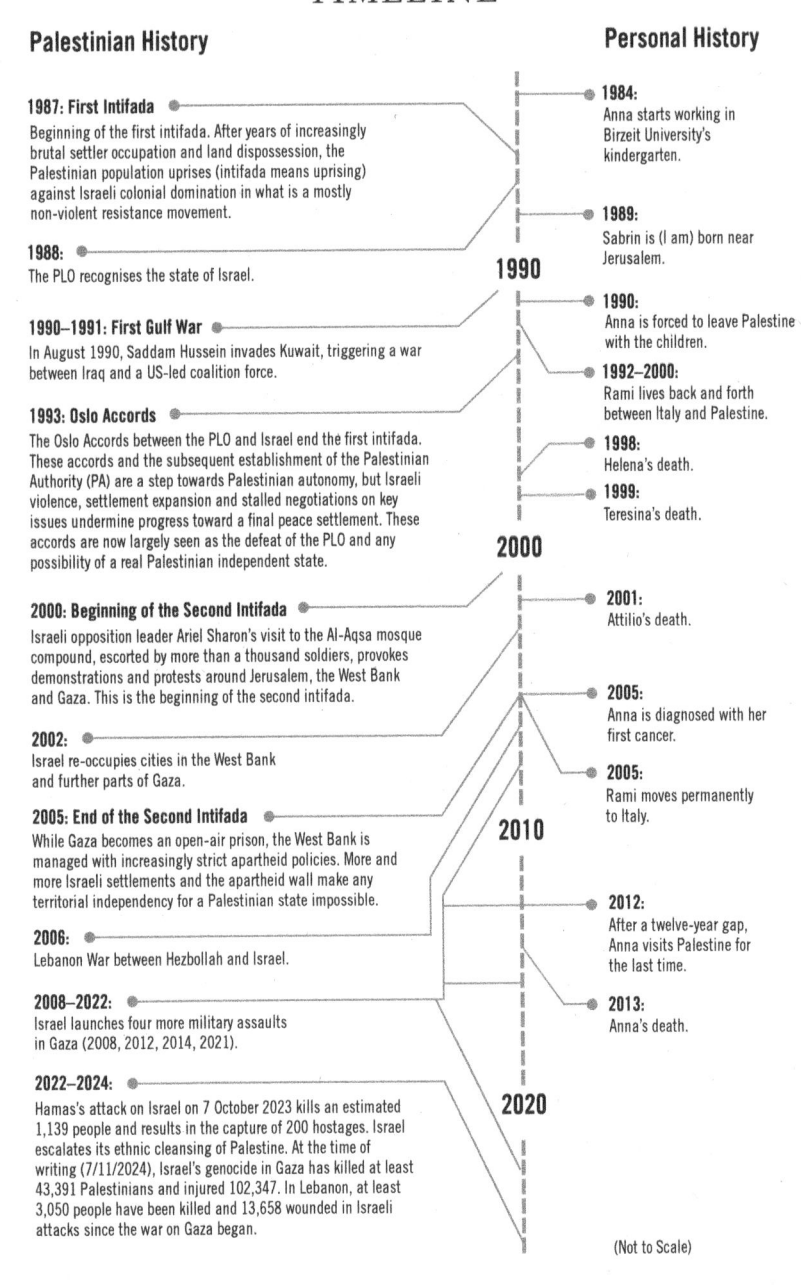

Palestinian History

1987: First Intifada
Beginning of the first intifada. After years of increasingly brutal settler occupation and land dispossession, the Palestinian population uprises (intifada means uprising) against Israeli colonial domination in what is a mostly non-violent resistance movement.

1988:
The PLO recognises the state of Israel.

1990–1991: First Gulf War
In August 1990, Saddam Hussein invades Kuwait, triggering a war between Iraq and a US-led coalition force.

1993: Oslo Accords
The Oslo Accords between the PLO and Israel end the first intifada. These accords and the subsequent establishment of the Palestinian Authority (PA) are a step towards Palestinian autonomy, but Israeli violence, settlement expansion and stalled negotiations on key issues undermine progress toward a final peace settlement. These accords are now largely seen as the defeat of the PLO and any possibility of a real Palestinian independent state.

2000: Beginning of the Second Intifada
Israeli opposition leader Ariel Sharon's visit to the Al-Aqsa mosque compound, escorted by more than a thousand soldiers, provokes demonstrations and protests around Jerusalem, the West Bank and Gaza. This is the beginning of the second intifada.

2002:
Israel re-occupies cities in the West Bank and further parts of Gaza.

2005: End of the Second Intifada
While Gaza becomes an open-air prison, the West Bank is managed with increasingly strict apartheid policies. More and more Israeli settlements and the apartheid wall make any territorial independency for a Palestinian state impossible.

2006:
Lebanon War between Hezbollah and Israel.

2008–2022:
Israel launches four more military assaults in Gaza (2008, 2012, 2014, 2021).

2022–2024:
Hamas's attack on Israel on 7 October 2023 kills an estimated 1,139 people and results in the capture of 200 hostages. Israel escalates its ethnic cleansing of Palestine. At the time of writing (7/11/2024), Israel's genocide in Gaza has killed at least 43,391 Palestinians and injured 102,347. In Lebanon, at least 3,050 people have been killed and 13,658 wounded in Israeli attacks since the war on Gaza began.

Personal History

1984:
Anna starts working in Birzeit University's kindergarten.

1989:
Sabrin is (I am) born near Jerusalem.

1990:
Anna is forced to leave Palestine with the children.

1992–2000:
Rami lives back and forth between Italy and Palestine.

1998:
Helena's death.

1999:
Teresina's death.

2001:
Attilio's death.

2005:
Anna is diagnosed with her first cancer.

2005:
Rami moves permanently to Italy.

2012:
After a twelve-year gap, Anna visits Palestine for the last time.

2013:
Anna's death.

(Not to Scale)

PROLOGUE

Back and Forth

WHEN WE OPENED THE door, the smell of mould sucked us in.

Everything was exactly the same, everything in the same place. It was as if someone had always lived there, but had remained seated on the sofa, immobile, while mould, dust and time did their work.

Ramallah, 2012, our house. In that moment I didn't even know if I could call that place home.

So why did I recognise every object? The black chairs around the glass table, the Japanese paper window between the entrance and the living room, on the left the glass door cracked in a ball game, and, through the door on the right, I could already imagine all the different objects in the kitchen: the cups, the fridge, the old gas stove, the smell of toasted bread. There, among everything, I saw the movements of my brothers, my father, my mother as we were the last time we stayed here, in December 1999.

The smell of mould brought me back to the present. This house was not mine. I was just a guest of the objects we had left behind: I recognised them, but they didn't recognise me. The last time they had seen me I was a little girl of ten, short enough to sleep on the sofa my father had built, leaving the big bed to my older brothers. Twelve years later and I had to sleep alone in the room we had once fought over.

The veranda, my favourite room in the house, with its windows and doors overlooking the garden, was totally unusable. It was impossible to open the door without being forced back by the smell. In the kitchen, the oven, sink and window refused to work. The stove released a strong smell of gas.

I looked at my mother. For me, after all, this was more a home for my imagination, somewhere I had cherished as a summer playground, a small box of memories: sitting eating on the carpet in the living room, the shade of the living room when my mother used to close the curtains to let me sleep during the early afternoon, the shadow cast by the lemon tree on the kitchen terrace, the kitchen terrace transformed into a swimming pool during the hottest days of July.

But for my mother, this house had been her real, actual home for ten years. A home that she had never expected to leave, a home in her chosen country. This house had helped her to not feel homesick. The living room was the place where she used to host friends, musicians and writers, all avid smokers, who filled the space with sounds, words and smoke. It was in this kitchen that she had learnt how to prepare Palestinian dishes. She was the one who, blocking the drainage hole in the stone kitchen terrace, had transformed it into a swimming pool for us to play in during the hottest days of July.

My mother hung around the entrance hall and the living room for a while, looking around her, and then moved on to the kitchen. She opened all the cupboards, touched all the cups, the plates, the forks, the knives, the spoons, the blue glasses, the pans, my baby bottle, the sugar jar. She held the sugar jar for a bit longer, then put it back and closed the cupboard again.

I looked at my mother. She looked at the objects in the same way the objects looked back at us. She didn't want to recognise them. From the moment we had entered the house for the first time in twelve years, she had immediately seen a deeper change. As if the furniture was not just covered by dust and mould, but somehow shaped into something that she couldn't recognise.

'I love these plates. I want to take them with me!'
'Don't be ridiculous, we can't put them in the suitcase.'
'We can find another way.'
'No, we can't.'
My mother refused to encourage my desperate desire to take everything in our Palestinian house back home to Italy. She came to the kitchen only to get a glass of water and went into my brothers' room to rummage through the wardrobe. She discarded clothes and shoeboxes onto the floor until she took out a red box, opened it, and whispered something. She quickly closed it, put it back in its place, and closed the wardrobe.

She did this over and over again for the two weeks we stayed in Ramallah while I kept on going between rooms, trying to fit the things I wanted into the only suitcase I had with me. She ignored me and I ignored her; I in my stubborn desire to keep hold of everything, she in her desire to let everything go.

'Mamma, look what I found in this chest!'
'I know what you found there. We can't take them to Italy.'
'But all these ...'
'We can't bring all those books back to Italy.'
She said no, but she nevertheless joined me in the living room, to inspect the books I had found in the chest. Books had always been her weak point. She started taking them

out without paying attention, emptying the trunk as quickly as possible as if to end the matter. Then her eyes started to read the titles. Her hands began to linger on the pages, and she paused to smell them. She leafed through them, finding between the pages the remains of a bookmark made from a receipt, a piece of paper scribbled on by my brothers, a birthday card from Italy, a photo.

Each book released not just the words and stories inside it, but also the stories she herself had put there: stories of the moments when she was reading those books, twelve years ago, twenty years ago, thirty years ago. Some food needed for the house, my brothers drawing for her while she was cooking, her mother missing her on her birthday, a kiss between her and my father.

These books reconnected her to her old life in that house, the life she had chosen for herself when she was in her twenties. She recognised them and they recognised her. They gave each other their stories.

'We can find a place for them in my suitcase,' she eventually decided.

When we went back to Ramallah less than two years later, my father and I refused to stay in the house. There was too much mould and dust, too many things. Instead, we rented a room in one of the new hotels in the area, and went to the house for just a few hours, to see if there was anything else we wanted to take back to Italy. Now I could understand my mother: those objects were a presence of an absence.

I went into the kitchen and started opening all the cupboards, touching all the cups, the plates, the forks, the knives, the spoons, the glasses, the pans. My baby bottle and the sugar jar weren't there.

'Babbo, where are the baby bottle and the sugar jar?'

'Mamma took them last time.'

Everything else was in the place they had always been, but they were no longer the same. I didn't recognise them, and they didn't recognise me. They no longer brought back my childhood memories. They just reminded me that my mother didn't want them, and so I looked at them with the same detachment she had.

I walked around the house, going back and forth between the rooms. I was trying to find something that my mother would have wanted, something that could help me find her again. But I couldn't find anything.

Then I remembered my brothers' bedroom. I went to the wardrobe and opened it. Rummaging around, I found the red box, took it out, and opened it. The box was full of letters, my mother's letters. The letters she had written to my father during the first years she was back in Italy with us, while my father remained here for work. The box was full of her words, her stories.

The stories of those moments when she was writing those letters, twelve years ago, twenty years ago, thirty years ago. Some food for the house, my brothers drawing for her while she was cooking, what she did on her birthday, a missed kiss between her and my father.

Those letters reconnected me to her life, to the life she had chosen, to the life she had lived in that house, far from that house, going back and forth between two countries.

CHAPTER ONE

Baccalà

Ventoruccia farmhouse, 1991

TEN YEARS FROM THE DAY that she closed the door behind her, Anna opened it again and climbed the narrow flight of stairs to the first floor. The familiar smell of tomato sauce greeted her.

At the top of the stairs on the right, Anna entered the main room of the farmhouse. The large, blackened fireplace dominated the whole space. Coal black from the smoke and ash, it seemed to Anna like a doorway into another world: everything revolved around that fireplace and its smudged red stones. It was used to warm up the winters, to cook, to prepare the bedwarmer, to boil water to sterilise cloths from period blood, to make soap, to clean the linens with the ash, and there was enough space to sit right by the edge of the fire and fall asleep. Bent over a copper pot, Teresina was there. She was mixing ingredients and tasting them with a long wooden spoon, her lips puckered in a kiss over the ladle. From the shiny red of the spoonful Anna knew that Teresina was preparing her baccalà. The boiling sauce and the steam must have hidden Anna from her grandmother's sight and hearing, because Anna was nearly touching Teresina's shoulders when she turned around, alarmed.

'Sei te?' In shock, Teresina looked at her granddaughter as if the image of this young woman was a trick of old age.

'Nonna!' Anna called her, touching her shoulder and face.

'What are you doing here?' Teresina touched her face in turn with her coarse hands. 'Che ci fai qui? Che ci fai qui?' she repeated while opening her arms to receive her granddaughter's body.

The women hugged and for a moment it felt as if Anna had never left. Then Teresina grabbed Anna's shoulders and, taking a step back, looked her into her eyes the way she used to do when the little girl was hiding something. Anna knew Teresina was looking for answers, but she wasn't ready to tell her granny why she was back.

'Ho fame, Nonna. Is the baccalà ready?' she asked instead, hoping to gain some time over a plate of warm food.

Teresina understood and nodded. She put two plates down on the table and took out the week-old bread so that Anna could wipe the sauce from the plate the way she liked. Then she went back to the fireplace, and lifted up the pot of baccalà. She took the three steps from the fireplace to the table and placed the pot on the wooden surface with a thud. She filled the ladle with baccalà and poured it onto the first plate.

When the pieces of white salted cod had settled on the bottom of the plate and a layer of oil covered the surface of the stew, Teresina tried the same question again.

'Allora what are you doing here? Did something happen?'

Anna wanted to tell her everything, everything about her life over the past ten years, but she couldn't. The taste of baccalà brought her almost to tears – so much has changed … Moving her eyes to her grandmother's face, Anna noticed the marks of time on Teresina. Until that moment she had just seen her granny, as she had always been, but now

Anna saw the trembling of the hand lifting the spoon, the back curving to one side, the nose becoming bigger and bigger over the shrinking body. Anna tried to look for the woman who had given her an untamed desiderio di lontananza – that urge to be somewhere far away, a need for a larger life.

The first time Anna had felt that desire she was maybe five, cycling from the farmhouse where she lived with her parents and grandparents and her uncle's family all the way to her school in the village. Her grandmother was the one pedalling, while Anna, sitting on the back, opened her arms out wide. They raced down the gravel road, passing the shrubs and yellow broom flowers, the other farms, an old military post, the cypresses, the campo santo, wind and leaves on their faces. There was a sort of obstinacy in the way they rode the bike down to the village.

Anna knew it was not easy to withstand that resolute drive, not her own, not her grandmother's: eventually she would have to face the reality of being back. But for now, sitting near the fireplace with her grandmother, she let her mind drift back to when everything had started, all the way back to the years spent in that farmhouse and in that village, trying to see through all her choices.

Ventoruccia farmhouse, 1967–77

The graveyard marked the end of the main road and the everyday activities of the village and announced the beginning of uncharted territories. From the cemetery a long, dusty road led towards hills of olive trees, vines and scattered farms. The farmhouse where Anna lived was the last, remote dwelling before the dense woodlands of holm and cork oaks. After their farm, the road became a footpath, winding through the trees and mushrooms and the smell of humid leaves. Anna would play in the fields, then stop there, where the woods began, and listen to its call: right there, between the open land and the line of trees, the air suddenly became cold and quiet like a whisper from afar.

From the farmhouse, past the stables and the henhouse with their smell of acidic manure, a small rusty gate opened with a whistle onto a wasteland, and then uphill with the scorched hay for the horses and the unplucked weeds, which made Anna's legs all itchy. Turning left, downhill, there was a well: a round, stonewall structure, low on the ground, recently covered with a plank. All Teresina's stories were about that well and always ended with someone dying in an unpleasant way. At night Anna would pull the covers over her head, sure that her grandmother's stories would reach her all the way there in her bed, in that house set apart from the normal life of the village.

There was a story about a great-great-uncle who loved to ride horses without a saddle. One day his horse was nervous, the uncle was drunk, and they both fell. Although the horse had the worse outcome, with a bullet to its head, the man suffered too. A back injury left him unable to move anything below his belt, except for his left leg – useless with horses or with women. He would try to walk and drag his heavy right leg, but that only helped to attract the scorn of the family, who called him a 'cripple'. It would have been better if they had shot him too. He eventually found relief at the bottom of the well. Handling his right leg over the rim, he looked for an instant down into the darkness before pushing himself in.

There was another story about the daughter of a third cousin who had spent all her youth on the farm and wanted more from life than just wine diluted with water. She fell in love with a man from the village, gave him her trust and virginity, and ended up pregnant and alone. Her family lamented her lost honour, considered more disgraceful than being a cripple. The girl felt like a cripple too, dismembered by that misplaced love. One night, she found her way to the well, climbed onto the edge and, without hesitation, jumped in.

Then there was the child who fell into the well, but Teresina never said any more than that, warning Anna that the only thing to learn from this story was that she should stay away from the well, do you understand? Stay away from the well. Anna didn't need any warning: she would have done anything in her power to stay away from it, and from that farmhouse too for that matter.

The farmhouse and the fields surrounding it were known in the nearby village as 'Ventoruccia' because when everything in the village stood still, not even the faintest bit of air moving through the branches of the trees, the Ventoruccia could already feel the breeze of summer's end. And when the breeze finally reached the village, the Ventoruccia already shook with autumn gusts.

In winter the wind was so strong that it seemed made not of air but of flesh and bones. During those nights when Anna couldn't sleep, she would imagine the wind as someone coming from afar, a ravishing stranger rattling the doors, knocking at the windows, begging Anna to go with him.

Those winds meant that the grapes and the wine made on the farm were not the best. The only exception was the vine on the pergola in front of the farmhouse. Its uva fragola, the foxgrapes, were so sweet you could eat them with bread, just like that, still warm from the sun's heat.

On the farm, working and sweating on the land was the only way to live – there were animals, crops, olives and grapes to attend to – and it was even busier at harvest time. Men and women from nearby farms would come and help.

The work started at dawn, the men in the fields, the women in the kitchen. Every woman who could reach the kitchen counter – sometimes even those who couldn't unless they were standing on a brick – would start by mixing eggs and flour, and then rolling the pasta, cutting it into long ribbons, and letting them dry, hanging from a broomstick set between two chairs. These tagliatelle were served for lunch on a never-ending table set up in the barn, made of large wooden boards, standing over pressed hay. Anyone over the age of seven drank wine, which was responsible for all the stains that didn't wash away, the dirty songs, that irresistible dozing-off heaviness and, every now and then, the quarrels. It was always the same old tiff, and Anna used to get so bored by those drunken arguments. It seemed like they couldn't talk about anything else but what happened during the war.

'Can they not talk about something else? The war ended twenty-five years ago!' Anna protested to Teresina once.

'Zitta Madonnina!' Teresina shushed her. 'Things like that never end!'

Anna didn't know what Teresina meant, but as she grew older, she realised that every piece of news was a good excuse to open up the wounds of the war again.

'Ma cosa ne sai te what it means to resist? You have always been a fascist, everyone knows that!' someone would start shouting while discussing the student strikes taking place all over the world against the war in Vietnam.

'What do you want to protest? You have your socialists in the government, don't you? And our mayor ... a communist!'

'Have you seen what they have done in that school in Rome? People can't protest anymore! And what happened in Avola? Shooting strikers! Fascismo!'

Religion often added to the tension and Anna lived the conflict directly at home, where the battle was being fought by two women. On one side there was her grandmother, Teresina, who, if she could have, would have slapped every single priest and nun she bumped into. On the other, there was her great-aunt, Messinella or the baciapile, as Teresina liked to call her: a stoup-kisser, who spent most of her time in church, adoring whatever was holy.

Messinella and Teresina were sisters, but they couldn't have been more different. Teresina was at least a head taller than most women, and several inches taller than many men, including her husband. She would lift baskets full of logs for the fire and walk uphill whistling effortlessly. At the end of the day, her hands would be stained with the soil she had hoed and with the blood of the animals she killed. She didn't like to take orders from anyone, certainly not from a distant god. Despite being unceremonious to the point of rudeness, Teresina was in fact mostly known for her largesse and for her habit of indulging in simple pleasures: she loved to eat and drink, let Anna try cigarettes when she was just eight years old and bread dipped in wine when she was only five. Teresina was neither elegant nor graceful, not a beauty either, but she knew how to hold you in her arms at just the right time and dry your tears, like a fireplace sharing its warmth.

Messinella was a little, weak woman. She always complained of migraines and aches and pains, and how she couldn't really bend to pick the tomatoes or help with the chickens – that smell was making her migraines even worse. Instead, she spent her days whispering rosaries and embroidering altar cloths for the churches and convents of the village. She had a sort of reverence for everything and everyone who was high up, because that was the position of God. For that reason, she had never disliked Benito Mussolini, whom she always referred to as 'Duce'.

However, unlike her god, to whom she could pray all day long if she wanted to, Mussolini could not be mentioned at the Ventoruccia.

Things got worse during 1943, when Teresina promised to feed Messinella to the pigs if she mentioned the man's name again. That summer Mussolini clung to power with his Nazi puppet state, while the German troops were militarily controlling all of north and central Italy, conscripting as many men into the army as possible and killing anyone who tried to resist. Those who refused to enrol in the army, or to collaborate with the Germans, were left with no choice but to join the resistance or go into hiding by escaping in the woods.

Among those who hid was Pietro, Teresina's husband. He was a slim and graceful man who could recite by heart entire lines of great Italian literature, despite being hardly able to read them. He was a sweet man and knew how to use his sweetness to handle his strong-willed wife, who became as tender as warm bread under the foxgrape-blue eyes of her husband.

Teresina thought that it was the fault of Messinella and people like her if men who should have been working the land were instead forced to die like flies or hide like cowards.

To religion and politics, sex added another point to the sisters' list of reasons for hating each other. Teresina, who grew up with and bred animals, didn't feel any shame talking about sex. For her it was a natural thing, so she never stopped her son-in-law when he used to jump from the first floor of the farmhouse and walk all the way to the village to visit one of his mistresses. But after the birth of his daughter Anna, she placed a pitchfork just under his window: sleeping with every single woman like a horny rabbit was no way to raise a girl, and if his wife – Teresina's own daughter,

Vittoria – was not going to do anything, she would. Teresina was the first one to show her naked body to Anna, telling her where all important bits were, and explaining where children come from by showing her a pig giving birth.

Messinella didn't want the words sex, or nipples or birth to even enter the house, just as much as Teresina didn't want the name of Mussolini uttered. Messinella never had children. She made her husband pay the price of having married her, and ruining her idea of chastity, by treating him as the worst of her disgraces, belittling and mistreating him, and warning him of the hell awaiting at the end of his life. After her husband's death, her contempt then transferred to Anna who, as a teenager in the 1970s, was starting to enjoy the freedom of wearing short dresses and skirts. That was the first sign that the devil had got hold of Anna, and Messinella didn't let a minute pass without warning her that hell was waiting for her too.

Not knowing if she should pay attention to these warnings or enjoy her body as Teresina encouraged her to do, Anna spent most of her adolescence trying to find a way out of that dilemma. Like wearing short skirts, but then volunteering to play the angel in the Christmas recital. Or dancing with boys, but then helping Messinella with her embroideries.

The solution came to Anna by chance, one summer night, when she was almost seventeen. She had spent the evening out with friends and had come back to the farm late. Her parents would probably not notice, but Messinella would always wait for her and force her to kneel down and pray to God to ask for forgiveness for her sins. That particular night, Anna took off her shoes and entered the house silently, on tiptoes. When she reached the top of the stairs, Anna saw a feeble light coming down the corridor. She froze, trying to quickly think up an excuse – she had stayed with a friend who felt unwell, for example, or even better, she had stayed to make sure a friend didn't commit dirty deeds. But there, in the silence, Anna heard the sound of agitated voices coming from Messinella's room. Was Messinella not alone?

Anna thought about grabbing her chance and quickly running to her room, but then curiosity made her turn around and walk back towards her great-aunt's room. The door was half open and the pale blue light from inside cut a line on the dark floor.

There, standing right in front of a small television and illuminated by the blue halo of the screen, Messinella was immersed in the wonders of the adult TV channels. At that late hour, it was not uncommon to come across one of the popular erotic television comedies of the time, but this was different. Messinella's attention and interest – usually reserved for her Bible only – were such that she didn't even hear Anna coming into the room. In that woman completely transfixed Anna saw through her aunt for the first time, and could not help herself: she burst out laughing and ran out of the room. Messinella, caught red-handed, jumped in fright, and ran after her.

'You see, you see what happens when you follow the devil's steps!' the great-aunt kept shouting.

Anna didn't know if Messinella was referring to herself, or to the people in the porn film, but if she had been given the choice of Messinella's life or the actors', Anna knew which one she would not have chosen.

Anna fell in love for the first time when she was seventeen. Edoardo, with his darker skin, the wave of his hair, and the longer lines of his eyes, looked like he was from far away – maybe from a desert of sand dunes or even further. It did not matter that he actually was from the village: through him, Anna still learnt that she had a propensity to fall in love with the geography of her lovers: a certain quality that inspired in her dreams of remote countries, of foreign smells, of nomadic winds, of incomprehensible languages. This fantasy was helped by the fact that Edoardo was one year older than Anna and rode a motorbike. They would drive fast up and down the hills and Anna could open her arms again, taking in all the wind and the leaves, and feed her stubborn desire for flying away.

Some days the only way to find relief from the call of faraway was to drive along the winding roads of the countryside – where the trees on both sides touched at the top – and to close her eyes, letting the light of the sun hit her eyelids through the vibrato of the leaves. Anna liked to imagine that beyond her closed eyes there was the ocean, with no horizon. In this way, Anna fell in love with Edoardo and started to come home later, discovering things that Messinella would not have approved of. She began to think that perhaps she could stay in the village after all, that Edoardo could offer her a different world, right there. All they needed to do was to take his bike and ride it through the wind and leaves.

'We need to talk,' said Edoardo one day, after their usual ride uphill, towards his house.

There was something in Edoardo's tone that made Anna sense that reality was about to come back into her life. Was he moving away? She could go with him, there was no need to even ask her parents, they would not understand or even care! Had he met someone else? But how, when? Weren't they always together, always happy? And they all knew each other in that miserable hole, how could he meet someone else? Was he tired of her? Did she do something wrong?

'If you want to break up with me, you better do it here.' Anna's voice sounded less controlled than she wanted.

'It's not about us.'

Inside the house, lying under what looked like a pile of clothes on the sofa, was Edoardo's sister, Francesca, emitting a sound that was barely louder than a final breath.

'Tell her! Tell her what you told me!' Edoardo was looking down at his sister, using a voice Anna had never heard him use before. A voice so similar to the other men in the village, to her own father.

'I told you I have no idea how it happened,' she answered from under the pile.

'Don't play with me. I am sure you knew exactly what you were doing when you did it.'

'When you did what?' asked Anna. She was trying to understand what was going on between the two of them.

She hadn't seen Francesca often. Edoardo's sister was a couple of years younger than them and she was always hanging out with her own friends, but Anna liked her: she had a kind smile, and the same eyes as Eduardo.

'She managed to get herself pregnant,' Edoardo answered for Francesca. In that moment Anna felt, there in the space between her lungs, where the ribs give up to the flesh, the first blow of disappointment.

Francesca had started to cry and Anna moved towards her, seeking out her face from under the covers. Francesca's eyes were red from crying and from brushing away the tears that kept coming.

Anna and her friends had often heard rumours about girls falling pregnant apparently without reason, but thought it was just a way to scare them and make them behave. Now, in Francesca's eyes, she saw all the girls from those stories, all those stories she couldn't understand, or know if they were true or not.

In Francesca's eyes she saw her friend Paola. Everyone

in their group of friends was saying that she wasn't just getting fat; she had managed to make that older guy, yes that handsome one, have sex with her – who knows how, with those crooked teeth and those hairy lips – and the poor guy had no choice but to marry her, that sneaky bitch. Anna had laughed too, because yes, that guy was much more beautiful than Paola.

And in Francesca's pile of clothes Anna saw Agnese too. She always came to school dressed in rags, clothes that someone had given her unmarried mother out of charity. She was very small, pale and always dirty. The nuns who ran the school didn't like her much and always made the wealthy girls play apart from her. They said that she was not good company for well-educated girls, that God had made an example out of her, that a woman without a husband had to pay for her sins. Anna had believed that story – it was God's word after all – and when their school days were over, she never saw Agnese again.

Then, in Francesca's tears, Anna also saw the bottom of the well. The well on the left, past the stable, the henhouse, the fields, and the rusty gate. The daughter of a distant cousin. The family lost its honour, she lost her mind and jumped. Anna didn't remember when Teresina had told her that story, but in that moment she realised it might be true, that maybe that cousin's name could even have been Francesca.

Through Francesca, Agnese, and Paola, the reality of the village found its way back into Anna's life – the spell was broken. In Edoardo's tone she recognised the family's disdain, the nuns' judgement, the laughter of her friends. He wasn't different after all – he was like everyone else, just another guy from the village who only cares about what people think; no matter how cool he might behave and talk about rebellions and revolutions and complain about the suffocating mentality around them, he would do actually nothing to change it.

'So can you tell us what we should do now, Francesca?'

'Stop talking to her like that!' Anna surprised herself – for the first time she had a clear sense of who she was and knew the right thing to do. Right, but not legal. They would have to find a safe way, get the right contact, invent credible excuses.

'I am going to do this to help her, not you!' Anna clarified to Edoardo.

Anna didn't see Francesca after those days, and she didn't see Edoardo either. She decided then that it was up to her to get away from the village, no one else. Edoardo tried to contact her again, but after a while he gave up. He was a nice guy, sure, and Anna would miss the rides on his bike, but she didn't know how to explain to him that he had betrayed the promises in his eyes.

If it was not for Teresina, Anna would probably have felt the allure of the well more strongly than she did. She had inherited her grandmother's obstinacy and intolerance of rules, and she found growing up in that farmhouse on the outskirts of a village built on alliances and rumours almost unbearable.

Anna would spend whole days with her cousin Silvana; daughter of her father's brother, she was the only one who could really relate to what Anna felt and who would plan with her how to escape that misery. It was their constant preoccupation, growing in between the disquiet about finding their place in the world, and a desperation not to become like their mothers. Anna didn't know what to think about her mother, Vittoria. Their relationship had never been more than minimal interactions, not because there were frictions (oh, Anna wished for something more, something to complain about like all her friends did), but because Vittoria never seemed to be there, her presence almost ghostly; it looked like the slap Teresina had given her, for singing a fascist song when she was just six years old, had left her forever insecure about using her voice.

Vittoria hadn't inherited any of Teresina's qualities. Teresina's fierceness to fight for what she wanted seemed to have completely bypassed her daughter, who was the exact opposite.

'It's because that girl grew up with Messinella, I'm telling you. I was out, working the fields, feeding the animals, trying to keep the fascists away from my pantry, from my children and from that prudish *baciapile*, and she was at home sewing her altar cloth, kissing her prayer cards, and putting all that religious stuff inside my girl's head. There is nothing more I can do for her.'

Teresina knew this wasn't all true. That Messinella's husband earned decent money, and that the money was needed to keep the farm working and the children fed. And that money could only be accessed with Messinella's approval.

That approval had a price that Vittoria paid for all her life, always obliging the whims of her aunt. Even when it was time for her to get married, it was Messinella who paid for the wedding rings. Not as a gift, but as another way of keeping Vittoria in her service, working for free, with the excuse that she hadn't paid back the money Messinella had spent on her. Vittoria never complained. A blind obedience made her love those who asked the most from her. That was the only explanation Anna could come up with to understand why her mother had married her father.

Attilio had grown up in an extremely poor family. His father had died of malaria, leaving three small children. The young widow had tried to do what she could to keep her children alive – resulting in more unwanted children – until Attilio and his siblings were old enough to start working in the pyrite mines. Anna was not sure her father had ever been taught how to be sweet. His big triangular nose turned bitter even his elegant face. Lean and proud, he was a great dancer, always wearing a bit of cologne, right between his jaw and neck, for the delight of his dancing partners. At village fairs, he would teach Anna how to dance and would never lose his patience when she kept stepping on his toes.

But back at home, his smile and charm would disappear. It was even worse when they moved out of the farm and into a small flat in the village. Away from the open fields and winds of the Ventoruccia, and the piercing eyes of Teresina, everything happened behind closed doors. He would close the door of the bathroom because he didn't want anyone to see him naked, and when Anna came in once by mistake he threw the glass soap holder at her. Behind closed doors there were shushed sobs, the shattering of crockery, the thuds of furniture and bodies. Every time a door opened for Attilio to enter or exit a room, silence would follow.

Already small, Vittoria would become even smaller in front of her husband, and tried to make any traces of her disappear. Even when food was not a problem anymore, Vittoria would always serve Attilio first and only ate what was left. She would fix all the holes in Attilio's clothes, wash all the stains of lipstick on his white dancing shirts, swipe away all the pieces of broken plates.

Anna remembered one night when the three of them were sitting at the kitchen table, eating.

'I will have a coffee with the others at the bar.' Attilio spoke his first words all evening.

'Do you really need to go out again, can't you stay at home for once?' Vittoria tried to protest.

That was probably Vittoria's first and definitely her last attempt to stop her husband going out for the evening. Attilio didn't stand up from the chair: he simply raised his eyes from his plate and looked at Vittoria, his head and body perfectly still, his jaw tensing.

'Donna!'

Attilio said that word, woman, in a long thundering tone to remind Vittoria of her place and not to dare to step out from it.

It was that *donna* that Anna had run away from all her life.

CHAPTER TWO
Radios and Onions

MY PATERNAL GRANDFATHER DIED before I was born. My paternal grandmother died when I was eight years old. There are some photographs showing a one-year-old me curled up on her lap while she is cleaning and cutting green beans. I don't recall that moment – or any other moment with her. Neither of my grandparents seem to have left any traces on who I am. But I know it is not that simple.

When I started to ask questions about them, I could see how their influence has passed down the family tree, visible through years of relationships, education, dynamics, quarrels, affections, habits, holiday meals, distances, gossip and reconciliations, all the way to me. Although I never got to experience the famous silent mood of my grandfather first-hand, I experienced it in my uncle's introverted character, my father's ability to hold silent grudges for days, and my brother's contemplative attitude towards life. My grandmother's impetuous affection, of which that photograph from my childhood is just a hint, made it to me via my aunt's cheeky dimples, my father's passion for cooking big family meals, and a kind of unquestionable adoration that all her offspring have towards her.

According to my relatives, my grandmother was flawless:

she never did anything wrong and was always there for those in need. Compared to her, my grandfather faded away from the family's core memories: that quiet man didn't leave many words behind and so people didn't have much to say about who he was. For everyone, the centre of the story had always been my grandmother. For everyone, except my father. He had a different view of his parents and so gave me the chance to rebalance the story.

I have been told many contradictory versions of my grandfather's life and that of my grandmother before their marriage. Someone told me about my grandmother's family in Honduras. Someone told me about my grandfather's lonely childhood. Someone told me about the healing powers of my grandmother's voice. Someone told me about my grandfather's unsettling gaze. Someone told me about an inexplicable restlessness in my grandmother's nature. Someone told me about the age difference between them, but someone told me it was less and someone told me it was more. Someone told me they loved each other. Someone told me that in those years, love was not a reason to get married. Someone told me about the catastrophe of 1948 – our Nakba, when Palestine was taken away from us – and the death and diaspora that followed. Someone told me that our family was lucky, that our house in Bethlehem was not touched. Someone didn't want to tell me about it at all. Someone told me everything they remembered. Someone told me what they wanted to remember. From all these voices my grandparents' past started to take shape. It is not much, but it is a beginning.

*

Bethlehem, 1943–67

People talked: they said she had hot blood. That when Helena was born, in the humid rainforests of Honduras where her family had migrated to in search of fortune, the sticky heat penetrated her skin and bones and blood. People told George that yes, they knew she was young and beautiful but this is how temptations come ... they come with the warm rain and they are young and beautiful like deceiving ghouls.

George dismissed the gossip as envy or superstition. He asked for Helena's hand in marriage and discovered that he was not the only one. Many of those ones who didn't believe in superstition – and a good number of those who did but found their inner scepticism for the occasion – had already asked for her hand too.

George was not as rich as Helena's father and not as educated and sophisticated as Helena, but his big, well-known family was good enough for Helena's father – who, having moved back with his family from South America, wanted to open a chain of shops in Bethlehem and needed a name people recognised and trusted. George's handsome face, on the other hand, was enough for Helena, and so in 1944, a few months after their first encounter, thirty-year-old George and fourteen-year-old Helena became husband and wife.

George was in complete awe of his young wife and considered her the unexpected reward of a life which hadn't, up until that point, treated him well. George had lost his mother when he was only three. His father had remarried immediately and the stepmother, after becoming pregnant, couldn't really see the point of looking after someone else's child. He already had the luck of being the first-born boy, with all the family privileges that it implied, and so, as far as she was concerned, he shouldn't expect any more than that. So George grew up pretty much by himself and learnt early on how to ignore the long silences at home. He got so used to his loneliness that it never crossed his mind that his thoughts and feelings were something to share with other people. Years later, his wife, and then his children and grandchildren, were left to guess what this man actually wanted to say from his enigmatic eyes and muted lips. Or what he needed when he slightly moved his eyebrow towards the sky, stretching all the lines of his forehead. Or what he intended when, instead, his eyebrows moved down towards the ground, wrinkles converging between his eyes.

All the silence and unshared feelings made him needy of things that could be touched with his bare hands and understood by the full use of all of his senses. He connected with the world by being practical and found his calling in the physical and at the same time philosophical art of butchery. He found an inexplicable pleasure in working with those big pieces of flesh, seeing how the muscles were inside, the nerves and the tendons, the connections of the organs. He even found something intimate in the smell of fresh blood.

Helena found it baffling. She couldn't understand how someone could be so connected with the tangibility of life and at the same time so detached from the mysteries of life itself. Her childhood unfolded on the opposite side of her husband's: like the two faces of an embroidery tapestry she only had to see the neat design appearing on the surface, and not all the entangled threads behind it. She was a loved child, but not a spoiled one and her beauty was only one among other qualities she had to attend to.

Her father believed in the blessings of a good, well-paid education; so by the age of fourteen Helena had not only a beautiful face and raindrop-shaped eyes, but other talents too

– the ability to paint a landscape, speak French and entertain her family and friends with her poetry.

Who could expect, then, that the girl didn't have just the eyes of the rain, but also the roar?

Helena was capable of all moods of rain. From the refreshing soft rain after a hot week to the cloudburst waiting for the morning busy bustle. She could be gentle as light rain shaped by the breeze, or she could be impetuous and threatening as a thunderstorm.

But her moods were never inexplicable. For example, Helena tried all that she could to break through the strange emotional detachment of her new husband, and when nothing worked she resolved to simply mirror him; and so it became a silent house, the air full of the undischarged things, the ground cracking dry under the feet.

When children arrived, Helena could finally let loose upon them everything she had kept inside. George instead became even more clumsy, the house full of these little people for whom he was now responsible. He had no idea how to deal with them or talk to them. Every time he tried, he could hear the heartless, unemotional voice of his stepmother and would immediately close his mouth, and frown.

And yet when he turned forty-three, with four children – three girls and a boy – he declared he wanted another child. He really meant he wanted another boy. His hope was to defend himself and his only son from the collective whims of the four women in the house. It was a strategic move, a risky one, for there was always the possibility of yet another girl instead. Helena thought she had enough children. She was twenty-six and she had given birth to four children in eight years. Her body and mind were tired, and she wanted something more than just raising children.

'It's not just a few seconds of pleasure.' Helena was

pushing back her husband. 'That's all you know about it! Then you ignore the rest, the nine months that come after – nausea, cramps, constipation, mood swings, frequent pissing, backache, swollen feet – and then hours, if not days, of deep indescribable pain, and yes finally a little thing comes out, which screams like hell. And then you have to feed them, change them, cradle them every hour, night and day. You stay there, in your butchery, you barely see them or talk to them. You should be content with what you already have.'

It was more than a matter of another child: George was finally ready to be present in his children's lives, and he tried to convince his wife every way he could.

Flowers and jewels at first, but Helena was too clever to be seduced by these things. He tried making her jealous. Helena said he could have a child with another woman then, before slamming the door of their bedroom. So George tried her patience: not coming home for dinner when Helena had spent the whole day preparing his favourite dish, refusing to visit her relatives, not going to church, entering the spotless house in his bloody shoes. But Helena didn't care, and if he wanted to behave like a child, well, this was just one more reason not to give the family a sixth one. George, finally, tried to persuade her by sharing his feelings, but Helena was already too entrenched in her stubbornness to be surprised, let alone moved, by the first candid words of her husband.

George needed time to understand that his wife had won the argument, but when he realised, he became more silent than ever before. He did want another child. He loved his other children, but it was too late to tell them.

In the end, even if she could stand her husband's oddities and tricks and rages, Helena decided she couldn't go back to a silent marriage. She decided that one more child wouldn't make any difference, and it would be good company for the youngest one.

'Tayeb,' she said to her husband. 'But after that, khalas, end, stop.'

Nine months later a second boy was born. And George was indeed more ready, and to demonstrate that – or simply because they were too many of them to live in too few rooms – he decided to use all his practical love to build a bigger house for them all.

Rami grew up with a different father and a different mother than his siblings. It is said that when it comes to parents, children never have a clear picture, and every one of them knows a different story, a different secret, a different pain.

If you asked Rami, he would tell you that, yes, his father was silent, but he was a strong presence, a bit enigmatic, yes, but reassuring. And that his mother was a woman capable of torrential love, but also of sudden periods of aridity when she could disappear for days from the house, often retreating to a family member's home or the local convent, until George managed to get her back. Rami's childhood was more animated and playful than that of his siblings, with more words said and feelings shown more openly. His sisters were transforming into young women and also gave him attention, filling the house with strange objects with fascinating French names – cologne, bigoudis, foulards – or turning the living room into a concert hall, with musical instruments and books all around. His brother was there too, and Rami looked up to him and nagged him to hear about all his exciting adventures.

But it was also a less stable childhood: his sisters left the house to go abroad to study or get married, his brother became a busy, grown-up man with no time to waste with his little brother, and the relationship between his parents, having emerged slightly from the protracted embarrassment of silence, brought brighter spells but became less predictable.

The first time history entered Rami's ten-year-old life – which otherwise would have been a completely normal life – was in the shape of a radio.

Rami realised that there was something strange going on early one afternoon in June 1967, when he was walking back home after school. There, in the school's playground, the older boys were being trained, but not for any kind of sport or competition. They were armed, and despite their bemusement at having to hold a rifle instead of the usual ball, they were trying to learn how to use it. Rami thought it was just a new exercise and that he needed to wait until he was old enough before he could try it too.

It wasn't until the next day, when his mother prevented him from staying out after school to play with his friends, that he sensed something was wrong. At first, he thought he was in trouble for stealing his father's playing cards again, and he braced himself, ready to spend the whole afternoon helping with the sheep and cows. But there was no punishment, or even household chores to do, and his father told him there was no need to bring the animals – cattle, goats and sheep – up the pastures on the hill. There, rising from those fields, Rami could see black clouds of smoke. That was the moment Rami felt for the first time, there in the space between his lungs, where the ribs give up to the flesh, a feeling that something had been lost.

'We have to bring our stuff down to the ground floor,' said George. 'Mish kteer, but the most important things.'

'We need to bring food too!' interrupted Helena.

'Rami, ask the neighbours if their radio works or if we need to bring ours.'

'Can I bring cards, Baba?' asked Rami.

'Shu injannet? Do you think this is an appropriate time for cards?' cut short his mother.

The ground floor was the original floor of their house. It was an old building of arches, high ceilings and thick walls. Rami's brother, sisters and parents had lived there before he was born, before his father had decided to expand it by adding a modern first floor, with more rooms, thinner walls to gain space, and a white balcony on the front. At one point George had believed that the family could use both floors, that in the future one of his children could raise their family downstairs, and that there would be enough space nearby to build another house. But then he had to use all his savings to build that first floor upstairs. He had made his wife sell home-cooked food to raise more money to build the stairs, had kept the children busy by making them take out the old nails from the unused supports so that they could reuse them for the new walls, and had finally ended up renting the ground floor, just for a short period, because he needed the money to build the ceiling.

After nearly ten years, however, the neighbour's family was still living downstairs, and they now shared the thickness of the ground floor wall with them. When George built the first floor he didn't expect to need a thick wall. They didn't need to protect themselves from the cold winter now that efficient kerosene stoves could be bought from the nearest shop; the summer heat couldn't harm them, not in the garden with the bulky shade of the olive trees and the little pool for redfish, quick plunges and children's games. George didn't really think he would need to defend his family from another war, as if what happened in 1948 hadn't been enough.

'Shu sar? What's going on?' asked Rami, when everyone seemed to have settled down.

'Switch on the radio,' said Helena to Rami, without answering his question.

For a time, they all listened to the radio silently.

'Our great armies are gathering together to defeat the enemies!'

'The courage of our generals is forcing the enemy to retreat!'

'The precision of the pilots is cutting the sky with the blades of their wings!'

But no one explained to Rami or to his animals what was happening up on the hill. Or why it wasn't an appropriate time to play cards. Or how long they would have to stay with the neighbours, in that awkward silence. Sunset came and went and no one moved from their places, no one switched on the lamp, or went to the kitchen to cook dinner. They waited in the darkening living room in complete silence, like neglected furniture in an abandoned house. Just the radio declaring its big victories.

'Why can't we turn on the light?' Rami asked.

'Shush,' they all hushed him, as though someone else were there with them, lurking in the shadows.

Then darkness took over, and they relaxed, with that naive certainty that if you can't see then you can't be seen. Feeling protected by the anonymity afforded by the lightlessness and forced together in that unusual proximity, they started a conversation. At the beginning, they just commented on the optimistic reports on the radio:

'Our army is unstoppable!'

'Weinhum? Where do you think they are?'

'Our planes are flying all over the sky!'

'La, I can't really hear them, can you?'

'The enemy is surrendering!'

'Emta can we switch the lights on?'

Then it became more and more like a normal conversation with the radio just an annoying, interrupting chatterbox.

'We should eat something ... Fi akel kteer. I brought so much from upstairs, and if we are winning, we don't need it all.'

'Sfiha, walla zakie, they are always so good when you make them!'

'The generals are triumphant and they are announcing that ...'

'The secret is in the meat, in how you mince it.'

"An jadd? I thought it was in the dough.'

'Rising against the enemy ...'

"An jadd 'an jadd. Believe me. I will tell you a story so you can understand!'

Gossip and anecdotes, and then longer stories started to pour out, as if the darkness had finally freed them from the silence that had hung over them for years. They could reveal themselves to each other in a way they never had before. George, who couldn't see the intimidating beauty of his wife's eyes, or the confused expression on his children's faces. Helena, who in the dark couldn't reflect her husband's silent image. The children, who were no longer required to interpret their parents' thoughts. They all let go to a downpour of words.

It was then that they heard it. Not from the radio, which was still celebrating a declared victory, but directly above them. A big boom, which made the thick wall tremble. And then a siren. Rami felt his chest expand in fear, as if a little explosion had happened right there between his lungs and his heart. But the radio was still cheerful.

'Our great army won, we destroyed our enemy, we took the sky and the land ...'

So when it was announced that the army had entered the town, they really believed it was that great, victorious army of theirs, which had finally arrived and saved them all.

But it was not like that. Despite all the big promises on the radio, the army, which had won what they then called the six-day war, inflecting what became the Naksa, was the enemy's army.

The new occupier came shouting at every door.

'You have an hour to leave, or we will bomb everything here.'

It was pointless to hide any longer. They needed to do something, make a decision.

'Mahaddesh yitharrak min hon! No one moves!' It was the neighbour's voice in the dark.

'Shu? What do you mean don't move, they said they will kill …'

'Hoss!'

Silence was back. They would not leave the house, not under any circumstances. The Nakba was a fresh wound: when using the same threats, the same weapons, that same army had scared almost a million people away from their land and into refugee camps from Gaza to Syria.

So this time: no. Let the bombs come. Let the killing come. We will not move.

After the last day of this new war, after the bombs and the lies on the radio, people started to come out from their houses and see what life would look like under the new occupation. Rami wondered what he was supposed to do. Should he still bring the animals up to the hill pastures? Was his father going back to his butchery? Could they go back upstairs, or were the walls up there still too thin, still too dangerous? But there was no answer. The silence, which had fallen upon them again after that night of stories, was thicker than ever, and Rami was left to work out for himself what was the right or wrong thing to do, like playing a new game of cards without knowing the rules.

But it was not only Rami: no one seemed to know what was right or wrong anymore. There was a strange ambiguity between the two. Everyone was left to figure out for themselves what they should be doing. For example, Rami's favourite uncle, Albert, couldn't decide the right thing to do with his rifle, and so he took it and hid it in the well close to his house instead of handing it over to the occupying army. That was Rami's time to learn that nothing ends as expected around a well.

What confused Rami more than anything, however, was how he was supposed to behave. When George discovered that his son had become friends with the soldier guarding the building opposite their home, Rami experienced one of the longest silences his father could keep up. But then George made him behave nice and politely when the new settlers came to buy meat from his butcher shop. Or his uncle Albert who, once released from prison for hiding his rifle down the well, made him sell souvenirs to the occupiers who had started to come to Bethlehem as if they were tourists.

Then came the new identity cards. The whole town was lined up in the main square, in front of the church, all waiting for their turn to declare who they were and what they believed in. Rami started trembling. His school was a Catholic school, but his mother kept taking him to the Greek church. His father preferred some of the Protestant groups: they were more practical, less wordy, a compromise between Helena's deep faith and George's useful empiricism. So, when his turn came, Rami didn't really know what to say.

He had never really thought about it. For him, anything was good. He thought about declaring his passion for the Greek style, for its dramatic ceremonies. But he also really liked his Catholic teachers. And what about his father's scepticism for *all* of these faiths?

The occupying authority made everything simpler – or more complicated.

'Christian or Muslim?' the soldier asked.

Rami, instead of rejoicing at the general label of Christian, was overwhelmed by panic. He had never really considered being Muslim, but many of his friends were. Could he come back another day? Reflect on it a bit more? Try them all and then decide? And what about Ibrahim, his classmate with a Muslim mother and a Christian father? What would he have answered?

'Christian,' his mother cut in, putting family loyalty over his deep questioning about faith.

Rami understood then that he was not supposed to answer, he was too young to have his own identity card, which was given only to people over sixteen. Nonetheless, Rami was never convinced about these new cards. They looked strange: they had the name of the new occupying state on it, even though they were still living in the same place; used an alphabet Rami didn't know how to read; and there was that word *Christian*, too general to be the truth, yet so precise that it cut through reality.

Rami, and everyone else, soon found out that it was not just a question of God. That there were some tangible, earthly privileges that came with being Christian but didn't come with being Muslim. Better business, shorter queues at the checkpoints, softer treatment in prison. People who probably knew, but who hadn't paid much attention to it before, started to ask their neighbours what IDs they had been given.

Even Rami and his friends played with their identities like cards at a game table.

You got Muslim, I am sorry for you.

I can give you my Christian one if you give me your sweets for the rest of the year.

But whereas for Rami and his friends it was just a game, for others that new word on their ID brought an awareness of difference into the town. They said it was just a word that had no value, that it didn't matter for them, they knew who they really were. But in the long run that word became more and more powerful, and drew a new, invisible border.

Birzeit 1974–76

The second time history entered Rami's life was in the shape of an onion.

Although some of the soldiers had tried to sneak into Birzeit University, most of them were outside, throwing tear gas at the students inside.

The campus had been built by repurposing the biggest houses and other buildings in that small town on the hills. They were bought up one by one. The first one for the high school, the second one when it became a college, and then more and more until it became a university, with various departments, a cafeteria, the student dorms and a theatre.

From the outside it didn't look like a university campus: the essential architecture of the village with its cream-coloured stones, the buildings surrounded by gardens and trees, and the traditional balconies and verandas created the placid atmosphere of a vacation retreat. It was hard for the students sheltering inside to imagine that just behind the vibrato of the leaves there was an army waiting for someone to make one wrong step.

CROSSING

It was November 1974, Rami was seventeen years old, and for the first time he had exchanged the thick walls of his father's house for the thin walls of a student room an hour away from Bethlehem. He had started university one month before and, for all he had imagined his first year to be, he hadn't considered the possibility of a full-scale siege. But things escalated quickly when demonstrations erupted to call for independence, now that the Palestinian Liberation Organization had just been recognised by all the Arab countries, and that the United Nations General Assembly had put the Palestinian Question back in their agenda for the first time since 1952. The occupying army charged the demonstrators, and several university students and schoolchildren were shot, wounded and arrested.

Then on 21 November 1974 the president of Birzeit University was deported to Lebanon, with no formal process, during the night. The excuse to deport people was always the same, 'security violation', but it was never clarified whose security or what violation. It was just another attempt to intimidate students.

The occupying army expected unrest and readied itself by posting soldiers around the university campus. At the first sign of commotion, the soldiers launched tear gas. Rami was hit by the first wave of gas and was trying to cover his nose, mouth and eyes without any results, when a hand – the rest of the body invisible because of the smoke and the tears – reached out to him, offering half a red onion.

'Khod! Sniff this! Tears against tears. It will help you wash away the gas and breathe and see again,' said the hand's voice.

Onions were a common cooking ingredient, and countless times Rami had seen his mother chopping, frying, pickling, stuffing, roasting, grilling and adding them raw or cooked to every single recipe she was preparing. And he also remembered the countless times he had been the one in charge of cutting them – into small perfect little squares, or in long, long strips, or minced. How many times had he protested against the task, and how many tears had he shed while doing it! He had never imagined that onions, protests and tears could go together in a different way to the one he had known in his childhood kitchen. He never imagined that he could smell an onion with relief and eagerly inhale its pungency to bring on tears to wash away the tear gas. After these attacks, the students couldn't find any of the meals that would usually contain onions in the cafeteria, and for a few days they had to eat dishes that Rami now found tasteless. These kinds of things can make life seem suddenly less ambiguous, and with all the moral clarity of a seventeen-year-old, an army right behind the leaves, and the sharp help of a red onion, Rami started to understand what was right and what was wrong.

Onions were right, tear gas was wrong. The radio seven years before had been wrong, but the occupying power and the soldiers were also wrong. The green eyes of Muna were right and their first stolen kisses under the university campus's trees were also right. The disappearance of people in the night was wrong and empty desks in September were wrong. Palestinian flags on the roof were wrong for the soldiers, but not for them. Forbidden books were right, but they were also difficult to find. The campus being closed by the generals for no particular reason was wrong. Clandestine classes when university was cancelled were right, especially when there was no other way to have them.

'Armed struggle is wrong,' some people said.

'Armed struggle is necessary,' said others, but it didn't make it any easier.

'Escaping is my right,' they said.

'Escaping is wrong and cowardly,' others said. 'Resisting! Resisting is right.'

The confusion about resistance was wrong. 'But it is also right,' said the professor, 'disagreeing is democracy, disagreeing is right.' Disagreeing was wrong for the soldiers. But also, agreeing with them was wrong. His mother's food was right. The onionless food of the cafeteria was wrong. The students from the villages told him about the things that were happening there. Torture was wrong. The students from Gaza told him about things happening there. Shooting was wrong. Demolition was wrong. Threats were wrong. Fear was right but it was wrong too. Rami remembered the first time he had felt fear, in the space between his lungs, when he could see black smoke rising up from the pastures on the hill. Black smoke was wrong. But smoking with friends, in the night, singing songs and dancing, was right. Music was right, but it was not always enough. Friendships were right, but it depended with whom. Discussing politics was right, if they kept it secret. But designing and distributing flyers was wrong, extremely wrong – especially if the soldiers caught you.

Being caught was wrong.

'But doing nothing is wrong, kaman.'

'They can catch you even if you do nothing.'

'Sahh, that's right, think about our university president.'

'So, what do we do?'

After a few months of clarity, right and wrong muddled again inside Rami's mind: he realised that right and wrong were not enough. Facing fear, that feeling growing uncontrolled under the undefended layer of flesh between the ribs, right and wrong were meaningless. Rami felt the same confusion he had felt in front of the church in the main square when he was ten years old, when in a matter of few seconds he had been asked to decide who he wanted to be.

Once again, he felt that there were many things he could be and no one of them was right or wrong.

It was again thanks to his mother that he found an answer: a seed she had planted during the war, seven years before, suddenly broke through the surface.

It was September of 1967. The teacher had asked the students to draw something representing their summer, and Rami had asked his parents for advice. His father, who couldn't see why the teacher should ask such a thing after what happened, hadn't answered, so Helena had stepped in.

'What do you remember of your summer?'

'When they said they were bombing the house.'

'But they didn't. You know why? When Florence was bombed fi il-harb il-'alamyye it-tanye, they destroyed all bridges, but one. It was too beautiful.'

'They didn't bomb our house because it was too beautiful?'

'Mumkin. Maybe,' Helena had ended, being careful that George could not hear and mistake that *maybe* for an admission of admiration for that house built out of love.

The next day Rami won the prize for the best drawing. A little plane flying over a beautiful bridge. Seven years later, that plane indicated to Rami, like a finger pointing towards the right direction, what he really believed in.

CHAPTER THREE

Robiglio

WHEN I TURNED EIGHT, and for some years after that, my mother used to take me to Florence at least once every summer.

Even though Florence was just two hours by train from her home village, for me it was a real adventure. We would buy the train tickets a few days in advance from the only travel agency of the town, situated in the main square. My mum would check the train schedules with the man behind the counter and it would look as if the two of them were organising a long and perilous expedition around the world. The travel agency was located in a small room on the ground floor of a medieval building. All its furniture was made of dark wood. Pictures hung on the walls, showing enormous trees and blue seas in remote places. The yellowing borders around them made them look like old treasure maps of a disappearing world.

Florence became my mother's place, after she moved there when she was twenty. When we visited it together, she would make her way through it with all the confidence and the happiness of someone in their childhood playground. We would stroll for hours through its streets. She guided me along the lines of her story, the quick turns, the shades of the palaces.

She showed me with bright eyes and big gestures Via dei Servi, where she and my father had shared their first flat. She showed me where my brother was born, in the hospital in Piazza dell'Indipendenza. She showed me her favourite shops and corners. Her favourite food. We would always treat ourselves to lunch in one of the restaurants away from the tourist area. She knew where to go. That day in Florence every summer was our holiday even when we couldn't afford one.

Summer after summer we saw the town changing, welcoming more and more tourists. The food stalls in the central market gave way to souvenir stands selling little models of the duomo and fake leather bags. New residential areas sprung up to accommodate newcomers. Public transport cut right through the main squares to make it quicker to get around the city. My mother somehow never became disappointed. She accepted the changes to the town that had seen her young and in love and was now seeing her grow older year after year and would eventually see her disappear. They accepted each other's ageing. More than that, they enjoyed it.

I have always felt that my father was only an additional reason for my mother's love of Florence, and that my mother's relationship with Florence was rather a private one. I wonder how she felt when she eventually left the city. Did she think it was the right time, or was it more like an unavoidable split? Did she have to choose between Florence and my father?

What my mother used to tell me is that she was the one who fell in love first, when she saw my father, half-naked, at a friend's house. She also used to tell me that he was the most different person she had met up until that time and that eventually she realised she wanted to spend her life with him because of a language mistake. She said that she had felt a deep connection with him in that mistake, a sense of tenderness.

It is hard to write about my parents' romantic affair.

This is not how we usually imagine our parents. But there is something real about it, to see them as they were before they became ours.

*

Florence, 1977

Anna woke up in the middle of the night. The other young women in the nunnery were asleep. The silence was interrupted by the light snoring of the girl sleeping in the bed next to her. When Anna sat up, the first thing she could see straight in front of her was the big crucifix hanging on the wall with its agonised, long-haired Jesus. She released a breath held for too long. Here she was, at nineteen, back to a life of nuns, religion and vain men. When Anna had chosen to study to become a nurse, she hadn't expected nuns to be still so involved in the nursing-education business: they were the principal teachers and ran the cheapest and closest residence available for the students.

Arrogant men, they can be found everywhere really. It was almost impossible to avoid them. Catcalling you in the streets, a classic. Or leaning their shoulder towards yours at the bar, pretending there's no other space. Or what about when they offer to help with your bags but then get pissed off because they expect something in return?

But the most arrogant, Anna found out soon enough, were the doctors who treated the nurses as if they were their property.

That morning it had happened in the operating theatre. He had bent her over the operating table and tried to tear off her uniform. What an idiot! She liked him, they had been flirting for some time, he must have been able to tell she was interested. He could have just asked, she would have said yes.

So why did he try to force her? It was only another nurse coming into the room that had saved her.

How could she fall back to sleep? Anna ran to the bathroom, trying not to hit anything on the way, waking up her roommates or the warden-nun. The tiles of the bathroom floor were frigid under her bare feet. The cold helped her to hold back her nausea just long enough to reach the toilet. Hopefully no one heard her puking. She couldn't face the consequences if the nuns suspected she was pregnant. She was not, she was just disgusted.

She wanted to leave that place as soon as possible. Not Florence, which she loved, but that residence run by nuns and that hospital with its bloated doctors.

For a while she had thought it was not that bad: during their lunch breaks, trainee doctors and nurses would often share their frustrations and talk about how things had to change, how medicine needed a more human approach, for example, how doctors needed to work shorter hours, how nurses needed a higher pay, but Anna could still feel a distance growing between them. She guessed it had something to do with power. Doctors would always rank higher in the hospital hierarchy and eventually behave as though they didn't need the nurses.

Sitting on the floor of the toilet cubicle, Anna grasped what had happened with her young doctor: it didn't matter whether they were flirting, he was still a doctor and she was a nurse and power needed to be restored. She could hear her father's *donna* resonating in the little toilet space. To keep her in her rightful place. Kneeling in front of the toilet. Trying not to make a sound and bother people around her – the long-haired Jesus in the other room a reminder to accept her suffering.

It was 1977 and women were still having to demonstrate

for the right to have an abortion and were called 'puttane' – whores – for doing so. If she had been pregnant and tried to get an abortion, she would have been criminalised and yet nothing would happen to the young doctor for attacking her. How many other women were awake right now in the middle of the night and like her having to deal with the consequences of men's actions, asking themselves whether they had done something that prompted the unwanted attention, wondering if they were wrong.

She jerked up, wiped her mouth, and flushed her vomit down the toilet. She washed her face and looked herself in the old mirror.

Anna was done feeling wrong.

'Tu li devi lavare a fondo! Wash them properly!' shouted Alberto from the other side of his restaurant's kitchen counter.

'Cosa?' shouted back Rami.

During rush hour, restaurant kitchens sounded like big orchestras, thought Rami, trying to isolate the voice of his boss from all the other sounds.

But Rami had heard perfectly well, he just had no idea what *a fondo* meant. *Cosa* had quickly become one of his favourite and most-often-used words. People seemed to use it for everything. Give me that *cosa* – *that thing* – *cosa* do you want? – what do you want? – Ask *cosa!* – ask her! – *Cosa?* – pardon me? What did you say? Rami put *cosa* at the top of his vocabulary, especially that last meaning. *What did you say?*

'I said wash them well, well well!' Alberto, the owner of the little restaurant where Rami worked, was trying to explain *a fondo* to Rami while miming the rotating movement of a sponge in the air.

Rami nodded that he understood, and mentally noted: *a fondo* means *bene bene*, well well. *Bene* was among the first words Rami had learned. He learned it straight after *Come stai?* How are you? *Bene grazie.*

While washing the dishes, Rami was going back and forth through the pages of his mental vocabulary to find a space to squeeze the new word in. *Ciao, mi chiamo, vengo da, a fondo, cosa? come stai? Bene bene.* Rami stopped.

Was he fine? Was he fine really? Yes, he was doing okay. Bene, yes, but not bene bene. He was doing what he wanted. He was attending the Academy of Art, there were no soldiers waiting outside the classrooms to arrest those who had drawn flyers or waved flags, and the only onions he touched were the ones he cut up at the restaurant.

Alberto and his family were nice to him, and the job guaranteed one nice hot meal a day. Italian food. He liked pasta, of course, although Rami preferred punchy tastes. While he was playing with the chewy texture of cow's stomach of the Trippa alla Fiorentina, he wondered what his father would have thought. Would his father like it? And when he was sucking with pleasure the marrow out of the round bone of the ossobuco, he realised that he missed his father.

Rami missed his mother too. He tried to stop his thoughts before they carried him away and stopped him from washing all those dishes. So he focused again on his vocabulary: *Ciao, mi chiamo, vengo da, a fondo, cosa?* ... but *cosa* sounded too much like *casa*, home – another of the first words he had learned, but he didn't have the chance to use it as often.

Rami was doing okay, but he missed home. He missed the white balcony, and the garden with the olive trees and the pool where he would play his games. He missed the light. Even when studying the importance of light during his art classes, he could never capture the light of his homeland.

And then there was the embarrassing situation when he tried to express himself but nothing came out. Yes, he could say *come stai? Bene*, he could say where he was from, more or less, he could say what he was doing, he could go alone in the streets and survive, but he couldn't express himself deeply, *bene bene, a fondo*. That yes, he was okay, but then how could he say that he missed the light? Or yes, he was from Palestine but how could he explain the radios, and the onions and the blurred lines between right and wrong? He could say he was in Florence to study art, but he couldn't explain why. Yes, and he could survive in the streets, ask for help, say what he needed, but he couldn't really tell them *who* he was.

After work, when he didn't have to walk back to the Accademia for another class, Rami would stroll back to his friends' flat where another Arab guy and his French girlfriend were putting him up, until he could find somewhere permanent to live.

Rami would use these long strolls to find places he might like to live, see how far they would be from the restaurant or the Accademia, and to understand the town, literally.

He had soon found out that the Ponte Vecchio was called that because it was the oldest bridge in the city, as simple as that, but there were streets and squares whose names puzzled him and triggered his imagination.

He liked Via dei Leoni, just behind Palazzo Vecchio – because apparently the town had kept its lions there – and he tried to imagine how homesick those animals had been. Or Via del Fico, figs like the ones he would eat directly from the trees in the streets of Birzeit, big like his mother's hand and with a red heart. Via dell'Ulivo, because it reminded him of the olive trees in his father's garden.

Rami added all these words to the vocabulary in his head and there he created his own map of Florence, taking longer paths just to get home.

*

When Anna and Rami met, Attilio, Vittoria, Helena and George also met. Also Edoardo, Francesca, Agnese, Paola, Alberto and Muna met. Also the nuns and the soldiers met. Also the religious dilemma of Teresina and Messinella and the queue in front of the church to state your identity met. And also the farmhouse in the windy countryside, and the white balcony of that first floor built out of love. And also the wells met. And the bicycle rides and the onions, and the boring political conversations and the protests met. And some porn actors and some schoolteachers met. And the long silences, the submissiveness, the nights out, the distances, and that desire for lontananza and the homesickness.

Anna knew her and Rami's destinies were not easy to put together: there were too many things that could go wrong. But she didn't care. When she saw Rami for the first time, returning her gaze through the neck hole of the t-shirt he was trying to put on, in her own obstinate way she could only see the one path to happiness.

She was falling again for the geography she could see in someone's eyes, but this time that geography was real. Rami did come from far away, from across the sea, and he spoke a language that she didn't understand. And it was through a language mistake that Anna knew the exact moment she fell in love.

It was a winter afternoon a few months after they had met, and, at four, the sun was already setting. They had walked for hours back and forth along the River Arno. It was so cold that they had to keep their hands in gloves inside their pockets and still the tips of their fingers were starting to numb.

Anna kept moving her fingertips inside her pocket, rubbing them up against each other. She didn't know if it was just because of the cold, or because of the urge to reach for Rami's fingers, through all those layers of gloves and pockets. Anna was wondering if his fingers were doing the same: fighting against the urge to challenge the same cold and reach out to hers. She was trying to detect traces of that battle in his face, but he was concentrating on trying to talk, though hardly any words were coming out. Anna kept staring at the side of his mouth and at the warm breath escaping his lips, like cigarette smoke, hitting the cold air. She shivered and moved closer to Rami. She felt a bit guilty because even if she was giving all her attention to him, she wasn't really listening to what he was saying.

He probably noticed her inattention or was frustrated with the words that weren't coming out, or maybe it was just a way to fight the cold: he started to sing Sinatra's 'The World We Knew'.

He didn't know why that specific song came to mind. He knew it was flattering for his voice and he liked the perfect scenes the lyrics evoked around them: the endless walk, the street turning into gold under their feet, the world they knew, Anna beside him, and that word *love* hanging there. He kept singing, as they walked along the river, from Porta a Prato, passing by Piazza della Signoria and Ponte Vecchio. That was the moment Rami understood he was in love. He was in love with that city on the river, where you could walk from side to side. He liked the nights out, when the streets seemed to be all for him and the other students who gathered on the balustrade of the Ponte Vecchio to sing, play the guitar and dance. Now he could add the smell of Anna walking beside him. Her nose red from the cold, and her casual way of moving closer to him, without really listening to him but nonetheless giving him her piercing attention. So close he could feel Anna's fingers in her pocket play an invisible piano.

Anna would always remember those songs. Even if she couldn't understand the English words, she could understand

Rami's voice. It was something unknown to her, a male voice singing for her. They walked and sang until it was time for Anna to go back to the convent. Spending the whole night out was too risky and the next morning she had her shift at the hospital. Rami walked her all the way to the train station and it was then, when they said goodbye, that she understood she was in love. Not because of that last kiss, or those romantic songs, or even Rami's eyes that promised a different world, but because of a mistake.

'Okay, I'll see you soon. Remember you can't call me after 9 pm. The nuns won't let me take the call.'

'Don't worry, I will call you on time,' answered Rami and, looking in her eyes, he added with intensity: 'See you last week!'

Maybe it was the contrast between the serious tone of his voice and the mistake. Or because that mistake together with his accent made her feel far away from what her life had been in Italy. Or because time really could stop when they were together. But it was in that mix-up that Anna saw how their lives could mix up too.

'We are all in the same fight, capito?' said Rita, adjusting her jeans before squeezing onto the sofa. The movement of her long legs wafted the smoke away and Anna could see, for a few seconds, Rami's eyes looking for hers. He was sitting on a chair, on the opposite side of the living room, closer to the door

Anna had moved up a bit, to make more space for Rita, and when she looked back at Rami, he was hidden again behind a curtain of smoke.

Rami and his friends' flat was a very popular meeting place and Anna could always find someone there no matter what the time of the day. She never knew who was actually living there, who was a guest staying for a few days, or who was just a friend visiting for a coffee and a cigarette.

'What do you mean we are all in the same fight?' asked Ali from his cushion on the carpet. From the tone of his voice it was clear that, whatever the answer, he was not going to agree.

'Cioè: we are all fighting against the same system, after all.'

'La … Y'ani, maybe, but we have to focus on our own specific struggles and rights!'

'This is your problem, tesoro. You can't see that it's always about the same rights: human rights!' intervened Luisa, leaning forward from her chair to tap her cigarette ash into an empty wine glass.

'And that's your problem, habibti, you are … y'ani, come si dice …'

'Ingenua!' Rami tried to help.

'Oui, ingenua, naive,' added Marianne, Ali's French girlfriend.

Anna rarely spoke but absorbed all the different facial expressions and language tics and felt like she was in the centre of the world. That living room was a hub of people from everywhere, Italians, yes, but mainly students coming from abroad – France, Spain, Iran, Jordan, Chile, Argentina, Palestine.

'I am not naive,' Luisa kept on. 'Al contrario, it's you: you don't understand that if we unite, we have more chance of winning, all the minorities, the women, the Iranians, the Palestinians, the Kurdish, the Black people fighting apartheid!'

'Walla, we believed once that people would stand with us, and look what happened!'

'Yes, Ali is right.' Sharif was sitting on the table, behind Rami's chair. 'Look what happened in Tal al-Za'taar.

Three thousand of us killed in a refugee camp. Who was there with us then?'

Sharif's tone was sombre, as it always was. The line across his forehead wrinkled with the effort of explaining his opinions.

'Yes, bizzapt, and now with Sadat going to speak in the Knesset, we are more alone than ever!'

'Noi siamo sole da sempre,' Luisa came back. 'Last among the lasts, our needs are always less important than the common good. Only last March they called us *puttane* here in Florence, just because we protested for our right to have an abortion!'

'Aspetta, guys, you are putting different things together.' Rita was trying to take back the discussion she had started. 'The only way to improve society is to all work towards the same ideal. If we try to solve each problem separately, we will still have flawed societies. We can't keep saying *let's solve one thing at a time*, we have to solve them altogether as part of the same architecture, otherwise the building will keep falling,' she added in one breath.

The whole room had fallen silent as though everyone was trying to work out whether what Rita had said made sense or it was just nonsensical utopia, stuff you read in books, you know, powerful, yes, but not something you can actually make happen.

Anna still didn't know how to react in those moments. Was there tension? Did she need to say something to break it? Where did Rami stand? What did she herself think? In a way, it was no different to those political quarrels back at the Ventoruccia, but now Anna could see how, for some people, there was no choice, no way out, their mere existence was a political issue.

'Ovvia giù, chi vuole un caffè?'

The silence was soon broken with chatter as though the word caffè was enough to resolve all their dilemmas.

Ali and Marianne offered to make coffee and left the room.

Sharif stood up and offered his hand to Luisa and they walked towards the kitchen, laughing and talking.

'Do you want something?' Rita asked Anna, before leaving the room as well without listening for her answer. In her tone, Anna could sense that Rita didn't like the way the conversation had gone.

Rami was still in his chair, listening to Hooman and Pedro whose conversation had moved on to university classes and exams. But Anna could see that Rami was just pretending to listen. She could recognise when Rami became distant. When he had left the room, but his body was still there.

She stood up, took a chair, and dragged it next to him, but it was only when she touched his cheek with the back of her fingers that Rami realised Anna was there.

'Scusa,' he said. 'I was thinking.'

'Yes, lo vedo.'

Anna expected Rami to say more, but he said nothing.

'What are you thinking?' she asked.

'Niente, you know, the same.'

'No, non lo so, I don't know what you think. I am not in your head!' Anna wanted it to sound like a joke, but for some reason her voice came out serious.

Rami looked at her surprised, as if, for the first time, he realised that people couldn't read his thoughts. He smiled.

'Why do you smile?'

'Perché, I just thought about my father. He does the same, thinking that people can read his thoughts!'

Anna looked at Rami, more in love with him than ever.

'He doesn't talk much, but it's because he can't find the words. Not even in Arabic. I used to find them in Arabic, but in Italiano, la, I can't and my thoughts have begun to stay in my head, like my father's.'

'I can help you, at least with the language.'

'But I sound stupido.'

'No you don't. You speak well!'

'I speak well, but not well well. I can't say difficult things. I can't say anything deep, like Sharif and Ali. We can't say more than the surface of it.' Rami lowered his eyes, away from Anna's.

She knew that if she wanted to understand, she couldn't let his eyes move away, and with her left hand she moved his face back to hers.

'Try to tell me. I want to know more.'

Rami's sigh was so strong that it could have twisted away the lid of a jar.

'Non lo so, it's like missing something and at the same time not missing it. Does that make sense?'

It was Anna who needed to find the words to tell him that, yes, it made perfect sense to her. That she too missed the bicycle rides, her granny, and even the farmhouse a bit. And yet nothing would make her go back.

'I would like to go back to Palestine, be there and discuss these things with my people, with the people who have to go through it. Here, we are just talking. But really are we *doing* anything? When I was at university back home, people did all sorts of things, yes they talked too, but then we needed to *do* things if we didn't want to completely disappear under oppression, if we wanted the world to remember that we – Palestinians – existed.'

'What things?'

'Everything: protesting, marching, playing music, organising, trying to coordinate politically.'

'Are we not doing that here?'

'Yes we are, but I wasn't happy there about it and I am not happy here, but at least I was there with my people, not trying to play the artist away from them. And yet I didn't want to be there because I wanted my life to be more than just surviving. I don't know, it's so difficult.' Rami put his hands on his eyes. 'Cioè, I want to do something, but I want to do the right thing.'

'Like what?' pressed Anna.

'Non lo so, I don't know what is right or wrong, I have never known. I just feel powerless. Like there is nothing I can do that can really make a difference. Sometimes, when we talk about how we can resist, and I say that I want to ... how do you say that? Without violence?'

'Pacifica?'

'Yes, when I talk about nonviolent resistance, I feel like a coward. When I was at the university back home, there was plenty of nonviolent resistance. Flyers, flags on the roofs, singing and dancing. But what did that bring us? More violence! And we are losing more and more: they are coming in our houses, in our schools, taking our land, deciding what we can say, what we can sing, eating our food, yet I can't make myself believe that taking up arms is the only answer ...'

Rami let out a sob and Anna recognised his frustration. Was it not the same frustration that Teresina had felt when she talked about the war and the fascists? Yes, it was, and it was the same frustration that Anna had seen in the foxgrape-blue eyes of her grandfather Pietro, when Teresina reminded him that he hadn't had the nerve to join the freedom fighters on the hills. Anna knew that rather than accusing him, it was Teresina's way of trying to excuse him. But she also knew that Pietro didn't want to be excused: once, reciting to her – a bit by heart, a bit adding his own imagination – the riots of Milan from the novel *Promessi Sposi* of Manzoni, he had paused.

'Ricordati, never be violent,' he had said, the phantom of two world wars in his voice.

Anna, through Pietro and Rami, felt that frustration too. What can you do when you are born into violence, when wars, occupations, injustices, destructions keep coming, and yet you don't want to use violence against violence?

Anna didn't know what to say. She had never had to choose, but she knew she had inherited Teresina's anger. The anger which would have probably led her to embrace armed resistance.

'Why did you come to Italy then?' Anna asked, to break the silence.

'I know I should be there, helping to free my country, but at the same time I want to be freed *from* it. I want a life where I can be just me.' Rami stopped, surprised by what he had said.

Lying on the sofa in Rami's apartment, Anna lit a cigarette. She took the first drag and, resting her head on her left arm, exhaled the smoke. She was alone, waiting for Rami to get ready to go to the cinema, and thinking about the conversation of the day before. They had lived their lives in completely different places, grown up with completely different families, speaking different languages, eating different food. They had entirely different histories, and yet they were at exactly the same point in their lives, carried there by a similar chain of events. Rita was right, they were all fighting something. No matter where they came from, they all carried with them the conflicts of their homes. But were these conflicts the same? Could they be fought in the same way? Anna doubted it.

The cigarette had burned too much, and she had to shake off the ash before taking another drag. She looked around through the haze of smoke. Days' worth of newspapers were piled on the floor, along with empty wine and coffee glasses. There were books written in different languages. Rami's art books left untouched on a paper bag on the table. Cigarette butts everywhere. The brown paper wrap of a panino was open on the coffee table, the breadcrumbs mixed with cigarette ash. A guitar was propped in the corner, next to some cassette tapes. She stood up and walked towards the cassette deck. Anna started to go through the tapes, whose labels and songs, like the books, were in different languages.

She was tempted to play Battisti, her favourite. Then she recognised a tape that Rami had played again and again and she put it on. Anna liked the scratching sound on the tape at the start, before the music started, because she could imagine the people recording it. The first notes played and then the first words, that she could now recognise as Arabic but was still unable to understand.

Anna went back to the sofa swaying her body to the music. She lay down and closed her eyes, letting the cigarette smoke swirl around her. She thought about her battles against her village, where gossip, religion and men kept suffocating women's lives; she thought about her family, her father's cruelty and her mother's submission; and she thought about Teresina and her stubbornness, how her grandma's desire for lontananza, her belief that life could give more, had encouraged her to leave and saved her from all of that. For a second Anna believed – no, more than that, she *felt* – that she had won. Right there on that sofa, alone yet surrounded by all those people and *their* battles, she felt at the centre of the world. Right there, she could imagine herself being everything, everywhere: in a French boudoir with Marianne, smoking on an Iranian takht with Hooman, reading Neruda with Pedro, and in the garden with the little pool that Rami had described to her. But also in Paris in the aftermath of the student revolution, between disillusionment and new ideas, in Teheran to talk with the people who were striking, with the resistance in Chile fighting against Pinochet, and finally in Palestine to understand the pain of Rami over the theft of his land. All this pain and these struggles going on all at the same time could be overwhelming, but they could also be empowering, strong in the conviction that they could at least imagine a better world together.

'I thought again about what we talked about last night.' Rami interrupted her reverie.

Anna hadn't heard him enter the room.

'Cioè?' she asked.

'You asked me why I came here?'

'Sì ...'

'I came here for the Ponte Vecchio, to make ponti vecchi for my country.'

Anna looked at Rami, amused and confused. Maybe it was his Italian.

'What do you mean "make ponti vecchi"?'

Rami sat down next to Anna on the sofa and took some time to put his thoughts in order.

'During the war, the Ponte Vecchio was the only bridge the Nazis didn't bomb in the whole of Florence. Mama told me that even Hitler couldn't destroy such an artistic masterpiece. Ecco, this is why I came here: to study an art that can't be destroyed. To make beauty my way to fight against the oppression of my people. But then, when I came here, I found out that what my mother had told me might not be true. That it wasn't the Nazis who didn't destroy it.'

'So who was it?'

'Maybe it was the guardian of the bridge's shops, who cut the cable of the explosive charge. Quindi vedi ... nothing is indestructible. So why am I here?'

'I see,' said Anna, pinching the skin on her neck like she did every time she was nervous or pensive. 'I mean, yes, but also, no, non capisco ...'

Rami remained silent, waiting for Anna to explain which part she didn't understand.

'Cioè, after all, Ponte Vecchio is still here. It *is* indestructible.'

'Yes, but ...'

'Yes, but the fact that it might have been one of the people of Florence, rather than one of the German invaders, makes your point even more important.'

Rami smiled. He could see where Anna was going.

'Sì!' he said, encouraging Anna to keep talking.

'Art is indeed indestructible, but it's more so if its people take care of it and use it. It was like that also during the flood of the Arno in 1966. It was the people who saved the works of art and the books from the mud.'

Rami's smile became broader. 'Quindi, are you saying that I have to make people love the art of my country?'

'Sì,' said Anna, looking back at him.

'I can start doing something here and now. I can show people here that we Palestinians have our own Ponte Vecchio, that this is what we are fighting for, that we should cut the explosive charge!' Rami stood up, rapturous. 'Hai ragione! I need to tell the others, *all* of us should bring our culture *here*. Show our dances, our music, our poetry. Showing what can be lost if we don't act. We need to organise something!'

Anna jumped and landed on the stage on her toes, as Rami had instructed her to from his seat in the first line of seats below. Holding hands, twenty people formed a line, alternating men and women. They were dancing dabke, rehearsing for the performance that night. Rami had been quick to convince his friends to put together a show featuring all of the music and traditions of their group of friends, from Santiago to Jerusalem and Teheran. He was enthusiastic: this was the first night of the tour around Italy that he had organised. He hadn't expected so many people to say yes, and the shows were going to go on for the whole summer. He was glowing.

'Forza, come on, faster!'

Anna struggled to keep the beat. Dancing was not her forte. She had thought it was, when she danced alone, humming her own music, moving her fingers and arms in the air. But on the stage Anna had to follow the beat coming from the speakers, the beat to which everyone was dancing. Counting. Counting was the problem. One two three. One two three.

'Eh, eh, eh ...' Rami was choreographing their movement and keeping the rhythm by singing short syllables, snapping his fingers and moving his shoulders up and down as though he were unable to keep his body still while the music was playing.

Anna tried to keep up, but it was not easy.

The show was taking place at the Loggia del Pesce, a square covered by an arcade right in the middle of Florence, just a few steps from Rami's restaurant. Alberto and his family were coming, and so were some of Rami's friends from the Accademia – the organiser had told him that they were expecting the square to be full.

In the way that he was instructing the dabke dancers, in the way that he played the oud with the other musicians, in the way that he explained the meaning of the poems of Mahmoud Darwish, Anna could see that Rami had found his calling. Anna wanted to be part of it, and she had learned Rami's songs even if she understood only some of the meaning, and learned more or less how to dance in the traditional embroidered dresses that Ali had shipped from Palestine.

Sharing the movements of those dancers and the words of their songs, Anna soon found herself part of their world: she shared their disillusionment, the displacements, their hope too, their waiting for letters, the interrupted phone calls, and she shuddered at the news coming from their countries, felt their homesickness, believed in their fights for liberation.

When Anna told Teresina that she was marrying Rami, she knew that her grandmother would look at her a certain way. The problem, Anna knew, was that Rami was not Italian. Foreigners to Teresina meant German soldiers, commands given in strong accents, fear and famine. Or they meant American soldiers. The American soldiers who visited Graziella's house.

Graziella, a friend of Teresina's, lived in a one-room flat at the end of the narrow alley between the second-biggest church of the parish and the clock tower. She was a widow and she always wore a black skirt. Her hair was chestnut brown and she had light eyes. A good trait to have if you are working with Germans who missed home.

Nobody had complained when Graziella's clients were German soldiers. Even when queuing for sex, the next in line with their belt open already, people were silent in front of the soldiers' piercing eyes, or the squared eagle on the uniform. But their voices had come back once the American troops came to the village. Suddenly her neighbours found that queue inappropriate, especially so close to the second-biggest church in the village. But it was not a question of morality, rather it was the fact that some of the American soldiers were Black, and the villagers had never seen a Black face before – apart from the black faces of the men coming out of the mine, but that was different: it could be washed away.

Teresina didn't care what the neighbours thought and,

unlike others, continued to visit her friend. She knew that, in times of war, you need to scratch out a living any way you can. She simply found Graziella's way more honest than the people who knelt down in front of the soldiers for other reasons.

But Teresina's attitude towards her granddaughter was different. Anna was the first one to bring a foreigner who didn't wear a uniform to the village. Teresina had never believed the rumours about foreigners, about Arab men and their brutality, but now she was worried that those rumours might actually be true. Was Anna putting herself in that situation just to follow her restlessness, her dreams of a faraway life? Was she just doing it to defy her parents and the entire village? Teresina feared Anna's stubbornness would lead her to make a decision she would soon regret.

In a certain way, it was true: Anna had spent her whole childhood plotting her escape from the village. But, during those first years in Florence, she believed she had already left the village behind. Her love with Rami had nothing to do with it.

When Rami and Anna finally moved into their first flat together, she felt she had accomplished something. It was a little flat in Via dei Servi, right behind the famous cathedral of Florence, on the fourth floor of a nineteenth-century building. It had a bedroom, a kitchen and a little basin and toilet, but nowhere to bathe. Every Sunday Rami and Anna would go to the communal baths close to the train station to take a proper shower.

On the ground floor of their building was one of the oldest pastry shops in the city, Robiglio. They could smell the fragrance of pastries, cream and coffee from the early hours in the morning before dawn to late at night when the other shops had already been closed for hours. Anna used to spend long minutes standing in front of the shop window before opening the front door and taking the stairs up to their flat.

Rami had built all their furniture, using leftover pieces of wood from the joiner's workshop at his art academy, and reusing pieces of discarded furniture found in the street. The bed, the sofa, the chairs, the table, everything was handmade by Rami. It was not much but it was theirs. Now that she had her certificate Anna went to work nearly every day, doing shifts at a small clinic, and Rami had kept his job at Alberto's restaurant while finishing his studies. Anna helped him write his essays and his dissertation to avoid those language mistakes for which she had fallen in love. They ate prosciutto and melon during the summer evenings to avoid the heat of the hob and would then go to Ponte Vecchio, to sing and chat with friends. There wasn't much more than that to their days, but Anna didn't want anything more.

One evening, going back home, the smell of Robiglio was impossible to ignore. She had to go in. She had to stare at the rows of sweets, and cakes, and biscuits, and pastries. She knew she would regret the expense, but she had to choose one or two – one for Rami for when he came back from the restaurant. She chose a Fruttodoro and a Bombolone. She paid with the few coins in her wallet and flew up the stairs with her pastries. She sat on the chair that Rami had built beside the table that Rami had made and opened her box, finally touching the pastries with her fingers. She grabbed the Bombolone with both her hands and brought it to her nostrils. The granules of sugar stuck to her skin. That smell of fresh sweetness was all hers. She smiled. She hadn't wanted to eat the pastries straightaway, she had wanted to wait for Rami, but the temptation of the sweetness overwhelmed her and after the first bite she could not stop.

Rami arrived a few moments later to find his wife, still at the table, the cake wrappers in front of her, the cream on her fingers and a satisfied expression on her face.

'What happened?' he asked, taking the pastries as a clear sign of celebration.

'I am pregnant.'

CHAPTER FOUR

Ma'amoul

Bethlehem, summer 1979

When Anna saw the house for the first time, she stood mesmerised by its whiteness. She was not used to all that white.

It was not a dirty white, or a yellow white, more a changing white. A whiteness for the light to play with during the day. The bright white of noon. An opalescent pink in the early morning. A warm amber in the late afternoon, holding all the heat of the ending day. At night, the reflection of the moon made it blue.

Anna saw the house for the first time at its whitest, when it was hard to look at without being hurt by its glare. Behind the main gate, the lemon tree offered the only shade at that brightest hour. Anna found relief from the light in the shade of its leaves and green fruits. From there she caught a glimpse of a vast garden.

Her eyes were led there by the grape vines overlooking a strange little pool. She recognised that place from Rami's stories. He had told her once that as a kid, he had tried to baptise the family's chicks. Anna smiled. She had expected something bigger.

Beyond the pool she could see the familiar shape of olive trees, and there were other fruit trees too. But her eyes were drawn back to the imposing shape of the building. It was not what she had imagined when Rami had told her that it was a house over two floors. It looked much taller than that. The columns surrounding and supporting the balcony proved that there was a certain pride in that house.

'Let's go!' said Rami, leading her out from the shade of the lemon tree.

Anna knew they were all waiting for her. To see the woman who their son, brother and nephew had brought from abroad. This was the reason for that summer trip, so that Rami's family could meet his wife.

Rami opened the main door of the house and Anna inhaled the smell coming from inside. It was particular, a mix of soap and herbs. They climbed the stairs to the first floor, which had been built for him, and before Rami could knock at that second door, the entire family was there welcoming them in. Anna was at first impressed by what looked like an excessive number of women. She couldn't even count them, taken by the energy with which they welcomed her, their different voices, the colours and cut of their hair, their dresses, the way they moved their hands around her, their words, the line of their eyes. It took a few minutes for Anna to see that there were also men in the room, hidden by the women's bodies. At the back of the room Anna spotted the timeworn features of someone who could be Rami in forty years' time, and of someone else who could be Rami in ten years' time. They could only be Rami's father and brother, and she wondered why there was such variety of femininity in the family but such uniformity on the male side. It seemed as if the women took up all the space, and the unbound stream of their words was met with a resigned silence from the men. Helena, Rami's mother, was standing in the middle of the room. Her beauty was inescapable, and Anna could see the imprint of it in all the faces surrounding her: in their lips, in their cheekbones, and of course in those green eyes. Anna sensed that Helena was intimately connected with every other person in the room, including her newly arrived youngest son, and she could not help but feel drawn to that woman too.

'Ta 'ali hon, you must be tired,' said one of the female voices.

'… and hungry,' added a second.

Helena's hands led her towards one of the white sofas in what looked like a formal living room. The whiteness was the main element inside the house too, with high ceilings and arches dividing up the space. But the dominance of the white was diluted by the many colourful objects around the house.

'Do you want to drink some water?'

'Or probably you prefer some lemonade?'

'Was the trip difficult? Did they ask you many questions at the airport?'

They were all trying to speak slowly, using basic words in English, but Anna still could not follow, so Rami had to translate every question into Italian. She sat stiffly on the sofa, trying to process everything going on around her, the questions being asked, the looks being exchanged, the food being served.

On the large coffee table Rami's sisters were arranging trays carried in from the kitchen, one after the other. There was a small bowl with salted seeds and pistachios, almonds, cashews. Another tray for the fresh fruit, loquats, figs, grapes. And then a tray of pastries smelling strongly of cinnamon and nutmeg.

'Ahwe?' said Helena, offering a small cup to Anna.

Anna knew that this word, so similar to her Italian *acqua*, water, didn't mean water at all. It meant coffee, as Rami taught her. She also knew the grainy taste of that coffee, because

Rami had prepared it for her a couple of times. It was so rich and dense, sharp and sweet at the same time. She grabbed the cup with a grateful nod of the head.

Through the forest of bodies, legs and arms moving all around her, setting the table, bringing more food, serving coffee, Anna could see a hand reaching for a green marble box and opening it to take out a cigarette. Rami's father, George, was looking at her while she was looking at him. He smiled, and then, stretching his arm, offered the green box to her.

She accepted it without thinking and took out a cigarette. She was bringing it to her lips when she suddenly stopped and put it back in the box. George was still looking at her, but with a questioning gaze. She put the box back on the table and picked up the cup that had been filled with more coffee.

'Tutto bene?' Rami asked her.

'Sì, all good,' said Anna. It was true, she was feeling overwhelmed, and she didn't know how to answer all the questions or whether to accept the things she was offered, but she felt an innate sense of excitement.

'Shukran,' she said to everyone, wanting to thank them but worried about getting the pronunciation wrong and saying the worst word ever.

'Ahlan wa sahlan, habibti!' said Helena, with enthusiasm, and everyone followed with little sounds and words of what seemed approval for Anna.

The excitement gave way to the enjoyment of the food and company. Anna pretended she was following the conversation, even if they were all aware she couldn't, so after a while her attention moved from the people to the food. She was hungry, and her love of sweets took over. The pastries looked like fat biscuits of different shapes. She lingered with her fingers before choosing one. They felt like sand to her touch, and the smell was irresistible ... across the aroma of flowers, butter, spices, sugar, she could see the family she had just become part of. They were all talking and sipping their coffee and eating their pastries with the natural manner of many years of talking that way, sipping their coffee that way and eating their pastries that way. She was there trying everything for the first time, trying to find her own way and make it hers. She bit into the biscuit. Her teeth sank into it, through the powdery layer of crust, to a soft brown paste. Dates. It was like nothing she had ever had before.

She closed her eyes in delight and when she opened them again George was looking at her, clearly considering this new woman in his family's life. Anna thought minutes went past without George moving his eyes, so she decided to ask for help and with her elbow she poked Rami's side.

'What happened?' asked Rami.

'Should we not tell them that I am pregnant?'

Anna didn't know exactly which of the words Rami had just used with his family meant that she was pregnant, but it didn't take long before Helena and the other women jumped up from the sofa, hugged her and told her who-knows-what and touched her hair and her belly. She had now the full attention of the family, as if she had only become part of it in that moment. George stood up and came over to hug his son and daughter-in-law, and Anna noticed that his inquisitive eyes had softened. She wondered if that silent man would be a good grandfather, thinking about the detachment of her own father. But Anna could feel that George had a different role in that family: his silence was not threatening. Behind those eyes there was an enjoyment of the movement and noise around him. That gaze was a way of telling her that he saw her; he knew she was there even if she couldn't speak to them yet.

*

The following days were a continuous back and forth of people coming to meet Rami's pregnant wife, and then of going out, visiting relatives and different places, taking photographs and shopping for the food that Rami couldn't find in Italy – including ma 'amoul, those fat, fragile biscuits, filled with dates, pistachios, walnuts, soaked in flower water and spiced with cherry-seed powder.

The house was always full of people and Anna was never left alone. People talked to her continuously, asking her questions, caressing her and touching her belly, offering her food and drinks, bringing her gifts, showing her dresses and baby clothes, and she could only nod and smile and say thank you.

Anna soon learnt that the best place to sit at those long tables of food and gatherings of relatives was next to George. She learnt that those deep gazes were George's way of communicating. In those days of continuous chatting and greetings, and sipping and eating, the silence of this man provided solace to Anna.

There is a photograph taken on one of those days of a big meal eaten among the columns of the terrace of that first floor. Rami took it, standing at the end of the long table, and at the other end George is looking directly at the camera – white hair, short-sleeved white T-shirt, the old skin of his arms wrinkling under the weight of his shoulders. Next to him Anna is looking at the camera too, but without posing. Her thoughts are untouchable. The August sun is strong even in the photograph, and the chit-chat of the table can be heard, through the years and the family camaraderie: people are sitting around the table, others are standing, there must have been so much movement to and from the kitchen, the women bringing salads, bread, lemonade, arak, then rice and meat, and then coffee, tea, sweets. But all the movements are suspended. Yet the stillness doesn't belong to the camera, it seems to belong to the silent understanding between George and Anna.

Rami never really knew what Anna thought of her first trip to that faraway place. Was it what she expected? Rami had never seen her so quiet. He knew it was not just a matter of language because she was quieter with him too. Was it because of all the attention being paid to her? Or the pregnancy? Or was she absorbing the reality of his land? Rami knew she liked being there because of the way she was looking at everything around her, and the joy with which she was eating the food, and smelling the smells, and how she played with the light, uncovering and covering her skin to see the effect of that strong sun on her white, white complexion.

Rami showed her around, not just his hometown, with its square and its church, his old school and the market, but also his old university, with the villas turned into classrooms, hidden and protected by green leaves. They also travelled all the way north to Tabariyya and the lake, and west to the sea, to the old port of Akka and its Ottoman public bath. Anna had even persuaded George to go with them, to everyone's surprise.

Anna learnt that George had not been to Akka since 1948, but that before then, when he was young, he used to love to spend time in that ancient town on the sea.

'He would take his motorbike and leave Bethlehem early in the morning,' Rami told her, 'and he would reach the sea between Haifa and Akka in under two hours and stop for a coffee in the old port. Can you believe it? My father on a motorbike?!'

Anna knew well the feeling of freedom you could get from riding on a motorbike and yes, she could believe that her father-in-law loved that feeling too.

'Three more hours and he was in Beirut,' Rami continued. 'It is incredible that you could do that before! Then there was the revolt of 1936–39 against the English administration, then the war, then in 1948, with the Nakba, our world shrank. My father refused to leave Bethlehem after that. I can't blame him. Whenever we try to go around, we are just reminded of what the occupation has done to our land.'

Anna saw George from far away, through the crowd of women in their embroidered thobes and men selling produce from the villages surrounding the town. Piles of fresh vegetables towered all around: small, chubby aubergines to stuff and cook in tomato sauce or to pickle; ya'tin, a greenish-white vegetable between an eggplant and a courgette to stuff and cook with white dense yogurt; fa'ous, like cucumbers but fuzzy and sweeter; fresh herbs and green leaves, scented parsley, maramia, a sweet sage for stomach ache, mulukhya, a wild mallow to boil in broth and eat with yellow rice and meat. The air was full of the slightly rotten smell of summer-heated fruit – grapes, figs, prickly pears – and the sounds of overflowing markets. Anna loved the intimacy of the market, a place of shade after the white light on the white streets, where people were pushed towards one another in the flow of the crowd and it was possible to touch and whisper.

George was sitting on an old wooden chair, under the awning of his butcher's shop, and from the distance he looked as if he was living at a slower pace to the rest of the market. His movements were meticulous and unrushed. Anna drew closer and before he could see her, she watched how much care he took as he pulled a grape away from the bunch, directing it into his mouth, breaking a piece of flat bread and adding it to the mixture on his tongue. If she focused enough she could hear the pressure of his teeth on the pulp, until the grape collapsed. Time stopped for a while. Anna was surprised when a clear image came to mind – her grandmother eating bread and foxgrapes under the pergola in Tuscany – and she felt she was in the right place.

'Anna!' called George, bringing her back to the noise of the market. 'Shu bitsawwi? What are you doing here?'

Should she admit that she couldn't stay another second at the family home because it was too hard to make herself understood, to try to be part of the family, to show interest in gossip she couldn't understand? That the only thing she could do was smile and nod, and say la or na'am, even if she didn't really grasp what she was denying and affirming? Should she say that she just wanted to stroll around alone and find out where, for God's sake, she had actually ended up? Had she made the right decision? Was she right in being there? For what? For love? Should she say to that calm man that she had probably just found the answer in his measured movements and his grapes and bread?

'I got lost,' she lied.

'Yalla, sit here, we will go back home together,' said George, patting the chair next to him.

So Anna stayed. They just sat there, without needing to talk, looking out at the crowd, under the huge beef legs and shoulders, whole lambs hanging from the ceiling and the penetrating smell of blood and flesh.

Florence, 1980

'Go home, you have time to get her things ready and come back. She is not ready yet!' said the doctor to Rami.

The hospital was just a few streets north of their flat in Via dei Servi, so Rami ran. The doctor said that there was still time, but Rami didn't want to leave Anna alone.

He rushed down the stairs of that squared building. Once outside, he tried to calm himself down by looking at the name of the streets the way he used to when he had first moved to Florence. The main door of the hospital was in Piazza dell'Indipendenza – named after the insurrection calling for annexation to the new Italian state. Then he went south through Via Nazionale – still named in honour of the new nation – and then all the way down the long Via Guelfa – named after a battle won by the Guelf faction in 1289. He kept running straight to Via degli Alfani – named after the famous banker family that had lived in Florence in the fourteenth century. Then finally he turned right into his street, Via dei Servi. He reached number 42, the sweet smells of pastries from Robiglio welcomed him, and he ran up the stairs to the fourth floor. He grabbed the few things he thought Anna might need and rushed back to the hospital.

He had taken less than twenty minutes to go and come back, but his son had been faster.

'The doctor thought you would faint, he thought you were too young to see it,' said Anna.

But the doctor didn't know how far Rami had travelled in space and time to be there in that moment.

All the decisions Anna had taken so far had led her to that moment. She didn't regret them; she just couldn't believe how fast and full of consequences the last few years had been. Love was the problem, wasn't it? From the moment she had fallen in love, her decisions were not just her decisions anymore; her decisions also affected someone else and she, in turn, was affected by someone else's decisions. To love is to compromise. And that compromise, that complete entanglement with another being was at the same time a burden and a yearning. From the moment she had fallen in love with Rami, the decisions she had taken were because of love. In that blindness and yet determination to do everything possible to make that love work. And two years after that language mistake, they had Marwan. Because of her little boy too, already almost one, Anna's choices were not hers alone anymore.

So here was the crossroads: Rami had been offered a job back at his old university in Birzeit, one hour from where his family lived. That meant leaving Florence, the place that had given Anna so much freedom and happiness. Leaving the job she had chosen for herself. Leaving her country and culture for an unknown one. Raising her son, educating her son, feeding her son with the customs, the books, the food that were not hers. And yes, leaving her family. Her father who, for all his harshness, had still helped her when she moved away from the village, and had welcomed Rami without judgement. Her mother, whose meekness outraged Anna for years. Yet now being a mother herself, Anna understood why certain battles are not worth fighting. Her grandmother who was getting older – how could she give her strength from so far away? Moving to Palestine meant Marwan was going to grow up with none of them, not knowing the taste of baccalà, the winds blowing down the hills, the wild bicycle races.

The nostalgia surprised Anna: now that she finally had the chance to leave what she had always wanted to leave, a feeble bond with her childhood home appeared; perhaps, after all, she too belonged.

If love played a big role in Anna's final decision to move to Palestine, then so did that haunting desire for lontananza, that conviction that the world could offer so much more. At that crossroads, Anna decided to start anew. To do what Rami had done all those years for her, learning to speak her language, learning about her culture, eating her Italian food.

She felt a fondness, starting to grow stronger, for that country that Rami wanted so much.

'My father wants to come here,' said Rami, closing the door of their new flat behind him.

It was a more spacious place, located in a village outside Florence. They were no longer living among the palaces of Florence, the streets and the alleys named after those who made the history of the town and then the nation. There wasn't the duomo, just at the end of the road. And there wasn't Robiglio, with its tempting displays of pastries and biscuits. But there was a shower, in the toilet, just for them. A modern flat with everything needed to grow a baby. Marwan wasn't exactly a baby anymore. Almost two years old now, he was becoming bigger and bigger and the little flat in Florence couldn't keep up with his needs.

'Non capisco. Why does he want to come now? We are moving there in a couple of months!' answered Anna, standing up from the sofa.

'Non lo so. He said he wants to visit Italy, and since we are not going to be here for long, he thinks it is his last chance.'

'But where is he going to stay? And what is he going to do? I can't take any leave from work!'

'Ha detto di non preoccuparsi, that he can look after himself and can also look after Marwan.'

'But he has never left his town for more than one day, and he doesn't speak the language!'

'I am sure everything is going to be fine!'

When George arrived, Anna knew that it was not going to be fine. The man, who she remembered majestic with his white hair and deep eyes, was barely recognisable. He had lost weight, his skin had faded from a dark olive colour to the yellow of bad olive oil, his white hair, once full and pure white, had become thin and like old paper. As soon as George saw Rami and Anna, he smiled, his eyes sunken even deeper in his hollow face. He was meeting Marwan for the first time, and it was probably the idea of having another boy in the family that made him smile so much. But Anna, who had learnt to read so much in the silences of that man, knew there was something else. She wondered if that smile came not from the idea of having another boy in his house dominated by women, but from the reassurance that there would be someone to take his place.

'Keef halak?' she asked, even before saying hello. *How are you*. It had been nearly two years since they had seen each other, and she had made progress with her Arabic, getting ready for their move to Bethlehem. George looked at her with a surprised and amused expression.

'Mabsouṭ!' he answered.

Well, but not *well well*. George trusted Anna and trusted her intelligence enough to know that she had grasped something, but he behaved as if nothing was happening. He wasn't here to explain.

'Non credo, cioè, I am not sure your father is okay,' said Anna that night, sharing the sofa with Rami.

'Probably. He coughed the whole day, but he told me that these last few months the weather has been bad.'

'It's not just the cough, it's everything else. He barely ate today.'

'This is because we don't cook well enough, we don't have my mother's skill,' joked Rami, but Anna was right.

'Why don't you take him to the hospital tomorrow, and we can try to convince him to have some tests.'

This is not why I came here, thought George, lying on his hospital bed. He hadn't come to see Florence with its indestructible bridge, nor the river, nor the duomo, nor the museums, nor even the famous steak, la Fiorentina. He hadn't even come to see Rami, or Anna for that matter. He had come for Marwan. The little chubby boy. The last few days with his grandson had brought back the feeling he had had when Rami was born, when he had felt ready to take care of another human being. He wondered why he always realised he was ready when it was too late. Those hospital tests were not going to come back quickly, were they? It's not true that bad news travels fast. Bad news takes its time to strike you, as if you have time to waste.

But when Anna came back she had a big smile on her face.

'Buone notizie! It all looks okay, it probably really was just the weather, but the doctor says you need to take care of yourself anyway.' That was Rami, pretending to translate Anna's smile.

George tried to believe them, even for just a second, but he knew that they knew. He just wondered why they were lying. Were they trying to put the burden of breaking the news onto someone else's shoulders? Why then had they forced him to take those tests? No, it must be something else. Were they trying to leave him in peace to enjoy his last days in Italy without sombre conversations? Did they really think he didn't know?

How couldn't he know? He knew he was dying. He didn't need doctors or tests to tell him. His body told him. First the lack of sleep told him, as he lay in bed waiting for the sun as though it was never going to rise back again. Then the muscles left without strength. He felt like the pieces of meat that he sold in his butcher's shop. Hanging there, with no blood left. Then the cough had arrived, and he knew that his breath would be the next thing to leave him. Helena said he should stop smoking, that it was all those cigarettes which made him cough like an angry donkey. He didn't stop. It was too late to stop anyway. And then his appetite left too. He had never been a voracious eater, but he had enjoyed sitting at the table, looking at the clean tablecloth, trays and bowls scattered all over, the plates filled with rice, thick sauces and broths, the bright colour of the fresh salads, the smell of mint, parsley, lemon and the warm brown of the toasted almonds. And of course, on top of everything, the pieces of cooked meat that had been cut by his own hands. All that food shared by the hands and mouths of the people he had helped give birth to, he had fed and seen becoming adults, and his wife with the rainforest in her eyes, all the people he loved.

George could recognise when a life was reaching the end. He had seen it many times in his animals' eyes. They knew it. And he knew it too. And he was sorry. He could have done more for the people seated at that table. He could have told them stories instead of choosing silence. And what about that new little boy in the family? George would be dead before Marwan could remember him. This was why he was here, this was why he had left his country, his town, his butchery, his house built out of love. No other reasons but to be in some photographs next to Marwan so that the little boy could look back at them and ask about him. He tried to smile as he never had before. He didn't want his grandson to think he had been a silent, grumpy old man! But who would be able to tell Marwan who that man had really been? If only he could say now all the words he had never spoken before. He tried to talk to the little boy and tell him what he had never said to anyone else, but the little boy looked back at him with his joyful brown eyes and tried to grab with his little fingers George's breath and lips, gibbering and giggling at the old man. There was no need for words then, and a different, grateful silence came back to him.

CHAPTER FIVE
Cheese, Butter and Labaneh

I FIND IT REALLY HARD to imagine my mother during those first months in Palestine, when my parents and my one-year-old brother were living in the big white house with my recently widowed grandmother and my father's older sister.

They took the room close to the bathroom, the one sharing a wall with the kitchen. I slept in that room myself for a few months during the summer of 2018. While falling asleep on the hot white sheets, with the cold breeze of the night and the voices floating in from the streets, I kept thinking about them there, in that same bed, nearly forty years earlier. It's not a room for privacy. There are two windows, one facing the neighbour's house just one or maybe two metres away. The other looks onto a balcony, which can be accessed from the kitchen. I struggle to imagine how, in that room, my parents managed to start their new life and conceive their second son.

I wonder who my mother was then. So young, with one child, and pregnant with a second, in a foreign country, with no friends or language. I can't help but believe that she was too in love, naive. What was she thinking, following like this a man to a place of such instability and oppression? I can't visualise her: what she looked like at twenty-five, how she expressed herself, how she moved from room to room in that house or through the streets of Bethlehem. And yet I am sure she was happy – after all, she had followed her dream to see a bigger world, to be far away from her village.

When she told me stories from that time, she did so laughing. I try to put myself in her place: what would I do? How would I speak? Where would I go? When I try to answer these questions, I don't just use my imagination, I draw on my own experiences and feelings in those same places, and I find myself in the bewilderment of this Palestinian identity that has always been mine, but that I have never thoroughly lived. And I suspect this bewilderment matched hers. When I walk the streets of Bethlehem I can see her steps in my own; in the faltering words that come from my mouth, I can hear the echo of her words, our voices sharing the same struggle with the language. In trying to understand her excitement and frustrations, I can feel our shared desire to belong and yet to be elsewhere. As I keep writing, it's not always evident what is mine and what is hers, or if there is such a thing as mine and hers.

*

Bethlehem, 1981–82

The first floor of the white house became Anna and Rami's home. They slept in Rami's childhood room, with the window facing the backyard balcony – the everyday balcony used for hanging the laundry and drying the wild mallow before making mulukhiya.

Anna liked that balcony because she didn't need to maintain any pretensions. She could go out there in her nightgown with messy hair and smoke a cigarette. She could go out into the sunlight, among the washed white linens and her mother-in-law's black dresses of widowhood. She could escape there, for just a few minutes, leaving Marwan in his grandmother's care. She would sit down on the floor, in the shade and with the smell of soap emanating from the washing line. She just needed a few moments for herself, to let her surroundings sink in: the tiles, the noises coming from the streets, the dust blown by the breeze were unfamiliar to her.

When Anna had come to visit Palestine for the first time – two years ago already – it had been for just a few weeks during the hottest time of the year.

Now her life was here. All the things that she had liked during her first trip, everything that she had looked at with curiosity, now needed to be learnt. Incomprehensible things needed to become familiar, names needed to be remembered, words needed to be memorised and then assembled to mean something.

Anna spent her evenings sitting at the kitchen table trying to decipher the conversations. She could see lips moving and emotions taking shape in the eyes and wrinkles of the people around her. They were all trying to communicate with her like mime artists, using great gestures and exaggerated smiles. She felt stupid and silence often seemed like the safest answer. She missed George, and without him Marwan became her refuge.

With Marwan she let out all the words she had accumulated during the day. She said them all to her baby, all in Italian, and all so fast that Marwan could answer only by opening his wide brown eyes even wider. But he never gave a word back. Marwan was nearly two and he hadn't spoken a word. Everyone was worried and tried to convince Anna to see a doctor. But Anna knew exactly how Marwan was feeling as she was tempted to do the same. No words, just a long line of *babababababa*.

You just need someone, just one person, who can understand your gibberish and then you don't need all the other words, Anna would tell herself, counting down the hours until Rami came home from work.

Rami was working as the artistic projects coordinator for Birzeit University. Maybe now, he thought, he would be able to make something of indestructible beauty. But the university, targeted as a place where resistance might brew, was still facing the same aggression by the occupying army as when Rami was a student – the soldiers bursting in, the imposed closures, arrests, protests, onions, flags on the roof. If anything it was becoming worse.

'I will be back at five,' Rami repeated every day, so that Anna would know when it was time to worry. Was it him that had been arrested this time? Had they stopped him on the drive home? She could wait a bit longer. Quarter past, twenty past, maybe there is traffic, he might have finished later, but every minute was a cloudy mixture of thoughts, what should I do, who should I call, am I worrying too much? Until finally the door opened.

During the day, before Rami came home, Anna would follow Helena around the town and the house. She spent hours observing her mother-in-law's way of walking, talking with other women in the streets, bargaining for the best prices for aubergines and beans, and then passing in front of the butchery where her husband used to sit beneath the hanging meat. She didn't say a word and moved on. They would then go back home, where Marwan would move from Anna's arms to Helena's arms with the same comfort.

Anna watched Helena being a grandmother. The connection that Helena seemed to have with her offspring was now there too, between Helena and Marwan.

Helena was peeling the green beans, sitting on a chair on the big balcony, the whiteness of the midday sun barely touching her skin in between the shade of the columns. Marwan, crawling at her feet, was playing with the green skins of the beans that had fallen onto the floor. Helena talked to him, speaking in long sentences, as if to explain the things around him.

The two women had their conversations too, in a combination of different languages and gestures. If Anna had found her way to communicate with George in shared silence, with Helena she had a dialogue made up of Italian and Arabic, with a bit of French thrown in from Helena's European education, and the Spanish she remembered from her childhood in Honduras. It was as if they both knew they couldn't speak the other's language but didn't care.

'Rami is not here, forse avrà trovato traffico,' said Anna, trying not to look too worried. And Helena touched her shoulder, looking at the clock on the wall, feeling what Anna had said.

Through Helena, Anna started to understand the world into which she had moved. She learnt who the best market sellers were, which ones you could bargain with, the best colour and shape of grape leaves, how to ask for the price, the best season for apricots and almonds. Or the tricks for washing away the stains from Marwan's clothes, or how to ignore people in the street looking at this strange couple of women talking their mixed-up language, or how to win a fight with Rami, when to compromise and when not to.

Anna found in Helena what Teresina had taught her during their bicycle rides from the countryside down to the village. Anna could see the same rebellious stubbornness in Helena's eyes. And Helena must have recognised it too, a certain obstinacy in her daughter-in-law, because it was from there that their connection started.

*

When Anna discovered she was pregnant again, it was the white cheese that let her know. In Italy there was nothing like it. There were cheeses like parmesan, dry and flaky. There were cheeses like ricotta or gorgonzola, creamy and fresh. There were cheeses like mozzarella with its stretched fibres. But, however hard she tried, she couldn't think of anything to compare with the jibne beda, the white cheese. It was a stubborn cheese, a cheese that needed to be worked before being eaten. Small hard white squares, salty like sea rocks. Anna loved them.

'La habibti! Mish tokli hek! Inti lazim wash it with warm mayye, water, agua caliente, plusieurs fois before you can eat it,' Helena tried to explain, miming the movements of the hands under the tap of warm water.

Anna knew the process, but she wanted the cheese now. It was true though that the jibne became a different cheese after a good bath. The white faded into yellow at the edge, the small blocks became less hard, and the saltiness became bearable. After the warm wash, it was no longer hard, or creamy, or stringy, or oily. It was rubbery. She pressed the surface with her index finger, and the white layer pushed back. Anna ate jibne at every meal, and with everything. Cucumbers and tomatoes. Bread and olives. But her favourite combination was jibne and watermelon. She had looked at it with terror the first time she was offered some, but there was something romantic in that strange combination, almost like her and Rami. That was her favourite way of eating it for a while, then she learned to cook it.

Jibne didn't melt. Never. It stayed strong in the heat, making little squeaky sounds as it fried. But it never melted. When Anna put it in her flatbread and bit down, she realised that she didn't know any words to describe this new texture – in Italian, let alone Arabic.

CHEESE, BUTTER AND LABANEH

It was while cooking a slice of jibne that Anna experienced her first morning sickness. She was pregnant again. When she had been pregnant with Marwan, she had never experienced any sickness. It was as if Marwan was enjoying the food she was eating. But this time she couldn't go near anything without needing to run to the toilet. Even jibne became untouchable.

'It's all normal,' her women-in-law kept telling her, with giggles and other comments Anna felt too sick to even try to understand. They were all excited about the new baby and had already started betting on different names for a boy or a girl. They looked at her with tenderness and pity. The Italian woman, crawling onto the sofa, trying to keep her nausea under control.

Anna wondered what they thought of her. She wanted to tell them, that yes, she knew it was normal, she was a nurse, she had already had a child, she had been alone then too. But she couldn't really answer, partly because if she opened her mouth, she would probably need to run to the toilet again! Partly because she still couldn't put together a sentence longer than ana biddi mayyee.

It was when the fever came that Anna no longer knew what was normal and what was not. Rami started to ask her medical questions she couldn't answer. She tried to think back to her nursing books and regretted having left them back in Italy. She tried to remember the pages about pregnancy, scanning her memory for something about prolonged fever and sweat and those strange pains along her shoulders and knees. But nothing came to mind.

'It's brucellosis,' Rami translated from the doctor, when he finally convinced Anna to take some tests. 'It's usually caught from unpasteurised milk and the soft cheeses made from the milk of infected animals.'

Anna could see big images of jibne beda all over her nursing books.

'We need to start treatment immediately if you want to have a chance with the baby,' the doctor told Rami.

'Do you know what he is talking about?' Rami asked Anna.

Anna knew and put her hands on her belly as if the child knew too. She could find, suddenly clear in her memory, the page in her nursing book listing the symptoms, causes and effects. Abortion, preterm delivery, low birth weight, foetal death, congenital malformation, maternal death. Raw unwashed jibne, jibne with cucumber, jibne with watermelon, fried jibne. Anna missed home.

*

Bethlehem to Ramallah, 1982

As part of the cure, the doctor prescribed Anna as little movement as possible, to lie in bed, to get complete rest. With the summer approaching, that was more easily said than done, the bedsheets becoming unbearably hot under her sweaty body aching with the illness, the stillness, and for the baby. And how could she ignore Marwan's need to play and for cuddles? She couldn't even lift him up.

'Mish mushkile habibti! I can do it!' Helena said, luring Marwan away from Anna and towards the kitchen.

Anna could hear her boy's and her mother-in-law's giggles. Forced into bed and into inaction, Anna could clearly hear the cutlery being set out on the tables, and the songs coming from the radio, the call of the peddlers – ka'ek, ka'ek! Khamse il kilo il batata! Ta'abored Ta'abored ta, ta, ta, ta, ta, ta … Or the arguments of the neighbours – la! Mish zay hek! La, wallahi? Yin'al abuku! She felt she could map the whole area by sound. She swore she could even guess the direction of the prayers: recognising the churches from the ringing of their bells and the mosques from the call of their muezzins. After a few weeks of inactivity in bed, she had mapped the house, the neighbourhood, and finally the town.

She felt she knew the life of the town better than anyone: what time the bread vendor would pass by with his wooden barrow, when the best songs were broadcast on the radio, what made Um Ali – the woman next door, mother of five – mad, which muezzin could hold the longest note.

Soon, however, Anna realised that somehow those sounds had detached themselves from what had produced them and entered a reality shaped by her own imagination, making her wonder what was real and what was not. Was he selling ka'ek, the sweet bread? And had Um Ali really said *damn your father* to her own children? Was she sure that it was Fairuz's voice coming from the radio? Was the bell coming from the north or from the east?

All the sounds and noises which had started to become familiar were once again surrounded by mystery. A bit uncanny even. That room was too small, the noises were starting to haunt her, her baby was too quiet. Anna needed to do something.

She started to think about those first months living in Bethlehem. She had enjoyed the presence of her mother-in-law, the way Helena had introduced her to this new life. In the beginning Anna had felt natural to be there, led gently into this new world. But there was something awkward about staying longer in that big white house, stuck in bed, while the household was busy and its women were all around her, like in a beehive.

It was time to move out.

'Dobbiamo spostarci,' Anna said to Rami one night. He had come back home an hour later than usual and came to sit on the bed to see if she was okay.

'What do you mean moving?'

'Finding our own place, la nostra casa, vicino, closer to your job.'

'Ma il dottore ha detto ...'

'I know what the doctor said, but I am nearly out of the most dangerous weeks and with the medicines and a bit more attention I will be okay, bene, anzi bene bene!' she added, smiling. 'I can even ask my cousin, Silvana, to come and help me. She would love to come and visit me!'

'Ma ...'

'I don't need to do much. You can make most things!'

'Ma ...'

'Rami, I can't take it anymore: worrying about you every day! And with the invasion of Lebanon and the protests against it, and all the people the occupation army is arresting. No, I can't go on like that! Every day is more and more dangerous. I don't need one more reason to be agitated!'

Anna knew she had won the argument, just as Helena had taught her: insist until you find the soft spot.

So in the summer of 1982 they moved to a flat in Ramallah that they could afford, with Rami's brother's physical and financial help. They also managed to buy and install a small TV just in time for the World Cup final, which Anna was excited about watching.

In front of that new television set, Anna, Rami and Silvana, who had come to help as promised, celebrated the three goals scored by Italy against West Germany and lifted up Marwan as if he were the gold cup. A few days after that victory, Marwan started to finally say his first proper word after weeks of saying only bababababaa and mamamama. Palla, tabeh, ball he kept repeating in his two languages, pointing at Anna's belly. Anna had put her hand and Marwan's on it, and they felt the baby kicking.

Relief. And it was a relief that Rami could go to work and come back so easily – commuting in less than fifteen minutes. Their new flat was midway between the centre and the university, at the very edge of the town. After those last houses on the outskirts, there was nothing but hills. They were on the ground floor of the building with a big garden surrounding them, with bushes of pink and yellow roses and a tall lemon tree. They spent long evenings listening to the calls of the cicadas, drinking fresh lemunada, playing with Marwan. Anna showed to Silvana all the reasons she fell in love with Rami's land. The orange sunsets and the smell of bread toasted on the fire. People's kindness at the market when they were trying to explain to Anna how to cook the vegetables they were selling. The big gates of Jerusalem and how domes of churches and mosques emerged together from the roofs of the old city. That was the life she had always wanted, what she and Silvana had dreamt and planned for all those years ago back in the village.

It was a new life but it was not less tense: when, in September that year, thousands of Palestinian refugees were massacred in Sabra u Shatila, the university and the whole town exploded in protests and demonstrations. The occupation forces assaulted the students and the protesters, shooting on the crowds, closing the main university buildings and launching tear gas. Anna could now see what Rami had told her for years and, for the first time, she could feel the fear, the frustration, the sense of injustice herself.

Ramallah, close to Rami's university in Birzeit, was completely different to Bethlehem, the town of his childhood. She could see why Rami wanted to be here, attracted by the job, and by the town itself. It was a growing town full of life: students were adding to the population and staying on as young professionals, and artists started to move in too, attracted by the university's facilities, the hopeful atmosphere, and bringing with them their music, their paintings, their poetry. Through Rami's friends and colleagues, Anna could experience all this too. In their living room, they hosted rehearsals for the university theatre and dance performances, games of cards and neighbourhood meetings. With people sitting at the table, on the sofa, on the floor smoking and discussing what they could do, Anna felt again the excitement of her years in Florence, but this time it was not just the big dreams of young people. Here, every gathering was already an act of defiance. The occupation soldiers could storm the flat and arrest them all at any moment if they wanted to. But still they kept going: people in the West Bank were starting to organise. They formed students' committees, women's committees, workers' committees. They created festivals so people could come together. They ran volunteer groups to look after their land, from picking litter on the street to helping each other during the olive harvest. Rami was glowing and if he was not organising one of the activities, he was the first one to participate. They all realised that they needed planning and cohesion if they wanted to survive under and against the occupation. They believed they could change things, shift the political situation, fight for their freedom, and Anna felt immediately drawn to this faith. It was the right place to be, not only for Rami, but also for her and their children.

When Amer was born he was very small, underweight and as white as uncooked jibne beda. But those seemed to be the only effects that eating too much cheese had had on her boy.

The doctor told them that Amer was a perfectly healthy baby, yes a bit small, but that's normal after all. Anna listened to the doctor and then looked at her first boy.

Marwan was nearly three, but he looked like a boy of five. Normal was relative.

Free to move again and go wherever she wanted, Anna explored her new town, Marwan trotting behind her and Amer in her arms. What she loved most was the long walk from the house to Ramallah's centre. Rami asked her if it was not too tiring with two children, but she said no. Making this long walk at sunset with the light lying over the hills, she would smell the bread toasting on fire, while children played on the streets free of cars and people gathered outside to enjoy the evening calm together. Ramallah became her town, one step at a time.

The doctor had told her that she was too thin. That a new mother couldn't be so thin if she wanted to breastfeed her baby. The doctor said it was normal after the brucellosis, but now it was time to bulk up. She needed to eat more. Anna thought about the jibne beda, and a wave of nausea came back. She wondered when she would finally be able to eat it again; or anything else, for that matter. After the fever and medicines, nothing had the same taste anymore. She looked at herself in the mirror. Her cheekbones, under the big lenses of her glasses, were even more visible.

She ate big round flatbreads, dipping them in zeyt and then za'tar. But it wasn't enough, and she didn't really know what to eat. She couldn't trust herself with her few words of Arabic to go out and buy fresh ingredients at the market the way Helena did, and cooking was not her thing.

Along the main road was her favourite place, a little supermarket. Everything was on shelves and most of it was packed and canned and some of the products had labels and even brand names she could recognise. She paused for a few seconds before going in. Her desire for lontananza felt frustrated. She was miles away from the village she had always despised. She was finally here, in her warm place, playing at being the ajnabye, the *foreigner*, and yet she felt safe in a supermarket.

'Ahlan wa sahlan Um Marwan!' the owner, Anthony, greeted her, when she finally entered. She was a trusted customer and he called her with the usual way of addressing mothers in Arabic: mother of Marwan, the first son. She liked it when they called her like that, because it made her feel part of the community.

'Marhaba, keef alak?' she answered, using the first sentence she had learnt back in Italy.

She was trying to learn more words. Every time she had to go out, she would write down and repeat to herself and her boys the two or three words that she absolutely needed for that day.

Qaddeish, how much

khubiz, bread, h pronounced like a little spurt of cough

haleeb, milk, the h pronounced like a breath of solid air

lahme, meat, with the same h of haleeb

bandora, tomato, that sounded like the Italian *pomodoro* but with a running nose.

batata, potatoes, easy one similar to the Italian *patate*, but with a heavy 't', as if it were tiring to say the word.

Shopping lists became lists of new vocabulary and every time Anna lost one, in the mess of the bags, torn apart by Marwan's hands, or forgotten somewhere, she had to start again, asking Rami over and over for the same words. She started repeating all the new words to Marwan, hoping that he could learn faster than she was.

Anna began to move around Anthony's shop. She had to buy the usual things for Rami and the children and would then see if she could find something that might whet her appetite.

There was an aftertaste on the back of her tongue, something

CHEESE, BUTTER AND LABANEH

Anna really wanted but couldn't pin down, until finally she recognised it, there in the middle of Anthony's supermarket.

The memory of bread, butter and anchovies brought Anna back to when she was fifteen years old, and would have done anything rather than go back home and sit at the silent table of her parents. A new bar had opened in the main square of the village and sold all kinds of panini with every sort of filling.

Anna started to go there for lunch, or sometimes an early dinner, rather than going home and she would survive for days on the bar's special offer: panini with butter and anchovies.

'Burro e acciughe!' she said to Marwan.

Could she put together a meal like that with Anthony's help? Or even something similar? She looked at her list: she was sure she had written butter many times before. It was something starting with 'z'. But nothing, she couldn't find or remember anything.

'Butter, burro,' she started repeating to Marwan, hoping that he could remember the word and help her. But he just smiled back, and soon became more intrigued by a can of meat.

She went to the counter, hoping that with some gestures Anthony could understand her.

'Shu biddek, Um Marwan?' asked the owner.

Anna thought a bit more, and then suddenly she remembered: zib, butter.

'Ana biddi zib!' Anna said with pride.

'Shu?' Anthony asked again.

'Zib, zib,' Anna repeated, her finger pointing at the counter with the fresh dairy products.

Anthony looked at Anna's finger and followed the direction, through the counter, toward him. He looked back at Anna, his eyes lost in translation.

'Um Marwan ... mish zib, it's not zib, what do you want?' Anthony begged, coming out from behind the counter to try to stop Anna from repeating that word. A little crowd was all around them. Anna looked at the butter, which seemed so far way. What was wrong with her asking for butter?

'Zibde, zibde!' said a little voice coming from their legs. Marwan had found his way to the counter, his little fingers pressed on the glass. 'Zibde, zibde!'

'Ah, zibde! Um Marwan: zibde, zibde!' Anthony was so happy, and he ran behind the counter to prepare her piece of butter. Anna looked at Marwan, then looked at Anthony, paid for her block of butter and rushed out.

Rami exploded in an irrepressible laughter when that evening Anna told him what had happened in search of explanation.

'Zibde, *zibde*, Anna!' Rami said, forcing the 'd' sound. '*Zibde* means butter, *zib* means dick!'

Anna blushed at the memory of her hand pointing at Anthony. Then she looked at Marwan. The right word at the right moment.

*

Tabariyya Lake, 1983

'Mish lazim itdallek honak, you will burn your skin!'

Anna ignored Helena's voice. And everyone else's. She was lying on the sand, just in front of the lake's water. She had dreamt about this light for years. She suspected that she had lived there in one of her past lives, if there were such things. She felt she was in her natural habitat. Maybe she had been a rich sultana, her body covered with precious oils and rose petals.

'Your skin is all red!' Helena warned again.

Her sisters-in-law would often touch her skin, pearly, hairless and soft, in admiration. And Rami had told her many times that her skin was one of her most sensual features. But not for her. So she was lying on the sand, trying to absorb the sun, trying to tan even just a little.

She looked at her naked skin and pressed her forearm with her index finger. It left a quick white depression and then came back to red. Maybe it was working: her melanin reacting to the light. Yes, her skin was red, not a dark olive as she hoped, but it would probably change with more exposure to the sun.

The heat of the sun was suddenly blocked by a huge shadow. She opened her eyes. A little head was hanging over her face, big loving eyes, and a smiling mouth drooling onto her nose.

Amer had crawled towards her and was asking for the attention she hadn't given him for the last hour. But Anna was not ready to leave her reverie. Her eyes closed again, dozing. A sticky hand smacked her cheek, and her eyes opened again. Amer was trying to walk over her face. She sat up and her imaginary life was gone. She took Amer into her arms. She had done her best to have that dream life, Anna thought, looking at the small body of her boy. After all, she was in a faraway place, surrounded by light, sand, the honey sweets. There was also so much more here than she could ever have imagined. She looked at Rami, playing in the distance with Marwan, Helena and the rest of the family. This was her reality. She stood up, holding Amer, and walked towards the others.

'I told you that you were going to burn your skin,' said Helena when Anna joined them in the shade.

Without the glow of the light, Anna could see that her skin was starting to turn so red it looked almost purple. She didn't look like her sisters-in-laws, or have the colour of Marwan's suntan. She looked like someone who got into a fight and lost. When she pressed her index finger on her arm, her skin cracked in pain.

'Mish battal! It's not too bad,' she answered, trying to convince herself more than her mother-in-law.

But by the end of the day, after her evening shower, the pain was unbearable. She couldn't sit. She couldn't lift Amer, even less Marwan, without her chest burning. She couldn't bend her knees or elbows without feeling the skin cracking. She looked at her face in the mirror. This was not the image of a rich sultana. She didn't know if it was the tiredness, sunstroke, the pain, or disappointment, but she started to cry.

'Habibti, la! Ma tibkish. No need to cry.' Helena came to check on her. 'We are obstinate, 'anidat! We stand still and face the sun. And if we get burnt, we just need to remember that grilled meat goes perfectly with yogurt!'

Anna didn't really get what her mother-in-law was saying. What did she say about lahme u labaneh?

Helena took Anna into the kitchen and helped her take her clothes off. Then she opened the fridge and took out the glass jar of yogurt. Before Anna could think about what was happening, her legs, belly, back, arms, chest and face were being covered with a dense layer of yogurt that her mother-in-law rubbed gently onto her skin with her hands. Her skin felt immediate relief.

'Lahme u labaneh zaky ktir, perfect combination!' Helena repeated and started to laugh.

Anna started to laugh too, a mixture of release and pain, big dollops of yogurt splashing from her body onto the floor.

In that moment, in the kitchen with her mother-in-law, Anna finally saw that her dream of finding a home in a faraway place had come true. Her naked body smelled not of precious oils and rose petals, but of grilled meat and yogurt.

CHAPTER SIX

Chicken Breast

Birzeit, 2018

Hoda opens the door and comes out into the garden. She doesn't expect to see someone like my father standing in front of her gate. She narrows her eyes to focus on the tall figure, to reconnect it with something in her mind.

'Msh ma'oul!' She lets out something between a whisper and a squeak.

She recognises him. She runs and kisses him and hugs him and asks why he is there, after all this time! Oh my God, why didn't you tell me you were coming?

Out of the corner of her eye she keeps looking at me. Hoda doesn't know who I am, and yet there is something familiar about me. When my father reaches out to me with his arm to introduce me, Hoda understands. She didn't know my parents also had a daughter. She hugs and kisses me with the same warmth with which she welcomed my father. It doesn't matter if we have never met before. As a daughter, I immediately receive the same affection and confidence.

We sit in her summer living room – the windows opened beneath the shade of the trees and looking over the white hills. Hoda disappears into the kitchen. She comes back with a tray of coffee cups and then starts to talk, fast. I try to keep pace, but I grasp only basic sentences and some names, including my mother's. I piece together the conversation. My father is talking about my brothers and Hoda is talking about her own children.

She keeps looking at me every now and then and asks me questions. I struggle to answer before my father comes to the rescue, explaining that I am still learning.

'Your mum didn't talk much either.'

After some more attempts at communicating with me, she gives up and I keep quiet on the corner of the sofa, sipping my coffee and trying not to lose track of the conversation.

Hoda stands up and disappears again inside the main interior of the house. It's my chance to ask my father about what I have missed from the conversation. He says that they are just formalities between old acquaintances. The usual. What happened afterwards. How the children grew up. I haven't heard from you for so long, what do you do now? I didn't know that she had died. Someone told me many months after. I am sorry I didn't call you. Here the situation is getting worse and worse. They do what they want, and we fade away.

The two of them went through the main events of their lives at this fast pace. Thirty years in less time than it takes to drink a cup of coffee. Somehow this summarising scares me.

Hoda and my mother had worked together for a few years. My father had been for a while the chair for the workers union at Birzeit University and had persuaded the board members to pay for a kindergarten for the children of staff and students. The kindergarten was in a small house, close to the main university building. It was a way of having parents and children in the same place. In case of a sudden curfew or yet one more incursion from the soldiers, they could at least all be together. My mother was offered a job: her nursing skills were highly regarded, and language wasn't a barrier for conversations with toddlers. It was the perfect position for my mother. She could finally work again, and my brothers could play with the other children in the kindergarten, all learning Arabic in the process.

Hoda was hired to work there too and that is when she met my mother. She was probably the closest thing my mother had to a friend at that time. Hoda wears black trousers and a black T-shirt, for her widowhood. Her hair is brown, but the dye gives it a reddish brightness. She smells of homemade food, but I can't pin down what exactly. Cooking is what she does now to make a living, preparing meals and banquets for events happening in the area. I wonder what she looked like when she was working with my mother, and what my mother would look like now, next to her friend.

When Hoda comes back into the summer living room, she brings a tray of sambousek. She stretches the tray towards me so I can take mine.

'La, shrukan.' I have to refuse.

'Tfaddali tfaddali!' She keeps stretching the tray towards me.

'Ma btikdar tokol minnu, 'yndha hasasie, an allergy, to gluten.' My father needs to intervene again.

I can't eat sambousek or anything else Hoda tries to offer to me instead. Eventually, she offers me orange juice and I need to say yes. She comes back and gives it to me with a half-smile, sits down and starts to talk with my father again.

I can see that she is ill at ease in my presence. I feel further and further away in the corner of the sofa, right opposite her. I don't talk and I don't eat. I am not part of her memories of the past. I am one of those events that my father needs to tell her about, filling in a gap of thirty years. There is nothing that connects us.

When my father tells her that I would like to come back, maybe with my cousin as an interpreter, to ask her some questions about my mother, she looks surprised. Even a bit irritated.

'Bus shu bidha t'araf?' she asks my father.

I try to explain, but at this point I am not part of the conversation.

'What do you want to know?' my father asks me in Italian.

'What Mamma was like when they worked together, her memories of those years, if she remembers anything in particular,' I say, and my father repeats it in Arabic.

I'm about to change my mind, though, say that I don't need to come back. People seem to remember her only through superficial details. It feels so hard to find out about my mother's life back then that I am contemplating making something up, but I can't. I need to at least try.

For my next visit, I came back with my cousin. Hoda speaks to me in Arabic with a bit of English, and my cousin translates for me in Italian, my mother tongue.

'Qalbha ktir kbir,' said Hoda, bringing her hands to her heart.

'She said that your mum had a huge heart.'

I didn't need a translation. Not because of Hoda's gesture, not because I understood the Arabic words, but because this is what everyone says, again and again. How can I tell Hoda that I want to know more, something else? That my mother must have been made of other organs, other muscles. She couldn't always be all heart, all love, all mother.

Hoda tells me all the best stories about my mother. How my mother endured pain and struggles, how she was always humble and willing to listen, how children loved her, how she learnt the language by herself. All things I already know, that everyone tells me. No one would say anything different, no one would say anything bad about her.

'My father told me that my mother didn't like to cook,' I attempt.

My cousin translates and, after a moment, Hoda starts talking again, looking at my cousin, but her body tilted slightly towards me.

'Bizzapt! Immek, *your mum*, didn't know how to cook. She spent all her money in that supermarket. So expensive because you buy everything jahes, ready-made. The day they paid us she would spend it all in there. At first, Dina, our colleague, and I couldn't understand what Immek was saying or wanted. She didn't talk to us. She only talked with the children. In Italian, walla, and with those baby words she picked up from them and their songs. She learned 'arabi hek. She used those words with us too – papa, bue, didde, dau. She made us laugh. She said that if children could learn like this, she could too. But, Immek bahlef fi alla, didn't need that many words. She filled the space without speaking. She did good things without effort. She never said no and everyone loved her. She made people feel better.

She often ate what the children turned their noses up at and when we asked lesh, why, she said she didn't like to waste the food. We thought that was her only proper cooked meal of the day, so we decided to teach her how to cook. You are spending too much in that supermarket, I told her. You have to buy the ingredients and cook at home.'

*

Birzeit, 1984–86

Anna knew how to cook pasta, but not much more. She and Rami mostly put together cold meals or ate from the many food stalls in the street. Every now and then they would cook kofta out of minced meat, tomatoes, onions and potatoes, but the results weren't satisfactory: sometimes the meat came out too hard, or they forgot to add salt and everything was bland, or for some reason everything became watery. So they didn't attempt it often. They waited to visit Helena for a plate of roz u loz or the filled pastries that they liked. It wasn't just a matter of skill – or lack thereof. Anna thought that cooking was a big waste of time. She enjoyed eating, but every time she went to the kitchen rather than staying in the living room playing with her children, or listening to the conversation of Rami's friends, or reading a book, she saw her mother at the kitchen hob.

But when she had assisted her mother-in-law in the kitchen, it hadn't felt the same. Helena was leading her family from there. She knew which dish to use to solve a quarrel. Which one to evoke nostalgia. She knew the favourite dishes of each of her family members and when to cook something special to call them back if they had roamed too far. In front of her cutting board Helena plotted and manipulated, the kitchen transformed into her seat of power.

Anna had noticed that power even before they had left Italy. When they were still there, Rami's thoughts had often left Florence, drawn back to his mother's kitchen table. He suffered from a nostalgia of the stomach, and Anna had suspected that her mother-in-law's recipes were one of the reasons why they were back here. Still, she couldn't get out of her mind the image of her mother, Vittoria, running around with her pots and pans, between the stove and the fireplace, trying to have everything ready before her husband returned from work.

Anna didn't want to spend time in the kitchen being like her mother, but she had to admit that being able to cook what she craved would give her a sense of control, like her mother-in-law. So, when Hoda offered to teach her, she accepted.

When Anna entered Hoda's kitchen, their colleague, Dina, was there too. On the table there was a whole chicken, the skin and most of its feathers still attached. An image of Vittoria killing and cleaning rabbits and chickens came to Anna's mind, but she pushed it away. This was not that kitchen in the Tuscan countryside.

'Inti lazim use it all,' said Hoda, lifting the corpse of the bird, 'otherwise it's a waste of money. Khsara. The breast is just one tiny part of the chicken. Y'ani, you can do much more with the rest.'

They taught her how to burn the skin over the flames – their hands moving as if they were cradling a baby – how to cut the chicken, how to marinate the best parts for the main dish, touching and stroking the flesh to make it absorb the spices, and how to cook them, grilled, roasted or pan-fried, covered with the dark red of the sumac.

'And what about the rest?' asked Anna, looking at the neck, the bones, the small bulge of the tail. So, they started to show her how to make the broth, simmering it for hours, taking away the white foam from the surface, and waiting for the marrow to come out. And then how to use the broth to cook the rice of roz u loz, or mix it with dried laban to prepare mansaf.

'And what about the rest?' asked Anna, looking at the giblets. So they showed her how to cook every last bit, everything down to the liver, the heart, the gizzards.

Anna went back and forth in Hoda's kitchen, her body getting used to moving from the counter to the stove, from the hobs to the pot of fresh herbs on the table, following the two women in that meticulous use of food, not wasting a drop.

Really, it was no different from her mother's kitchen, from the poverty of the Ventoruccia, that dependence on even the smallest piece of meat. Yet Anna, here with Hoda and Dina, didn't feel the same misery.

Hoda wasn't like Messinella. She didn't tell her that if she didn't clear her plate the devil would burn her little finger. That each crumb left was a sin to pay for – the image of her grand-aunt pointing her finger at six-year-old Anna, everything a sign of God's punishment. With Hoda and Dina as her teachers, necessity became a possibility.

After Amer's birth Anna's breasts had never been the same. It must have been something to do with all that cheese disease. Anna didn't remember this particular discomfort listed in her books among the effects of the illness, but she accepted it nonetheless. Breastfeeding Amer had been more difficult than breastfeeding Marwan; her breasts were in pain and Amer was not taking enough milk to give her any relief.

But then she started to feel a different type of pain. This time it was not around the nipples. It didn't feel like having too much milk in the breast. It was more of a prick in the side.

'Rami, can you come here?' shouted Anna from the bathroom.

She was in front of the mirror, the small light on, her left arm up, the right hand inspecting the soft flesh between her breast and her armpit.

'What are you doing?' asked Rami.

'Can you please touch my boobs?'

'With pleasure,' said Rami, confused and amused at the same time.

'I am not trying to seduce you, I just want you to tell me

if you feel anything different!' Rami was the person who knew her body better than anyone; he would definitely feel if there was something different.

'I can't feel anything!' said Rami, his hands still on Anna's boobs.

'Are you sure? What about here?' Anna moved Rami's hand on a specific spot. 'Don't you think that there is a small ball here?'

Rami took more time, paid more attention to what he was doing and then he felt it too.

The pages of her nursing books came back to Anna. She tried to remember if and where she had read anything about lumps. Cancer was the first word that came to mind, because it was the dramatic explanation that she and her colleagues had always jumped to in nursing school. But she remembered that there were many other possible explanations. A lump in her breast didn't mean cancer, not for certain, Anna told herself.

It was, though. The doctors told her when she went to the hospital. She remembered when the results of George's tests had come back. So this is how you feel when you actually hear the word.

'But it's a benign one,' they added.

Anna saw Rami's expression of relief before hearing his translation.

'But it needs to be removed, because you never know, it is a delicate place. However, we can't do this surgery here. There is a good private surgeon in Ramallah. You can have it done there.'

Anna heard only the word private. A benign cancer was not a problem anymore, the private expenses were.

'Do I really need to get it removed? If it is benign, can it not stay there?'

'There is too much risk of recurrence, and it's not a good thing to leave it there,' translated Rami.

'Is there nowhere else I can have the surgery? Ask them why they don't do it here.'

Anna was desperate to avoid going to the private clinic. She had worked in one of them, back in Italy, as her first nursing job, and knew about the expenses, the favours between hospitals and private clinics. She didn't want to go. She didn't want to pay for her rights. She thought about flying to Italy and having it done there, but the cost of the flights, leaving the children, and having to admit that she needed to go back, that her new country wasn't up to it, stopped her.

Anna told Hoda that they didn't have enough money. That the private doctor had given her a list of prices and options. The one without anaesthesia was the cheapest, because they didn't involve another doctor. Anna did the calculations, adding up or taking away, the income, the rent, the food. She thought about how many chickens she could buy with what was left, and if they cooked and ate every part of it, how much she could save. She thought about asking for a loan, but she didn't want to. She didn't know how to ask for money, and anyway she didn't want any debts. Anna told Hoda that she didn't have any choice but to do it without anaesthesia. She was a nurse after all. Nurses at school practised on each other in order to learn and she had experienced a lot of pain back then. They had learnt to take their own blood so she knew she could stand the pain. Anna decided that this was what she was going to do. Rami didn't need to know.

'This is the price of the surgery,' Anna told Rami.

She saw his face and imagined what he would have looked like if he had known the real price.

CHICKEN BREAST

'It's not a problem,' he said. 'We need to do this and we will do it. It's going to be all right.'

The breast is just one tiny little part of the chicken, thought Anna. You can do much more with the rest.

When she was in pain or when the day turned out to be one of those rotten ones – another university closure, a shooting, not enough money, an argument, friends and students being beaten and arrested – Anna couldn't help but think back to her years in Florence. Almost eight years had already passed from those first months in the city when she had met her friends in Porta a Prato and among them, Rami. What a great year 1978 had been! One of those years that you can look back on and say: see, that, that was one of the happiest moments of my life, you see, then, yes then, something important happened. One of those years when everything syncs, everything is fast and exciting, you are part of something.

Anna's memories of 1978 were so clear in her head. The long debates held in the living room of Rami's flat, when they would all stay up until the early hours of the morning, discussing politics, drinking, smoking, singing, dancing. Anna loved the feeling of exhaustion when she and Rami were finally alone in his room. Their eyes closing heavy while their lips still wanted to kiss.

Or walking the streets, every day a new protest. Important things to fight for! For years they had screamed in the streets, organised picket lines and sit-ins, collected signatures, occupied schools and university. And finally that May in 1978 two laws were approved, which deeply changed Italy. The Basaglia law – which closed all psychiatric hospitals and promoted fairer treatments and conditions for mental health patients – and the law to legalise abortions that, until then, had been punishable by imprisonment. As a trainee nurse and as a woman, Anna had celebrated those laws as a victory. They had finally made something concrete out of their ideals.

But some things take longer to change than laws. Some of the doctors and nurses at Anna's hospital refused to practise or assist in abortion procedures, declaring their moral objections. So Anna volunteered to take their place. She felt this was the first proper thing she had done to fight against the society of her parents.

How many women came to the clinic after the law was approved! Anna had to ask them so many questions, first to check their marital status and how long they thought they had been pregnant, and then to understand the reasons of their decisions. Sometimes the doctors would try to dissuade their patients and Anna would roll her eyes. Anna couldn't understand why they just didn't let these women make their own decisions about their own bodies. No matter how many abortions she had witnessed, no matter how difficult or how simple the procedure had been, how many tears of grief or relief she had helped to dry, Anna could always see in those women and girls' eyes the dignity that came from having control over one's own body and to be valued as a human being above all. That could never be wrong.

Anna brought her hands to her belly. The pain was strong. For a moment she wondered if she had done the wrong thing, if it was her fault. But she remembered those days in 1978 and those first women coming to the clinic, and that soothed her. She remembered the tiles of the toilet in the nuns' residence in Florence. After that doctor had tried to rape her. The disgust she felt at what had been done to her. She felt the same now, but just like back then she wouldn't let those men make her feel guilty for what they had done. The pain in her abdomen was not the result of her choices, it was the result of bad medical procedures. This was not her first abortion. She had already had one after Marwan. It was not the time then and it was not the time now. Anna and Rami didn't have the money for another child. After the breast surgery, her chest was still in pain and her doctors strongly discouraged breastfeeding.

But this second time was different. The doctor did not want to do it. She could tell – she had seen faces like his before, the judgement in the eyes, the smug grin of power. He hurt her with the bladed curette while cutting away the layer of the uterus. He didn't even say sorry.

The sense of injustice hit her again and again – years ago in that toilet cubicle, in the street protesting and being called whores, in front of those doctors who still treated women who wanted an abortion like they were not humans, and now. She took a deep breath and smiled to her boys playing on the carpet of the living room. Anna looked at Marwan and Amer and she thought that maybe that was it: those were her two and only children. She hadn't really thought whether or not she wanted another a child before, but for the first time she realised that probably it wasn't up to her. First the difficulty breastfeeding, then the cancer and now the constant pain in her uterus.

And the occupation was still happening, of course, more vicious than ever, ramping up arrests and assaults, using rocks to break the bones of schoolboys before handcuffing them. How many times had the occupying army closed the whole university with its students and the kindergarten children still inside, how many times had she invented games and stories to distract them, how many times had she hugged Marwan and Amer and the other babies, holding their heads to her chest, her hands on their ears, to calm their fear, to calm her fear?

It was better not to have another child. Yet the idea that she might not have a choice made her feel sick.

She tried to distract herself and looked outside. The pink roses in the garden were opening and the lemon tree was showing its first fruits. There was a smell of toasted bread coming from the kitchen. Rami was playing with their boys and laughter filled the house. The sense of injustice came back. For what had happened to her, for all the things they had protested for in 1978, for that precarious sense of home they had built in this country. There was still so much that needed to be fought for.

CHAPTER SEVEN

Cigarettes and Eggs

WHEN DO YOU KNOW that an uprising is starting? The tension is there, building up, but when do you know that it has become something more than just tension? People see this event, or that, as having been the last straw, but this is hindsight. In the moment, what makes you say, 'Here we are, something has just started'? How do you notice that history just took a sharp turn?

The intifada officially started in December 1987, when a military truck ran over and killed four people in Jabalia refugee camp. Demonstrations broke out in Gaza and then spread in the West Bank. But Palestinians had fought against the occupations for years, with strikes, protests, confrontations, appeals to international law, movements of peaceful resistance and of armed resistance. But nothing had changed. If anything, it just kept getting worse, with more settlements being built and land taken away from Palestinians, harsher economic conditions, more people arrested, tortured, killed. I ask my father how he knew that the intifada had started. The first thing he tells me is the explanation that everyone has been given.

'There was that attack in Gaza, that truck that ran over and killed those workers.'

'Yes, but how did *you* realise that something had actually changed?'

He thinks a bit and keeps on offering me reasons from the official accounts. I don't give up. I want to know how history actually steps into people's lives.

'I couldn't find cigarettes!' he eventually says. 'There were strikes, and shops were closing, but this had happened before. Still, we could find our cigarettes. Then the cigarettes disappeared, and you could only find them in this man's basement, who knows where they came from, and it's not that you could buy as many as you wanted.'

Here it is.

*

Ramallah, 1987

When history stepped again into Rami's life, it was in the shape of a cigarette. He'd seen clashes with soldiers before. Strikes, the throwing of rocks, schools and university closures, he'd seen those before. Accidents that didn't feel like accidents – like those workers who were run over – he'd seen those before too. Food shortages he'd also seen before. But Rami could always find his cigarettes. Now, it was so hard to find them that he regretted all those cigarettes he had only smoked half of and left unsmoked somewhere, thrown away before they could deliver their full promise.

He remembered the time Marwan had hidden his and Anna's cigarettes and wouldn't say where. They had exploited Marwan's habit of speaking in his sleep to ask, once again, where he had hidden them. Muttering sleepily, Marwan had confessed. They had found their cigarettes in the bottom drawer of the kitchen counter. Rami would never forget his boy's reaction when they had revealed to him the way he had confessed: Marwan had immediately put his hand on his lips as to stop any other word from leaving without permission.

Walking the streets of Ramallah, in search of someone who still had cigarettes to sell, Rami felt the same need he had felt that night at Marwan's bedside. Just one drag, just one drag. He knew something was going on because people didn't share cigarettes anymore. It had been easier before. If your pack had run out, you only had to ask your colleague for one. Not anymore: everyone was guarding their cigarettes and would look at you with suspicion if they caught you staring at their cigarette smoke. A few stopped smoking altogether, citing health reasons. They decided to quit and kept saying it was not because you couldn't find cigarettes anywhere. Not because the intifada had started.

Rami thought that the lack of nicotine was succeeding in weakening them into submission where other approaches hadn't. The occupying army had tried to wear them down with long curfews, forbidding people to go out and buy milk, rice and eggs, but they had still found ways – growing food in secret in their gardens, exchanging goods, making do with what they had. But what alternative was there to nicotine? Rami and all the other smokers were now a bunch of stressed-out people suffering withdrawal symptoms. He could see the occupation's strategy there. Paranoia was itself a withdrawal symptom.

For Anna it was easier. She had already given up smoking twice and she could do it again. It was Rami who searched high and low for a cigarette, just one. A friend told him about an underground trade. The man who owned the shop on the corner of Al-Ahli street had kept a stockpile and, although he was following the general strike and had closed his shop in protest against the soldiers' continuous harassments, he had opened his basement and kept a smaller business running from there.

When Rami turned into Dunia street and kept walking straight, towards that man's house, his heart was beating as if he were on a first date. He didn't like being so dependent and thought about quitting himself. One day. Not now. Now he needed a drag to release the tension. Smoking was the last escape.

*

So this is how it is, thought Anna. She had been in the country for almost six years, and for all that time she had told her family and friends in Italy that everything was normal. No one had believed her. But things *had* been normal. That word again. Yes, there were the clashes, the settlers' attacks, the random arrests, the checkpoints, the protests, the closures, but these things were considered ordinary here. Once she had got used to all of this, her life was not particularly different from the one she could have in Italy. That is what she meant.

Life had its own way of keeping going. For months she had been waiting tensely for Rami to come home from work every day, flinching at every louder sound, hanging back in front of armed soldiers blocking one road or another. But with time Anna's brain had simply gotten used to it. Passing the checkpoints had become a game. She knew that a nice pair of legs and a skirt moved at a strategic angle could do the job better than the right documents. The soldiers were young, after all. She herself was young, after all.

The most heated moments instead took place in her own living room, when Rami and their friends were discussing politics, debating what to do, organising. Rami had created a strong network around them. Before the intifada, he had even managed to set up an international festival at the university, with actors, musicians, dancers from twenty different countries, and an exhibition on freedom of expression to which famous artists had sent their work from Europe, Cuba, the US. Those were not just cultural events, Anna understood: Rami wanted artists from around the world to come and witness what the occupation was doing to them and bring that testimony back to their country, using their art to make it even more powerful. But the most important thing was how events like that brought people together. Thousands of people from all over Palestine had come every single day for the festival, and that coming together sent a strong message to the occupation that in response had set up a checkpoint right outside the festival and arrested local artists before they could perform. But Rami did not stop: he had supported choirs, theatre and dance companies in the West Bank and Gaza to teach teenagers how to move and work as groups. But now even gatherings for a quick card game were becoming dangerous. All they did was attract the soldiers' attention. Curfews became stricter, with shorter hours to go out, more patrolling and more arrests. Military orders closed the university indefinitely and they were out of work. So this is how it is. When it's not normal anymore. Anna wondered if they would get used to these things as well.

In a way, they already had. When you live in a state of constant occupation, violence does not surprise you: you learn that the violence of the occupier never ends, it only varies in intensity. The only possibility is resistance. So when the occupying army closed the university and the schools week after week and then month after month and then year after year, the people schooled students in their houses. A few words painted on the wall, some word of mouth, and classes were organised in living rooms. Maths just down the road, literature next door, politics and engineering behind the main square. Today here, tomorrow somewhere else.

When people were arrested, tortured, maimed, more and more every day, the family was taken care of by the neighbourhood. Someone would look after the children, someone else would prepare the food, someone would provide support. And life pushed on.

When the army started to extend its curfews for months at a time, hoping to wear down the population without food, people again found their way. Tomatoes grown instead of roses, onions grown in the shade of lemon trees, chickens kept as pets.

Rami had managed to find someone in Birzeit who could sell him some chicks, and now there were eleven grown-up chickens at the bottom of the garden. Anna knew how to kill them and cook them all the way to the bone, but that was not the aim. The aim was eggs. As many as possible, to supply the whole neighbourhood in exchange for a wide range of garden produce. They adapted to this normality. But how could she explain all this in a letter or over the phone?

Rami wanted to take Anna to the beach. On clear days, from the top of the hill in front of their house, they could glimpse the sea. Their eyes moved across the valleys of white rocks and deep green bushes, and at the end was a line of blue. The sea was so close that a glance could reach it, and yet it was inaccessible: if Rami wanted to take Anna to the sea, he needed to wait for a day when the curfew was lifted for long enough for them to get there and back. He also needed to somehow organise the logistics in advance, ask the right friends – the ones with permits and yellow car plates who could drive all the way to the towns on the coast – to go with them or lend them their car.

Rami wanted this day to be a special one for Anna. Something to distract her from the surgery, the abortion, the pain and now the intifada. Those had not been easy years, it did not look like things were getting any better soon, and Anna was every day a bit more silent, a bit more distant. He wanted to find some peace for her in the sea. He had even found a babysitter for Marwan and Amer, so the day could be just for Anna. Rami wanted to see her smile. Not one of her always-there smiles to avoid the are you okay? questions.

That day on the beach, Rami saw a proper smile. For a moment, Anna's eyes relaxed and stopped looking into the distance. Rami had wondered if her desire for lontananza had returned – was she dreaming of going away or going back to Italy?

Every time he tried to understand more about Anna, he found that he ended up understanding less. Why didn't she go back to Italy if she wanted to? She was the one who could leave, as the other few foreigners had already done. Why was she staying? Was it for him? Then why didn't she suggest that they leave the country together? Rami was trying to find the answers in Anna's eyes.

That day – for only that day – Rami decided not to wonder. He pretended it was one of those old days on the beach, back in Italy. He thought of the first time they had kissed on the sand on New Year's Day 1978. Almost ten years ago. Look how far they had come.

Anna had always been a bit of a mystery to him. He remembered that party, held at Anna's family's farm, to celebrate New Year's Eve together with the Florence friends. He had met Anna only a couple of times before then, but everyone was going so he went along too. They had all celebrated and ate and drunk and danced until the party simmered down in the early hours. Someone was sleeping on the sofa, someone in a sleeping bag they brought from home, and someone else directly on the cold tiles with a folded coat under their head as a pillow and another coat to cover themselves. Rami was on a mattress on the floor. He must have fallen asleep there, still wearing his clothes from the day before. His head hurt from the uncomfortable bed and the alcohol.

Everyone knew that Anna had organised that party and invited all those friends just to hit on Rami. He didn't understand why she needed to do all of that. Couldn't she just say that she liked him? Instead, she had decided to wake him up by throwing a bucket of cold water over him.

Was this the Italian way of saying I like you? He didn't really find it attractive, and yet he got up from the mattress feeling intrigued rather than angry. Rami didn't remember exactly what happened next, but he knew that later that day they were walking on the beach and kissing.

Ten years after that kiss, Rami hoped the beach would work the same magic. There weren't problems. Not really, not any that he could see. But he sensed that Anna was sliding through his fingers and he didn't know why.

At 9 p.m. that evening Rami was driving Mary, their babysitter, back home, when soldiers stopped the car just before the main road to the nearby town of Al-Bireh.

'Where are you going?' The soldier had a strong accent. He must have been in his forties. His beard, freshly shaven, was like a green halo on his firm jaw.

'I am driving her home.' He tried to keep his voice calm.

'Where have you been?'

'She was babysitting my children and I am taking her home.'

'And where have you been while she was babysitting your children?'

It wasn't wise to say he had been in the '48 areas, the areas occupied during the Nakba, because they would have asked why, and why, and why, until they could find a reason to arrest him. He tried to think of something else to say, but every answer was risky.

'My mother was feeling unwell. I went to visit her.' Rami thought he had come up with something that did not sound like a lie and was specific enough to avoid any more questioning.

'Get out of the car!'

Or maybe not. While the soldier searched his body for weapons, it occurred to Rami, for the first time that night, that his short trousers had been a bad idea and might give away where he had really been. How could he explain them in relation to the lie about an ill mum? But the soldier didn't seem to care.

'You, girl, go home.'

Rami felt better: at least Mary was being spared.

'There has been an attack. You will stay here with the other men until we find who did it.'

They marched him to the main square of Al-Bireh, ten minutes away from where they had stopped him. All the men of the town were lined up, sitting on the ground.

'What happened?' Rami asked a young man to his left, trying to not be overheard by the soldiers going back and forth.

'Wulad ... hjar ...' The man was trying to explain, but he kept his voice so low that Rami couldn't catch the whole sentence. He caught enough, though, to understand what was going on. It was so frequent now that he could have guessed anyway without asking.

It was always the same story. Boys throwing rocks at the armed soldiers and tanks – what the soldiers called an attack – and then the soldiers rushing into the town, gathering up all the men for collective punishment. The only thing that changed was which punishment they would get.

'If you tell us who did this, it will be simpler for everyone.' Always the same offer, over and over again.

Silence. No one would talk. No one had ever talked. The men of the villages refused to play the game forced on them. It was going to be a long night.

Anna looked at the time. 11 p.m. Rami should have been back hours ago. She started to think of all the possible reasons he was not home yet. First the most acceptable ones, a flat tyre, heavy traffic, a chat with a friend. But she knew that these were not possible. She tried to think of other reasons, absurd ones, rather than jumping straight to the worst-case scenario. She even hoped he was having an affair with the babysitter. At least then she could be angry at him.

She waited another half hour, pacing the house, checking that Amer and Marwan were still fast asleep. What could she do? The curfew was now back on, and she couldn't leave the children.

Before lighting a cigarette, she counted how many were left for Rami. She went closer to the window, moving the curtain slightly to peer outside, in case he was on his way down from the top of the hill. Of course he was not. How stupid it was, her habit of waiting at the window for people to come, as if it could make them any faster. It was even more stupid now that a movement at a window, an open curtain, the red glow of a cigarette could easily attract the attention of the soldiers. Anna immediately stepped away, but had had time to see that Yosef, their neighbour, had a car with a yellow plate. How could she have forgotten? Yosef lived on the floor above them with his pregnant wife. Anna didn't even need to go outside the building to ask him for help. She rushed up the stairs and knocked at his door. Nothing. She knocked again. He couldn't be out. No one was out at that time but Rami.

She knocked again.

'Oh my God! You scared us! We thought it was the soldiers!'

Anna thought about Yosef's pregnant wife and regretted having knocked so hard and so much, like an angry soldier.

'Scusa, Yosef, aiutami, I need your help!' Anna spoke as fast as she could.

'Shu?'

'I said I am sorry, scusa, but I need help.'

'What happened?' asked Yosef, trying to understand.

Anna tried to explain in the simplest way possible, but her words didn't come out clearly. However much Arabic she learnt, her Italian came back when fear, joy, love overcame her.

'Did you say Rami went out and hasn't come back?' In his mouth her words sounded simpler.

'Na'am! Sì!' confirmed Anna.

Yosef went inside his apartment and came back out with his shoes, a jacket, and his car key.

'Okay. I am going to look for him. You go back to your children, and please, if it takes me long, come up and check on my wife.'

Anna ran back downstairs to her flat and went straight to her boys. They were as she had left them a few minutes before. She felt selfish for asking Yosef to go out and look for Rami, but he was the only one she could reach out to, and the only one with a yellow plate. Yosef was from the '48 areas, which meant that he had a different identity card, and a document that allowed him to travel in his car in all the territories and avoid being stopped and interrogated at checkpoints. The yellow plate meant freedom of movement even if, under curfew, it was risky for him too: soldiers could shoot at anything moving and then make up an excuse later.

Anna sat on the sofa that Rami had built for them when they first moved into the flat. She hadn't liked the combination of lilac and white at first, but Rami was right, it absorbed the dark colours in the room – the petrol green of the armchairs, the black walnut of the bookshelves, the wine red of the carpet. The cigarettes were still sitting on the coffee table, close to the window. Anna lit another one.

Less than half an hour later a car stopped in front of the flat. She moved the curtains. It was Yosef. Why was he back already? It could mean that everything was alright, and Rami was just behind him. Or it could mean the opposite. She ran towards the door before he could knock.

'What happened? Did you find him?'

'Yes, laqetu. Te'laish.' Yosef paused. 'But he has been held by the soldiers. Some boys threw rocks in Al-Bireh and so they are holding all the men. Inti bti'rafi keef btimshi il umour. I saw his car – they left it on the side of the street. There is nothing we can do now. Jarbi tnami. He will probably be back before you wake up.'

Yosef spoke fast. Anna wondered if he did it on purpose so that she couldn't get the meaning of everything that was happening. There was nothing they could do. Or maybe Yosef just didn't want to do it. She regretted thinking that straight away. After all, Yosef was the one who had gone out, risking arrest and leaving his pregnant wife. She was the one who had stayed at home, not sure what to do.

'Shukran, Yosef,' she said, and closed the door.

At 1 a.m., Rami was still sitting on the pavement. All the men were still there. The cold on his thighs made him regret those short trousers for the second time that day. He had thought it was just going to be a short drive, no need to get changed. With his left hand, he was playing with the hairs on his leg, clotted together by sand and salt from the beach. Every now and then he stretched his neck, stiff after hours of sitting on the tarmac, and tried to look around. He tried to count the men lined up against the walls of the houses, but his eyes couldn't see them all. In the darkness the mosque was like a crouching bird, its dome like the arc of its crown hidden under its wings. Its shape made Rami look at the men once more. They all had their heads down, in torpor. He guessed there must be two hundred of them. The stone walls were merciless for their backs. Rough, hard and cold. There was no way a back could adjust to that. The young man next to Rami was trying to find a more comfortable position. Rami was sitting against a door and felt guilty. Doors were more comfortable. The wood kept the sun's heat for longer and the surfaces were smoother.

Rami rested his cheek against the door. It felt warm, like the sand.

At 5 a.m. Rami found Anna asleep in Marwan's bed. She was hugging their oldest son, her fingers reached out, touching Amer's arm on the opposite bed. Rami let out a big sigh and felt his tiredness deep in his bones. All night they had been kept on the tarmac, waiting. No water, no talking allowed.

When the older men or teenagers nodded off, the soldiers woke them with the stock of their rifles.

Towards dawn, the soldiers got bored of their own games and let everyone go. Rami couldn't find his car so he got a lift with someone else to get home as quickly as possible, to calm Anna down. Everything was fine.

He wondered again why Anna hadn't gone back to Italy. To a safer place, where she didn't need to wait the whole night to find out whether or not her husband was alive, where she didn't need to worry about food for the following day, or about who of their friends was arrested and when would be their turn, where she didn't need to fear that her children would be caught in the middle of gunfire. Maybe Amer was too young to understand, but Marwan was not. They were more or less the age of those children in the streets, throwing rocks at the tanks, not sure whether it was a game or not.

Why hadn't Anna just left?

His deep sighs woke her up. He watched her eyelids move slowly at first …

She saw the blurry images of the bodies of her children, the sunlight hitting the wardrobe, a white T-shirt on the chair – and then she recognised the figure sitting there. Her eyes opened wide, and she jumped out of bed towards Rami.

'Come stai? Che è successo? What did they do to you? Are you hurt?'

Anna didn't let him answer and kept touching his body in search of an injury. Rami took her out of the boys' room before she woke them up.

'I am all good. They just kept us during the night. Some boys …'

'They had thrown rocks. Lo so. Yosef came to look for you!'

Rami looked at her with a glare.

'Che c'è? Cosa guardi? Why are you looking at me like that? Do you think I would just stay home and wait?'
She said it fast, in Italian, her emotions spilling out.

Words had appeared on the wall during the night, as they often did. Sometimes they were messages for the community.
Do not give up.
Keep on.
Free, free Palestine.
Believe in the struggle.
Sometimes they were messages for the soldiers, of fight and rebellion, challenging them.

The messages were painted in colours – red, green and black – during the night.

It happened everywhere. Anna thought about the protests in Florence, the same white walls, the same graffiti and statements of youth and struggle and freedom. Even in her little village in the countryside, some of the boldest boys had painted messages, graffiti and a huge penis on the school principal's house. Anna could still remember the scandal.

Here in Palestine it was not the same, Anna knew. But it felt the same. A stunt. Yet with a pinch of bravery. The same feeling of powerlessness. Writing on the walls was all about that, maybe: a way of saying something when no other form of public expression was permitted. It was an old practice. More than old, it was ancient. All civilisations had their share of writing on walls, but in most cases it was an informal act, like a release. A moment of defiance. From the drawing of big dick shapes to freedom-for-all mottos.

Anna woke up that morning at the sound of loud voices coming from the road in front of the house. She got up,

CROSSING

trying not to wake Rami, and went into the living room, with the window facing the street. Against the morning sun and through the grey curtains she could see the shapes of a group of men and hear the foreign language the soldiers were speaking.

She froze, then walked carefully towards the window and barely touched the cloth of the curtain. A small movement to see more. The soldiers were looking at the house, at the wall. And Anna immediately knew what they were looking at.

She had to wake Rami and the children before the soldiers did.

'Rami svegliati.' She tried to make her voice calm, but her hands gripped his shoulder too tight.

'What happened?' He sat up in one precise movement.

'The wall. There is a group of soldiers outside, they are looking at it.'

'Go and wake up Marwan and Amer.'

Anna needed to find an excuse to wake them up and give them something to do, away from the front door. She needed to prepare a great breakfast.

Breakfast to cover the sounds of voices:
Fry the butter in the pan, lots of it for more sizzling.
Break the eggs in the glass bowl instead of the plastic one.
Whisk them energetically, making sure the metal spoon hits the sides as much as possible.

There were lots of eggs to break open. There wasn't any milk, but she could use water. She could prepare pancakes, or pretend that she was. A surprise for the boys.

But the soldiers knocked at the door before she could reach the children's room. Bang bang bang. The bangs echoed louder.

'Quick, go to the children. I'll open the door.' Rami didn't want the soldiers to knock again.

Anna ran to the bedroom and crashed into Marwan and Amer, running towards her. She tried to push them back into the room, but the children wanted to see what was going on.

'Did you do that?' The strong-accented voice of the soldier spoke to Rami.

'That what?'

'Did you write on the wall?'

'Which wall?'

'Your wall!'

'Why would I write on my own wall?' Anna knew that Rami was playing a dangerous game, but these were the last moments he could answer back and try to stand up to them before being taken away at gunpoint.

'Get out!' The soldier took Rami by the arm and pulled him out of the house.

Marwan tried to run to his father, but Anna stopped him again. She knew that she should have gone to the children's room, closed the door and stayed there, for as long as it took. She should not let the children try to go out, try to see. But she couldn't. She couldn't stay there in the room, not knowing what was happening, while Rami was outside.

They all rushed towards the living-room window and opened the curtain. Rami was out there, standing in front of the group of soldiers. Anna could count four of them, three young men, weighed down by their boots, and an older man, pointing a gun at Rami.

Rami looked at the window and saw Anna and their children. They should not watch this. But then again, why shouldn't they?

'Paint it white again!' the soldier with the gun shouted.

Rami felt eyes on him, not only Anna's, Marwan's and Amer's, but all of the neighbourhood's. It wasn't an uncommon sight. Everyone went through this at some point. Yesterday Rami had been the one watching and today he was being watched. There was nothing else you could do, not when you were the one without a gun, not when your children were looking at you. He had never felt as bad, not for the humiliation or the fear, but because he couldn't do anything to show his children that what was happening was wrong.

Anna watched Rami painting the wall white and remembered the older boys being forced to cover the graffiti on the principal's house back in her village all those years ago. No, it hadn't felt the same.

*

Why didn't my mother leave the country? When she saw that things were getting worse and worse, why did she stay there? Love and children are not an excuse. She could bring both love and children with her, or at least the children. I want to believe that there were other reasons, and from what I know of my mother there probably were. There was probably a certain stubbornness. That obstinacy that had been passed on to her from my great-grandmother, through my father's mother, and kept a strong hold on her. That obstinacy was probably coming from a certain pride. She didn't want to go back, admit that she needed to go back, admit that there was failure. But that obstinacy was also a connection to her chosen country.

In the struggle of Palestine, my mother recognised something of herself, something that could sum up her whole life. She recognised a sense of injustice, the same one that had haunted her all those years, all the way from her village in Tuscany. For the unwanted pregnancy of Francesca, or the poverty of Agnese, or that great-grandaunt who jumped into the well. For the fascists who had beaten Teresina's husband nearly to death and after the war, pretended that nothing had happened and paid Anna's mother to clean their houses. Or those people who complained that the prostitute of the village had too many Black soldiers as clients, but who had never complained when the soldiers were German. The young doctor who had tried to rape her, and the doctor who made her pay for her decision to have an abortion. And all the strikes, the starving, the raids.

My mother recognised herself in that uprising led by women.

Men were arrested or killed, and women took their places. Women were the ones working, feeding the family, coordinating the community, taking initiative and keeping the intifada widespread, united and popular. They were also the ones who raised the next generation. The ones preparing the stones to be thrown. And for that, they too were arrested and killed.

My mother knew all the revolutionary songs of those years, and used to joke about my brother who, as small as he was, wanted to join the other kids and throw stones at the tanks. And she was keeping the chickens to provide eggs for the community. But she never told me anything about actions, participations, what she actually did. Yet she stayed. When she could have left, she stayed. And she stayed with two children. Eggs for the community.

CHAPTER EIGHT

Feeding

WHEN WE WERE CHILDREN, my brother used to tell me that our parents, or rather, *his* parents, had found me in a sewage discharge close to my father's office. He called it the frog pond – mind you, this was down to a lack of vocabulary on his part rather than an act of kindness.

In the main street of Ramallah, the one that ran parallel to my mother's favourite supermarket, and towards my father's office, there was what looked like a bridge. We used to lean over it to inspect what was flowing underneath. The green water was still, the surface became thicker in places, forming black lumps of what seemed like seaweed. I don't remember the presence of frogs but, somehow, I remember the sounds of them. The croaks and the splashes. This is where my parents had found me, this is why I was so ugly, my brother said. But I have never really believed him.

Yet last night I dreamt that I was adopted, and in my dreams I could clearly list all the reasons why that must be the truth. There is a big age gap between me and my brothers. After the breast cancer surgery and the abortions, there was a high probability that my mother could not conceive. She even admitted that she had thought about adopting. I have never seen or found any pictures of my mother while pregnant with me and my birth certificate seems to have disappeared.

I would have never paid attention to any of these details were it not for my brother's childhood mischievousness. Or were it not because I have to write this chapter. I have gone back and forth, writing the chapters that have come before and after, coming back to this without any success, asking my father again and again the same questions about the events of those years, and trying to convince myself that it is time to put myself onto the page. Not only as the voice sewing together the memories but also as the baby I was about to be, part of the story myself, together with Anna and Rami, Marwan and Amer, part of their world that is the world I created for them.

*

Ramallah, 1989

Rami wanted another child. He was thirty-two years old, with two boys and, after seven years, he thought it was about time for another child. In fact, he meant a girl. Even if it was just to rebalance the numbers, like his father George years before him: George would have been happy to see that the majority of his grandchildren, with a stunning seven against three, were boys. But Rami wasn't. Rami wanted a girl, and he wondered if that desire growing in him was Helena's final revenge on her husband's old whim.

Anna had mixed feelings and wasn't sure that having another child was the wisest decision. She was thirty-one and her body was not as it used to be. It had been easy to get pregnant, before, but Anna knew that the breast cancer and the pain in her uterus weren't good signs for another pregnancy. Not to mention the ongoing occupation and the intifada.

FEEDING

Did they want to raise another child in that situation? They didn't even know if they would be able to reach a hospital in time with all the curfews and the checkpoints. Or if they could find enough food to feed all of them. Or a shelter if the soldiers started to shoot in the streets.

And what about the whole situation with her passport?

For nearly ten years Anna had been staying in the country as a tourist. Every time her tourist visa had expired, she had left the country: she would stay in Jordan for a few days and would then come back in on a new tourist visa. Back and forth, in and out. Everyone was doing it, every foreigner who wanted to live in the West Bank. It was easier to do that than start the process of applying for a permanent visa. Once you were on the occupying government's radar as someone who wanted to stay in the occupied territories, it was difficult to get off it. Sudden house controls, interviews and interrogations, changes in the documents needed for the application, new rules for permanent visa-holders to leave or come back to the country, were just some of their kindest ways to let foreigners know that they were not welcome. So people would go in and out every time their temporary visa expired, and so did Anna. Not every single time, though: there had been occasions where she couldn't be bothered with the expenses and hustles of going in and out of the country and had just overstayed her expired visa a bit longer, making sure to avoid the roads where controls and checkpoints were likely to be. If they encountered one and the soldiers were young, she would show her legs instead of her passport. Or pretended to play hide-and-seek with Marwan and Amer in the back of the car when the soldiers were not so young. There were times when she had to hide in the car boot.

Last time she had left the country to come back on a new visa, the soldiers told her that she couldn't stay any longer without a proper permit; she needed to legalise her status. To make sure she was actually going to do it this time, they took away her passport. They would give it back to her when she had sorted out the documents she needed to be able to stay, or if she left the country.

How stupid, how naive she had been. Anna thought back to the first time she was pregnant, when neither she nor Rami had a proper job – and yet, they didn't even worry about it, they were so happy. Or when they discovered she was pregnant the second time, in Rami's parents' house, with no place to call their own, and that virus threatening her and her baby. Reckless. Anna couldn't understand how they could have been so carefree. Yet she didn't remember being scared or regretful. In fact, those were the moments she was happiest. So what had changed? Why suddenly all these fears?

But now that Rami had put the idea of having a girl in her mind, she caught herself daydreaming with the possibility of new joys. She hadn't thought about it before, but she could now see herself taking care of a daughter, to whom she could be what her mother hadn't been for her. All that love that she always looked for in her mother, she could pass it down to a daughter: the attention, the complicity, the communion of being women together.

'Va bene,' she said to Rami. 'Let's try!'

Anna held a bag of bread in her right hand. It was still warm from the bakery, the warmth from the flat loafs adding to the heat of that August day. A small crossbody purse bounced up and down on her bump with each step. With her left hand she caressed her belly.

At that time of the day, the sun started to go down and the light softened to orange. Anna loved walking back home, facing the sunset. The orange light would first flood the hills and the valleys, then all the way to the coast. The sea was so close she could stretch out her arm and grab the coastline. Yet the occupation pushed it away, making it almost impossible to reach it with all the checkpoints, the permits, the military rules.

How many times had they walked along that street together – she, Rami, the boys – hand in hand or busy holding the sticky ice cream from the famous ice-cream shop, Rukab's, or a shawarma? Why couldn't life be always as simple as a sunset walk with the winds bringing dust from the rocky hills and people chatting and sipping coffee on the street? Since the beginning of the intifada, every little pleasure counted, like the warm bread hanging by her side, or the singing of the cicadas in the dry grass.

Would all these pleasures still be there for the child she was expecting? Would she and Rami and the children still be there, together in that land? There were two months left until the end of her pregnancy, and they didn't know the sex of the child and couldn't think of a name. Anna tried to imagine a baby, any baby. After all she didn't need to know if it was a girl or a boy, all babies looked the same. But for all the effort she put in, she couldn't picture this new baby and its coming to life.

It was not just because she herself didn't know what to expect, but because no one there knew what to expect from the life they were leading. They were pretending to go on every day, organising for liberation, fighting for years for the dream of a country. But the whole country was like Anna: having this life inside her without knowing anything about it, unable to promise anything to it, unable to guarantee safety, stability, peace.

Anna felt the summer day become heavier and gloomy, as if someone had just shuttered the windows.

The sun was still there, though, fading slowly for the sunset, but no clouds. The street had fallen silent, the shops had closed and no one was around, as if the town had been swallowed up by her thoughts.

Then, Anna heard gunfire.

She was mad at herself. After so many years when she had learnt to recognise the sudden empty streets, the silence, the heaviness as the signals before an aggression; and she had learnt how to look for the best place to hide and where to avoid, now, after so many years of cautiously living with the brutality of the occupation, she suddenly found herself right in the middle of it.

The noise of bullets was getting closer, the engines of the army jeeps louder. She looked around, quickly, her left hand on her stomach. Fuck. There was nowhere to turn. There were no bins or stalls to hide behind. The streets of Ramallah had never been so clean and tidy.

This is what Anna meant: what was the point of bearing that child, and then putting it directly in the middle of the fight?

The bag of bread was still hanging from her right hand. She didn't want to let it go. Its warmth was the only reassurance of normality, or what was left of it. She hadn't moved her left hand from her belly either. The purse was still there too. Anna didn't move. Was she really going to die like this? For having not seen this coming, not recognising the signs? Because her mind had wandered at the wrong time?

She felt a kick in her stomach and ran towards a door. Anna knocked, but she knew that no one would open. Not if she knocked like an angry soldier. But how else could she knock? She tried to flatten herself against the door, but that belly didn't really help, did it?

What a sight for those heavy-booted soldiers to find a big

belly protruding from a door, and attached to it this woman with her eyes squeezed shut, like a child playing hide-and-seek. I don't see you, you don't see me.

'Wala yhimmik, madame.' Anna heard the voice of a man.

He put his hands on her shoulders and turned her around so she faced the door. Then he leant forward and covered her body with his body, his hands on the door and above her head. Anna kept her eyes closed and her forehead on the wood of the door. She embraced her belly, the bag of warm bread still dangling from her arm between her legs. She stayed like that, trying not to move.

The man smelled of tobacco, but not cigarette tobacco. It was the apple-scented one of the argileh. Anna inhaled that familiar aroma and felt the warmth of his breath against her hair and ears, the movement of his chest going up and down. He was so much taller and bigger than she was. Anna opened her eyes to look at him, but she couldn't move her head freely, protected as she was by the man's shoulders and arms. From that angle she could only get a glimpse of part of his arm.

He must be young: the skin on his forearm, the dark hairs, the fingers, indicated that he was young. Why was he doing this? Why was he risking his life to protect her?

Anna took a deep breath and her body relaxed, the rhythm of his chest a cradle for her and her child. It was as though this young man was shielding her from the whole of reality. She heard bullets in the distance, covered by the sounds of his long breaths, the rustle of his T-shirt against her hair, and his heart pounding just behind her nape. And then she didn't hear him anymore. His body lifted away from her and she could move once again.

By the time she turned around he was gone.

People were starting to come back out of their houses and

shops and the bread in her bag was still warm. Anna touched her belly to check if everything was alright. The baby seemed fine. She looked around to see if she could identify the man from the body shape she had felt against her. But no one seemed as tall, as strong.

Anna hadn't seen where he had come from or where he went. He could even have been the man the soldiers were looking for. The only one who had stayed on the road. She would never know who that man was, but in what he had just done, she saw a chance for their baby.

*

Birzeit, 2019

The air smells of jasmine.
Little white flowers surrounded by the green of their leaves, surrounding the gardens, the houses with white verandas, arching windows.
It is hard to walk alone.
I get lost
a couple of times, taking the wrong turn.
I am looking for that supermarket,
my mother's favourite.
But I end up on the other side of town.
My father drew me a map. But I can't understand it.
Google maps doesn't work here.
I am left to myself.
How many times have I walked these streets?
But never alone. Someone was always by my side.
I can't ask for directions, my tongue will not help me.
What am I doing here?
Am I really playing at going native again?
If I could only place the door.

FEEDING

That door where that man saved my mother's life
and mine.
Would I find that half part of me there?
The way I know this place is through jasmine bushes.
The sugar of the lamunada.
The saltiness of toasted pistachios and loz.
The scent in the hall of my family house.
The sesame seeds of ka'ek.
The sound of battikh when it is ready to be opened.
I know this place
in the notes of the 'oud
the voice of my father.
My mother singing fishi lahme, fishi haleeb, binna za'atar uilla zbib
singing and dancing the revolutionary songs
Falestin arabie
Wein'a Rammalah wein'a Ramallah
I know this place
for the orange light of sunset
the smell of toasted bread on the hob
the zest of the sumac.
I know this place
from the movements of my father's hands
spreading the yogurt on the chicken.
Or dancing.
My mother's face behind the vapour
of a pot of rice.
She knew how to prepare
the perfect mansaf
'The best I have ever eaten'.
I know this place
for the ups and downs of the hills
the ones in my memory

the ones here and now.
I look towards west.
The big city on the sea
boasts a black skyline
so neat against the orange of the sunset.
It seems a city floating in another dimension.
It is a city floating in another dimension.
'se'a wahadeh btiwsali mashi'
Said the man.
Just an hour-walk
from these hills to that city.
If there were no borders
No passports
No checkpoints
If we were not natives
to be closed off in reservations.
So now
the taste of my lamunada is too bitter
the seeds too salty
the battikh opens rotten
the za'atar, the oil, the fruit of the saber
are battlefields for meaning
the 'oud has broken chords.
I can't hear my mother's voice
calling with the sound of little bells.
The petals of the jasmine are creased.
Why am I here?
Who am I here?
I leave half footprints on the ground.
I never belong entirely
or maybe we don't need to belong
to each other.
I don't need to prove

FEEDING

that you are mine.
Because I know how the za'atar tasted
before it became a symbol.
Because I know the surprise
of a glimpse of yellow lemons
even in the winter garden.
Because I know the touch of hands
that smell of garlic.
I don't get lost
in the vibrato of the air
before the summer night.
I don't get lost
in the songs of the cicadas
hiding around.
I don't get lost
in the milky tips of figs
picked from a tree
on the side of the road.
I don't get lost in the jibne beda.
I don't get lost
in the threads of the embroideries
in the warmth of the bread
in the smell of apple tobacco.

CHAPTER NINE
Baccalà II

Ramallah, 1990

Rami let out a big sigh.

'They will kill us with their bureaucracy,' he said.

Anna wasn't sure if that was a metaphor.

'We need to go to the military governor,' added Rami after a few seconds. 'We need to apply for permission for a family reunion so we can legalise your presence here.'

When the first refusal arrived, it wasn't a surprise. The occupying army never wanted foreigners to stay. Anna and Rami were prepared for it and simply filled in a second application and headed to the military governor's office.

'It's not the military governor's business anymore,' said the officer. 'You have your own organisations. You wanted them, so now you have them.'

The occupying army had for years tried to create groups of collaborators among the locals. Y*our own organisations*, as the officer called them. The village leagues, set up in the middle of the colonised to carry out the design of the colony, were a sort of administrative device to parrot a sense of independence, to pretend that the occupation was not there.

Rami compiled another application and went to the village leagues.

'Yes!' they said. 'No problem, we can have it done in a short time, but …'

Rami knew it couldn't be so easy.

'But you see, we are fighting for the same cause, so we need to work together. You know it's hard. People don't trust us, but we are on the same side. We are the same, aren't we?'

'What do you want?' asked Rami, hoping to cut the rhetoric short.

'It's not what *we* want, it's what's good for everybody, for the community.'

They told Rami that if he wanted his documents and wanted them fast, all he had to do was to agree to be filmed while he was handed the permit and testify to the efficiency and good will of the village leagues.

'I am not going to do it,' said Rami to Anna, when he got home and explained what was going on.

'Cosa? What do you mean, you are not going to do it?' Anna tried to make it sound like an actual question.

'I am not going to lend my face to this shame. I won't be an instrument of their propaganda!'

'Oh per piacere! Stop talking politics. Do you want me here?'

'Yes of course I do!'

'Then do it! Go and say how efficient and kind they are!'

'You can't ask me to do that. You know I can't!'

After that conversation they hadn't talked for days.

Rami thought about Anna's words. What was he doing? Was he going to let his wife be deported? For what? Dreams? Ideologies? Values? They are damn cold things when you are alone. He should have said he would do it. But then what? Put his face on TV for their propaganda when he had spent all this time fighting against it? All the humiliations, the interrogations, the chases, the cold nights, Marwan's eyes while Rami was painting over the graffiti on the wall, the chickens in the garden, the craving for cigarettes, the strikes, the lack of food and sleep, the fear, the grieving. Enduring all of that for what? To go on TV and support the occupation's machine?

Anna was right, he was talking like a politician. Anna, Marwan, Amer, and his baby girl! Could he stay there without them? After a few weeks he decided that he should try again with the village leagues, see if he could find another compromise. The radio, maybe: less shameful if it was just his voice and not his face.

When he got to the old building where the village league had their offices, he found it empty. The walls were covered with the word *Traitors!* written in red and black paint. The village leagues, *your own organisations*, hadn't worked. Rami let out another big sigh and sat down on a chair that had been left behind. He had nothing to decide anymore. The choice had been made for him. If he wanted to apply for a new permit, he would have to go to the occupying governor's office once again. And again and again.

Ventoruccia farmhouse, 1991

The smoke of the fire dying away and the flame reduced to orange coals brought Anna's senses back to the room. Teresina was cleaning her plate of baccalà with a piece of stale bread and was still waiting for an answer. Why was her granddaughter back?

Anna could give the easy answer, the one she had given everyone else. She couldn't stay in Palestine because her documents had not been renewed. Her application for a longer residency permit had been denied, and so had her visa.

That was true. She would not lie. But looking at her grandmother's fireplace, Anna felt guilty: she had done exactly what that fire did, wilt slowly. If the same thing had happened just a few years before, she would have been the first one to tell Rami, no way! You are not doing that for those traitors. But something inside her had faded away. It was not exactly like that, though. Rather, another fire in her had grown stronger, fiercer than her political commitment and more powerful even than her love for Rami. It was her love for Marwan, Amer, her new daughter, that had changed everything.

She could still feel the warmth of the bread and the smell of apple tobacco of the man who had saved her and her daughter's lives. The fear she had felt that day had made her understand: her body was not enough to protect her children.

The problem was that the occupation was more brutal than ever and that brutality entered every single aspect of their day-to-day life. Like that time she had waited the whole night for Rami when he had driven the babysitter back home.

Or when Helena had insisted on piercing Sabrin's ears. Although the child was only a few months old, Helena wanted Sabrin to have earrings for her christening. Helena forced the guy with the piercing gun to go ahead even when soldiers had started to shoot outside and the sounds of smashing, booms and shouting surrounded the small jewellery shop. The poor man's hands were shaking so much, and Sabrin's ears were still so small that Anna feared the worst.

'Oh come on!' said Helena. 'The worst that can happen is having the two little holes in different positions.'

And so it happened. Now Sabrin had two little holes, one much higher than the other. In the photographs of her christening, the earrings float at different heights, as though detached from Sabrin's head, or as if her head were heavier on one side. Marwan and Amer hadn't stopped laughing for days at their baby sister.

Then there was Amer: he was so restless. And since he had become an older brother, he believed himself to be a grown-up man. He wanted to join the other boys and throw rocks at the tanks and the soldiers. How many times had Anna had to stop him or chase after him!

More than anything else, Anna couldn't forgive herself for the scar Marwan had on his left leg. They had been walking towards her favourite supermarket when the soldiers started to shoot again. An army truck was chasing a group of boys who had launched rocks at it. Anna had pushed Marwan inside a butcher shop, the only shelter near them. A rubber bullet – rubber just a misleading word – had broken the glass of the shop window and hit Marwan's leg before Anna could cover him.

Anna could endure everything. She had made her choice to be there after all, to be there until that country and all of them – everyone in Palestine – would be free. But not at that price. She couldn't stand the pain, the tears, the blood of her son.

It was not about Anna anymore. Or Rami. It was not about that country anymore. It was about Marwan, Amer and Sabrin. They shouldn't have to pay for her choices. Anna needed to make sure they were safe, that she could always be there for them, not arrested overnight or shot on the streets. Why did Rami not feel the same?

Protected by Teresina's hearth, knowing her children were safe, with no army outside, she had finally found space to think about those years living in Palestine. She had felt hurt. Rami didn't want to sacrifice his political views for his family. But she knew it was not just about politics. It was more than that. She wouldn't want Rami to be a tool of the occupation's propaganda. That was why she had left his country, with their children, so that he could carry on with what he had started. He, but also Anna, had sacrificed so much, done so much, and Rami was involved in so much organising with his dream of using beauty to resist, finding alternative ways to reclaim life when the occupation has taken everything away from them, that he could not give up now.

*

My father explains it clearly and plainly to me. My mother had to leave because her documents couldn't be renewed. He tells me the story about the village leagues and how he said no to them. He kept his integrity and dignity. I believe him. I know how stubborn he can be, how important his values are to him. But then I think, *yes you safeguarded your dignity, but not your family.* So when I write about his decision, and my mother's decision, I try to imagine his struggle and hers. First she had to accept my father's stubbornness and then feel guilty for having asked him to betray his beliefs. I know that my father can be uncompromising, but I also know how obstinate my mother can be too, loyal to her own peculiar set of values. I know that at some point she must have understood my father's needs and embraced them. But I need to know more to help me understand my parents' decision. So I call my mother's cousin.

Silvana answers the phone in her strong Spanish accent. She has lived in Spain for so many years that her Italian is full of Spanish words and sounds.

I call her because, of all my family, she reminds me the most of my mother. They look alike, not so much physically, but in their way of smiling, talking, touching. They also shared similar experiences in their lives. Silvana too fell in love and moved to another country to be with the person she loved. And she and my mother were friends: they had been there for each other through a childhood in the deprivation of remote mining areas, the suffocation of religion, the pettiness of village gossips and the same family dynamics. She was the one who told me that they were desperate not to be like their mothers: resigned to the abuse of their fathers for the rest of their lives.

'Your mother had never been a front-line fighter. Even when I visited her in Florence, when there were those marches and demonstrations, she never fully took part. At first I thought it was because she was shy, then I got irritated because I thought she was one of those people who doesn't want to get her hands dirty. I was different, I wanted to be noisy, to be involved. It took me a while to understand that she simply had a different approach. She was silent, she stayed to one side, but she ended up making braver decisions than we all did. She thought that everyone had the right to build the life they wanted the way they wanted without judgement and that's what she did for herself. She seemed fearless.'

Big statements. If I didn't know my mother, I would hardly know what Silvana is trying to tell me. There are things in her speech that surprise me. I thought that my mother *was* a front-line fighter. She used to tell me about all those demonstrations in Florence while walking around the living room, showing me how they used to move their hands – her left fist pumping up and down in the air – and the things they sang – *tremate tremate le streghe son tornate* – and how she and her girlfriends didn't shave, and how they wore long skirts with no underwear. There was so much passion in her eyes while she was marching in front of me and in the way she taught me the revolutionary songs and slogans, or how to ululate the zaghrouta – a trill of joy. She was so proud when she showed me that she kept three keffiyeh in her drawer for me and my brothers. I believed she was there on the front lines. But my surprise doesn't last long. There is something in Silvana's words that I recognise: always being there, not abandoning her position. Standing up for it. Not judging.

'Your father amazed us. I mean, he amazed Italian people,' Silvana continues. 'We had a certain idea of how an Arab man should look and behave and he was nothing like that. We thought he was rather snobbish.'

'But did my grandfather accept Babbo straightaway?' I ask.

'Of course he did. He knew that your mother wouldn't really listen to what anyone thought anyway. She was already independent. And then, as I told you, your father was not what people expected. Your grandfather knew that he came from a more educated, wealthy family than ours. But we were still worried, we kept saying to each other, "If he asks her to go back with him, it's going to be a mess." We knew that your mother would have followed your father to Palestine without thinking twice. She was so in love, and she had fallen in love with his country too. It was her dream. She believed in what his country and his people were fighting for. She recognised something of her own struggle in it, the same sense of injustice she had felt all her life. If she was going to go, she would have ended up staying there forever. I told you, that was her way of making a point.'

'So why did she end up leaving?' I finally ask my question.

Silvana thinks about it. The answer must be more complicated than I expected.

'There were many problems,' she starts, and I know I need to take notes. 'When she was living there, I visited her twice. Once in 1982, when she was pregnant with your brother. It hadn't been an easy pregnancy and even though she tried to make everything sound okay on the phone, I wanted to go and check for myself. I found her happy. Yes, she had

had a hard time due to the brucellosis, but she was happy. She was at the end of her pregnancy and she was so excited. Your parents had just moved into their own flat. They were planning to open the kindergarten at the university. And the political situation wasn't so bad. I mean it's always bad when you live under occupation, but the people were nice and kind and they were going through it with such dignity. She felt part of the community.

'But when I went to visit her the second time, things had changed. It was at the end of 1986. She had talked to me less in those years, but I could see that she had gone through a lot. Again she tried to keep it to herself, but I could tell she was sad and dejected. And tensions then were high. The soldiers were always around, twenty-four hours a day, seven days a week. Waiting for a misstep, for any excuse to rush into people's houses and arrest them. She had done so much to be there, to stay there. She wanted so much to have her children and raise them in that land, for them to live in connection with that land.

'But she came back because she realised that you and your brothers were more important than anything else and she was scared for you. She once called me up crying. She didn't let me talk. "Arafat wants eleven children from each mother. But I am not giving him any. They are all mine. Let him make his own. My children are all mine."

I knew then that something had broken.'

*

Bethlehem, 1991

Anna and the children had left. They had gone back to Italy. Rami did not want to leave his homeland and family again, not in a moment like that, so he stayed but left Ramallah:

it was safer to join the rest of his family in the big white house in Bethlehem. It was unsettling to be there without Anna and the children. Alone in his mother's home, like when he was seventeen. No one demanding his attention.

Amer, don't hit your sister ...

Come down, Marwan that's not the moment ... wait, Anna che hai detto?

Sì, I can do it.

Responsible only for himself, he was not being constantly called for something:

Babbo, Babbo, Baba, amore.

There was no need to worry about every single thing.

Is that hill to steep?

This toy too sharp?

Did Sabrin sleep enough?

Did I say the wrong thing?

He should feel lighter. So why didn't he?

The small pool in the garden made him want to play with Marwan and Amer. The sound of frying jibne reminded him of Anna. He couldn't stop thinking about what was happening in Sabrin's life that he was missing.

Was she saying a new word today?

Had she learned to walk faster?

Were her eyes bigger with surprise at her new country?

Did she miss him?

Did she even remember him?

Rami questioned whether staying there was the right decision. But at least Anna and the children were safe. It was his mother and siblings who needed him now and he needed to be with his people. He had tried to explain that to Anna, but she kept trying to convince him to take the first flight out and join them. Wasn't it important for him to be with the children?

Rami didn't see why he had to choose between the two halves of his life: why couldn't he be both?

'Rami.' Helena sat next to him on the sofa, interrupting his thoughts. 'Habibi, we need this medicine for Basel.'

Basel, Rami's nephew, was ill, and after days waiting for him to improve, he was only getting worse. Rami thought again about Anna: if only Anna were here, she would know what to do. Instead, they had had to call the doctor.

'The doctor says Basel needs these medicines as soon as possible.' Helena had interrupted him again. 'He says we need to call the ambulance. It is the only vehicle that can move around the streets. We can give the driver the name of the medicines and he'll go to the pharmacist's house and collect them for us.'

'Come on, come with us!' said the driver of the ambulance. 'Yalla ya zalame, there's no risk! You'll be in an ambulance and with the mayor's nephew as guarantor here.'

The driver waved his head toward the man next to him.

'Marhaba, Abu Marwan. Yalla come with us. Just a bit of fresh air!'

Rami was tempted. The curfew had been in place for days, with just a window of two hours to go and buy food every three, even four days. A bit of fresh air would help to clarify his mind and shake off all those thoughts about Anna and the children.

'Tayyib, I am coming!'

'Aywah! But you both need to sit in the back,' said the driver.

In the back of the ambulance, an awkward silence fell. This was not exactly Rami's idea of fresh air or fun. It's not that they had nothing to talk about, it was just better to shut up and listen to what was happening outside. When the ambulance slowed down, was it being stopped by the soldiers? When it deviated from its route, was it to avoid a checkpoint? When the ambulance moved suddenly, was it because someone was shooting at it?

Those were the sounds and signs they were looking out for. To survive you had to develop sharpened senses. Rami wondered how long it would take to go back to being how he was before, not hiding every time someone knocked at the door, or looking for shelter every time something sounding like a siren kicked off, or sleeping through the night without waking up with every noise or because it was too quiet.

The ambulance stopped. Rami looked at the mayor's nephew. It could not be the pharmacist's road. Why had they stopped? They heard the driver talking to someone, offering explanations. And they immediately looked around for somewhere to hide or to see if they could open the door and escape. How could they explain two healthy men hiding in the ambulance during the curfew? Before being able to make a move, however, the door was opened for them.

'Get out!'

The soldiers didn't even wait for explanations.

The cell was made of two rooms connected together. They would have looked like two normal rooms were it not for the bars at the window and the presence of another seventy men. The prisoners were sitting on any available surface, on the benches, leaning on the walls, and on the ground. When some of them recognised the mayor's nephew, they made space for him in a more comfortable, less crowded corner.

Rami found somewhere to sit on the ground and rested his head on his knees. Through the only window, a hole in the wall with metal bars, the January cold and the silence of the town wafted into the cell. It was the first time that he had been properly arrested. He had been held sometimes or stopped and questioned, but he had never been locked in a cell.

He didn't know what to expect. Around him there were men of all kinds. Some were really old, others were as young as twelve, thirteen.

'First time?' asked the man next to him.

'Yes!'

'Oh, you could tell from your face!'

'My face?'

'It looks like you have been brought to your own funeral!'

A burst of laughter spread around the room like a wave on a pond.

'Shayef? You see? Nothing to worry about. Plus you came in with the mayor's nephew. You'll be out before you're able to remember that you've ever been here!'

That man was partly right. They came and called the mayor's nephew less than half an hour after they had been brought in. But they didn't call for Rami.

'Shayef? It looks like you have to wait like the rest of us!'

But Rami didn't want to wait. Wait for what? Why didn't they let him go with the mayor's nephew?

He wondered what these men had done to be in there, how long they had been there for and if they had any chance of being released. Rami wanted to know, but there was something about the laid-back atmosphere inside the cell that unsettled him.

'We all pass through here at least once.' It was the same man talking, but his voice had a different tone this time. 'Shayef Ibrahim? This is his eighth time!' Rami followed the pointed finger, towards a man with a white beard, a few heads away from him. Ibrahim waved back, raising his eyebrows with a mixture of resignation and amusement.

'This is my third time,' intervened another man. He looked Rami's age and was wearing what looked like pyjamas.

'Aywah! It *is* a pyjama,' he added at Rami's look. 'They broke into my house in the middle of night. I still have no idea why I am here, but I'm sure they will tell me!'

Another wave of laughter spread across the room.

'Ittala' 'alai!' said one man standing from the floor. 'They didn't even let me put my trousers on! I farted as much as I could when they pushed me into the truck!' He was showing a hole in his underwear. The heads of seventy men went up and down, shaking and vibrating as if an earthquake were moving the ground beneath them.

'They brought me in because I opened the window!' said one of the teenagers. 'My mother told me to. I told her it was too risky, "Not as much as not doing what I tell you to!" Another shudder of laughter went through the room before a siren kicked off.

'Shush. Stay quiet!' said the man in pyjamas.

They had expected it for weeks. Iraqi President Saddam Hussein had threatened to launch his missiles against Tel Aviv and selected targets in the West Bank if Baghdad was hit by the United States. He wanted to provoke a further escalation of the Gulf War that had started the year before, and there were even rumours that he wanted to use chemical weapons.

Rami looked at the open window with its metal bars, where the cold of the winter and the sound of the siren were coming in. How could he tell his brother that he couldn't get the medicines for his son? Or explain to Anna that it wasn't his fault if he couldn't call? She hated it when he forgot.

They could hear the agitated voices of the soldiers outside and then the sound of rushing steps. Then the noises stopped and more laughter shook the room.

'Why are you laughing?' asked Rami. He felt trapped in something worse than a cell. He felt trapped with seventy men, all completely out of their minds.

'They always do like this. The siren starts and they shout and panic and then they run to their shelter where they are as packed and squeezed in as we are, but with no windows!' Another burst of laughter.

'Then the siren starts again to warn that the danger has passed, but nothing ever happens! Nothing, not even a plane passes by. Saddam's weapons are less effective than ours!'

'My farts are more dangerous!'

The laughter took the room.

'And then what happened?' I ask my father over the phone.

'The mayor's nephew told my brother where I was, and he called the mayor again and explained what had happened, and after twelve hours they let me go!'

'Were you not scared?'

'Of course I was, but I wasn't alone, and after a while, those laughs became contagious. I guess it's the only thing you can do when there's nothing else to do. But after that I understood that your mother was right. I couldn't see why I was there instead of being with you in Italy. I realised I could not make any difference, not anymore, and I felt so impotent and alone.'

'So what did you do?'

'I went back to the occupation military headquarters. I had to. They were the ones releasing permits to leave the country.'

'And did they let you go?'

'Yes, they did. It was always better to have one less Palestinian in the country. Expatriation is as good as prison from their point of view. And the Italian embassy helped me make my case.'

'So what happened next?'

'I had to call the same ambulance to drive me to the military checkpoint in Jerusalem. But this time I had a permit, so it was fine, and from there I could use public transport to get to the airport.'

'Last time you told me that they arrested you on the day of your birthday, the 19th of January, and that you were in Tel Aviv airport for your flight the day that Saddam's missiles actually hit the town. I checked. The missiles reached Tel Aviv on the 17th, so two days earlier.'

My father thinks, trawling his memories again.

'You're right,' he then says, 'when I got there, it had already happened, but everyone was still walking around with their gas masks on. I mean not everyone. The occupying army had distributed gas masks to their own people, but not to us Palestinians.'

To Tel Aviv Airport, 1991

Rami was walking towards the bus station. From there he could take the shuttle bus to the airport and finally catch a plane to Italy. Around him, the only noise was the crunching gears of cars and buses or the sound of the steps of the few people walking around in the open. They reminded Rami of a fly, panicked, trying to escape through a closed window. An urgent buzz and every now and then the thud of the insect's body against the glass.

That image would have not come to him had it not been for all those gas masks. People in the streets, the ticket vendor behind the counter, the bus driver, they were all wearing them, ready to survive a chemical attack. Rami could hear the laughter of the prisoners back in the cell. But out here, surrounded by these strange beings in their masks, who knew he was not one of them because he was not wearing one, Rami forgot the reason why those prisoners found it so funny.

He looked around him to see if he could find anyone else without those flies' eyes and nose, someone like him. There was a woman who was walking fast, on the other side of the street. He waved as if she was someone he knew, but she just hunched her shoulders over and walked on faster.

Rami bought his bus ticket. It's about to leave, said a voice behind the gas mask, two big black eyes looking at him. He ran to find his bus, his steps loud in the silence, and Rami thought once more of an insect smashing against the glass, trying to escape.

The phone rang. Once, twice.

'Pronto?' answered Anna.

'Anna it's me, I don't have much time.' Rami's voice was calling her name from the other side. He hadn't called for days. It happened sometimes when the phone lines were cut, but even after months apart Anna hadn't got used to it.

'Come stai? What happened? Dove sei?' she was almost shouting at him.

'Sto bene, sto bene, Anna. I am here in Italy. I am calling from a phone booth, from the airport. I don't have much credit. I have just landed.'

Anna started to cry.

'So who came to pick you up?'

'No one came. Your mother didn't drive at the time. And it was so sudden that no one else could come. I took the train.'

'So who came at the station?'

'No one. There weren't mobile phones like now. I couldn't communicate so no one knew when I would arrive. I took the bus.'

'And was there someone to greet you at the bus stop?'

My father laughs. 'No, there wasn't anyone. No one knew when I was arriving. I needed the coins to pay the bus ticket, so I couldn't call. I walked from the bus stop to your grandparents' house, the one near the centre. You were all living there at the time, because we didn't have a house yet. I rang from the gate, and the front door opened straight away. The first thing I saw was you. You rushed out and threw yourself on the ground, and rolled over, and let out screams and giggles. You were like a little puppy. You were so happy I was there.'

CHAPTER TEN
Pasta in Palestine

The village, 1992–94

My mother used to wake me up at six in the morning, after her night shift at the hospital. My grandmother must have spent the night with me, but when I opened my eyes she was not there anymore. It was summer and my mother and I must have caught the first bus, because my mother still didn't drive. We were going to the beach.

It was just the two of us. My brothers had been sent over to Palestine to stay with my father, before we joined them at the end of the summer.

Those were the years of my most regular contact with my Palestinian side, made up of frequent visits to my father's country, forming bonds with the family there, the food, the events, the language. After the peak of the intifada had passed and the first talks of an agreement had led to the Oslo Accords – a sort of road map towards an independent Palestinian state – my father had started to go back to Ramallah; now that an end to the occupation seemed possible there was an enthusiasm for celebrating and highlighting the richness of Palestinian culture. All the work that my father has done during the years, all the organising, all the gatherings, all the theatre, the music, the festivals, could now become part of the reconstruction of his country. It seemed possible that we might all go back, and live there again. But for now my father was going back and forth alone, spending three, four months at a time in Palestine to work on his new projects and then a couple of months back in Italy with us who were trying to make the most out of our time with him. Then in summer, we tried to join him for our school holidays.

Despite this, since the age of two, when I moved back to Italy with my mum and my brothers, I spent most of my childhood in my mother's home village on the hills and I can only imagine now how hard it was for her to see me, us, growing up in the place she had struggled so hard to escape.

When my mother couldn't take me to the beach at dawn, she would take me in the evening, and we would have chips as our special dinner. There was this place close to the beach that sold them. Chips eaten this way – in blue-and-white paper boxes, with mayonnaise and ketchup squeezed from big bottles on the counter – were the absolute epitome of American modernity reaching the countryside of Italy, an area where big fast-food brands are hard to find even today.

We ate our chips on the bus ride home, stealing them from each other, eating them with our fingers and then licking the sauce left on our skin. My mother would clean my hands with the wet napkins she always had with her. The other people on the bus would stare at us because of the noise we made and the mess of food, sand and laughter. I would become quiet and so my mother used to whisper in my ear: 'They think that we are eating exactly like Arabs. But they don't know that this is the best way to eat food.'

Ironically, my father, the Arab, has always hated to eat with his hands – to the extent of even eating sandwiches with a knife and fork, and so I think this was a way for my mother to reconnect with her desire for lontananza, to remind herself that she had managed to run away from her village, at least for a while.

The entanglement of my two identities started then, in those years in Italy with my mother, going back and forth between two countries, on the bus ride home at sunset, with hands sticky with sand and food, and my mother proud to be seen as an Arab.

*

Sometimes words seemed to be far away, as if no one could reach them and there was too much to say and nothing left to say it with.

Anna stared at the blank sheet of paper. The lights in the living room were off, except for the lamp illuminating the white sheet. Outside it was even darker. The council hadn't installed any street lights in the neighbourhood yet and she couldn't afford curtains, so the window revealed that blackness outside. The house was the last one at the southern end of the village. No one was around. Everything was silent.

She had been waiting for that moment of quiet the whole day, when everyone would shut up and the children were peacefully asleep. But when it finally arrived, she was tempted to wake everyone up again. She told me many times that she wanted to write a book about her life, and I always wondered what she would have written. It didn't look to me like there was much to say. But in that moment, that night, in front of that silent piece of white paper, she didn't want to write her book after all. She wanted, and at the same time *didn't* want, to write yet another letter to Rami.

Anna hated it. She felt pathetic, asking her husband to come back, asking why he didn't write, why he was so cold during their weekly phone call. She didn't want to beg him for something she couldn't even define.

She stood up, switched off the lamp, and lit a cigarette. The little circle of red, glowing tobacco was the only thing Anna could see, a bright reflection on the window glass. She left the cigarette in an ashtray on the table before going and checking again on her children.

The two boys were asleep in an old red bunk bed, a gift from someone who didn't need it anymore. Marwan, now eleven, was putting on weight too fast, growing taller by the day, and it was difficult to find his shoe size in the shops in the village. Anna worried the creaky bed couldn't support her big son, so she had given him the bottom bunk and Amer the one above. Amer was still too small for a nine-year-old boy. He looked like he would never grow up. His legs were so thin that Anna had covered the manhole in front of the house out of fear that he would fall into it.

She was worried for her boys. She could see that they were completely bewildered. They had been back in Italy for nearly two years, and she saw that they still didn't understand why. Why were they here? Why had they abandoned their friends and house and father in another country? Anna tried to tell them that it was still too dangerous where they used to live, that she was a foreigner there, she wasn't allowed to stay there any longer, but that Baba had to stay because his job was there, and they needed the money. It was just for a few months. Baba would join them in their new house soon.

'But you have been saying that for years,' protested Amer.

Amer was the one who protested. His teacher said he was a difficult child, but Anna knew that he was already feeling the smallness of that village. Both Marwan and Amer were experiencing problems at school. They were the first foreigners in the village, with exotic names teachers couldn't pronounce or spell. Despite all Anna's efforts to teach them Italian, they had strong Arab accents, and when they didn't want the other children to understand them, they talked as fast as they could to each other in their first language.

At his new school, Amer had begun to tell the other kids about fights in the streets with rocks and stones, and scorpions in the garden, and how the school back home was always closed and people went to school in the neighbourhood houses, and how everyone grew food in their backyard, that his father was responsible for the eggs, and he wasn't scared of the curfew, and how the lemons in his garden were bigger than men's heads, and that once he had seen the head of a soldier looking out from a tank.

The teacher called Anna. Those stories were upsetting for the other children and the parents would complain. Sure, Amer wanted to impress his new friends, that's normal, that's okay, but there was no need to talk about those things.

Marwan was the more cautious of the two: he kept on pronouncing Bs as Ps, and tried to behave all grown up. He was the man of the family now, and he wanted to be taken seriously. His Italian was better than Amer's and Anna wondered if that was thanks to all the recipes they had written down together in Italian when Anna had finally decided to give cooking a go. She kept asking him if everything was alright at school. She knew the other children teased him, but he never spoke about it.

The teacher called Anna again. Amer had broken an older student's glasses.

'Why did you do that?' Anna asked him, in the principal's office.

'He called Marwan fat!'

Anna wanted to laugh and tell the teacher that she was the one to blame. She had told them not to accept arrogance.

But then she felt the whisper of loneliness inside her, and she didn't want her children to feel alone.

'Don't worry, I will pay for the glasses, and I'll make Amer understand the gravity of his behaviour.'

She wondered where she would find the money for the glasses, yet on the way home she bought her boys big ice-cream cones.

Now they were both sleeping, Marwan in that bed that was too small for him, and Amer in that body that was too small for him. Anna wanted to wake them up and tell them everything was okay, but she didn't believe it herself.

She went back to the piece of white paper and switched on the desk lamp again. The cigarette had turned to ash. She wanted to tell her husband that she couldn't stand everything by herself, that either he needed to come here, or that she needed to go back there. Fuck the distance, fuck the occupation, fuck the military governor and the family reunion, this was not what she had signed up for. She picked up the pen, thinking about Marwan and Amer. But then she felt the darkness around her closing in, almost dimming the light of the lamp, and she started another love letter.

My love …

*

Dear Babbo,

I scroll through Mum's letters. They span a period of two, three years. In some of the letters she said that she wrote dozens of them, but I only found eleven. You didn't keep them all. They were all in a shoebox in your house in Ramallah. You must have kept the ones that were the most important to you. They are all written on thin white paper, so thin that you can see through it and see the words written on the back. She used different pens, found here and there in the chaos of three children. Some are written in black ink, some in blue.

I can see her writing them, sometimes alone in the night, sometimes with us playing around her. She tells you when we are there, she tells you what we are doing, but just the nice things. She tells you how much we miss you, how much she misses you, and how hard it is to be alone, in that small village where people can't pronounce her children's names.

My favourite letter must be from around 1992. It is written in blue ink. It starts, as many others do, with My love. Then she talks about the weather. It's winter and it rains and rains. She is happy that your job is going well, but she would prefer being with you. She talks about how much Marwan hopes you will be back in time for his handball match. She asks what you think about sending my brothers to the summer camp. How hard it is making even simple decisions when you are not together.

Her neat blue calligraphy is covered with wild black squiggles. It's me. It's two-year-old me. I can see myself through the years and through her words. Mamma says I don't let her write, I keep calling Daddy, Daddy, *and kissing the paper, trying to write to you as she does. And then I run to the phone and say* hallo Daddy hallo, *waiting for your voice.*

Then the letter ends. Mum writes: Sometimes I would like to talk to you without writing on every line how much we miss you, but it's the only thing I truly think.

Sabrin, 2020

If I have to choose a soundtrack that takes me back to that time, it would be 'Heal the World' by Michael Jackson. I know that Michael Jackson is not the best singer to associate with childhood memories, but back then everyone worshipped him, and his music was played everywhere.

'Heal the World' was on the radio in the car that morning – the morning I experienced the power of music for the first time. I was already feeling sad. My father was going to take his flight back to Tel Aviv airport while I was at school, stuck at my desk. It was neither the first nor the last time that my father had needed to leave, but I only remember that one time. And I remember it because of the music.

My father was driving me to school, I was probably six years old, and the ride from home to school was exactly the same length as a song. We had a grey car, which could fit the five of us, me squeezed in the back, sitting in the middle between my older brothers. But that morning it was just the two of us. My father at the wheel, me sitting behind him. I was wondering what my father was thinking. He never said much about those long months he spent alone. He would buy dozens of long-lasting microwavable pasta and risotto meals to take with him because he said he missed Italian food. He would pack them all in his luggage and I wondered if all that space might be used better. For me, for instance. And I made plans for how I could possibly fit inside his suitcase.

He knew I was upset, because I had been silent and still for a whole three minutes. The radio was playing 'Heal the World', the saddest song ever, miraculously matching my sad, sad morning. My father was asking me questions, trying to make me talk, but I couldn't. I was making a huge effort to keep my tears back and to look like a strong girl. I was answering with muffled, mousy sounds. I was scared that if I opened my mouth, that song would come out with all its sadness and I would start crying.

When you drive somewhere you don't want to go, you hope the road will never end, that the car will never stop, that you can live all your life in the seat of that car and keep going for miles and miles until whatever is outside is not a threat anymore.

Once we had arrived at school, my father let me stay in the car until the music stopped and I hoped, for one second, that he had changed his mind, that he was about to start the engine again and take me away with him, like those packages of ready-made pasta. But he opened his door to get out, and then opened mine, and I got out of the car. End of the journey, end of the song. I looked at him, smelled his smell, and cried. I didn't want him to go, I wanted him to know that. I wanted everyone to know that.

I never asked what he was thinking during those moments. My father had to be the strong grown-up and so he didn't cry; he just held me tight, tight. The last memory I have from that morning is of my teacher trying to pull me away from my father's arms in the school hallway. My father telling me that he was coming back soon, my teacher telling me that he was coming back soon, 'Heal the World' echoing all around.

'He is not coming back!' shouted Benedetta, looking at me defiantly.

I thought she was my friend. Not someone who stabs you in the back.

She knew, like the entire school knew after the scene in the hallway, that to hurt me, to really hurt me, she just needed to mention my father and point out that he was not here, where all the other fathers were. A few years later, when some of my classmates' parents, including Benedetta's, started to get divorced, I felt a sense of justice. My parents were together, despite the distance, and despite what people had been saying for years.

But I didn't know that then. I didn't know that parents could get divorced. I just knew that my father was not there. He didn't pick me up every day from school like the other fathers. He wasn't there to talk to the other parents during my classmates' birthday parties. He wasn't there to cheer me on during school shows and competitions. I needed to say something back. I couldn't let Benedetta win the argument.

We were wearing our white smocks, and her brown eyes looked extremely mischievous. They made us wear that uniform, white for the girls and black for the boys, so that no one could tell if our clothes underneath were new or had been worn by our siblings for years before us. But you could still see the shoes, and Benedetta had always had the best shoes of the class. Her father owned the biggest shoe shop in the village.

I looked at the floor in search of the best answer I could give to Benedetta's mischievous eyes and shining boots, and I saw my shoes. They were old trainers, hand-me-downs from Amer. He was too small to inherit Marwan's wardrobe, but small enough to pass his on to me. I looked at those stretched shoes and knew I had to say something really clever.

'My mother is pregnant!'

This took Benedetta completely by surprise. At that age we all believed that if a woman was pregnant that meant that everything was okay, that everyone was happy and loved. And that I had won the argument.

'Yes, she is pregnant, and my father will come back!' I shouted those last words.

The matter was closed. I didn't think any more about what I had said until a few days later, after school, when Benedetta and her mother approached me and my mother in the car park.

'Congratulations!' Benedetta's mother said.

My mother and I looked at her, not trusting her smile.

'Your daughter told us that you are pregnant. Congratulations!' she persisted, noticing my mother's confusion. Her voice had a smugness to it that I didn't like.

My mother looked at me, and I recognised that glare. I was ready to lose the argument.

'Thank you,' my mother said, 'but she probably got confused. We are still trying!'

I looked at my mother standing beside me, covering up my lies and helping me win the argument. My shoes felt so comfortable.

'Why did you say such a thing?' my mother asked once we were alone. But there was no reproach in her voice.

I told her the whole story, about Michael Jackson in the hallway, about that day in school, and Benedetta's shining shoes, and what she had said about Babbo, that he was not coming back, was he?

'Of course he will come back,' she answered. 'Because he never really leaves us. Even when he is not with us, what do you think he does? He never stops thinking about you!'

The coffee had a weaker taste. For years Anna had learnt how to make coffee the Arab way – how to mix it with the powdery qahwe and add sugar and cardamom depending on her mood. The Italian coffee, and especially the coffee at the hospital where she worked, didn't have any effect on her. She even wondered if there was caffeine in it, because even after drinking cups of it she felt tired, like she was moving under water.

She turned the mixture of milk and coffee with the spoon and a drop hit the paper, right next to the full stop. Anna reread the sentence she had just written:

Ma quando tutto sarà finito saremo insieme 'per sempre' questo periodo sarà solo 'un brutto ricordo' e riusciremo presto a tornare tutti 'normali' – But when all this will end we will be together 'forever', this period will be just 'a bad memory' and we will be able to be all 'normal' again.

Normal, that word again – maybe that is why she felt the need to put it in inverted commas. Normality meant less for Anna now than ever before.

When they had moved back to her childhood village, she had dusted off her nursing degree and found a job on the psychiatric ward at the local hospital. During her breaks she found time for coffee and letter-writing, using the paper and the pens that the patients used for their activities. Normality was a sarcastic word to use in that place.

Anna had been working on the ward for a year and could clearly see that the boundaries between what was considered normal and what was not often became blurred.

At her locker in the changing room on the top floor of the hospital building, during the change of shift with the other nurses, she could sense that their eyes were on her. Or sometimes when she entered the staffroom, and the chatter stopped. Or when she phoned home to hear her children's voices and then turned around to be greeted with pitying smiles. She felt so tempted to slam the door, turn the table upside down, and punch those smiling faces.

How could they not see that it was not her choice to be there? If it had been down to her, she would have never come back, to the same people, the same names, the same stares, the same gossips. If she didn't punch their faces, it was only because she knew that those nurses were the mothers of her children's classmates. It was for her children's sake, not for her own, that she tried to befriend those women.

I can't go on like this (I am saying it like a joke, but I'm worried it may be true), she kept writing. *One day I might trade places with the patients and become one of those who now I have in my care!*

*

The Basaglia law on mental health was approved in Italy in 1978 and implemented gradually along the years up to 1998. When my mother started working at the hospital somewhere around 1991 and 1992, the effects of the law were starting to be felt.

Psychiatric patients were no longer confined to isolated asylums, and were now living in the community, monitored through the hospital where they had to go regularly for check-ins and rehabilitation. Some of the more serious cases would stay in the hospital for longer periods but were never sectioned, or treated like prisoners. The main idea behind the change in the law was that mental health should be seen as part of the social structure – even caused by it – and not as something to be hidden away. It was a revolutionary approach, one in which my mother profoundly believed.

She used to tell me stories about some of the people she took care of. How the majority of them had been driven to madness by their previous confinement in the asylum, how they would have been fine if only they had received the right care.

In that small village, with psychiatric patients living *in* the community rather than kept away from it, we used to meet many of them in the street, out for a walk, shopping, eating an ice cream. So I was able to put faces to the names in the stories, or so I thought.

My mother never kept us children away from the people she spent most of her time with. In the mornings when she wasn't there to take us to school, she was with them. When she wasn't there to pick us up, she was with them, and when she wasn't sleeping with us she was working her night shift with them. She had never ignored them or dismissed them. And when they came to greet her in the street when she was with us or ask for her help in the supermarket or at the ice-cream counter, my mother never stepped back.

There are three of them I remember clearly: Erminia, Giordano and Carlo. Erminia and Giordano were both old, or at least they looked really old to me when I was six.

Erminia had ended up in an asylum when she was really young. She suffered from narcolepsy, a disorder that makes it hard to control when you fall asleep, and once she had dozed off while cooking at the hob, setting herself and the kitchen on fire. Her family couldn't cope with her and her condition for many reasons including financial ones. And so, the cheapest and easiest solution was the asylum. In short, Erminia didn't have any psychiatric problems. What you can see now, said my mother – the fact that she barely speaks, that she always trembles and swings back and forth, the fact that she dresses in so many layers of clothes – all of that is the result of the kind of environment in which she was confined. We usually met Erminia walking around in her big bundle of clothes, swinging from one foot to the other, on her way home. Sometimes she wanted to be left alone, sometimes my mother would walk with her.

Giordano was in his sixties, maybe seventies. His only fault was to be born the son of an unmarried teenage mother who was confined for the shame she brought on her family. He had grown up in the asylum. That was his only reality.

He had nightmares about being chained to the radiators. We usually met him in front of the tobacco shop when he was trying to buy cigarettes. My mother offered him one of hers and they would smoke together while we were playing. Occasionally she bought him a pack.

Carlo would often come to our apartment at dinner time. Of the three of them, he was probably the one who needed the most help: I could sense that my mother was more careful around him. Sometimes she allowed him to come in and sit at the table and share dinner with us. Other times she would just give him a sandwich and talk him through the reasons why he needed to go back to his community house.

One of the first arguments between my parents that I remember was about Carlo. My father didn't like how often he came and rang at our door. One evening, as we were all sitting down for dinner, the doorbell rang and my mother let Carlo in. He took a seat at the end of the table, and my brothers and I instinctively moved away towards the other end. His face was red, his movements were slow, and it was as if his hands were not his own. My mother sat right next to him.

I remember fragments of the argument that followed, after my mother and my father had driven Carlo back to his accommodation: 'He is on medication, that is why he was so red' and 'I can't leave him alone' or 'You can't let him get his way' and 'What if he becomes aggressive?'

I don't remember Carlo coming again, or if he did, my mother didn't let him in. After that night I saw him during my childhood and teenage years and even when I was an adult: he would walk around the village or take the bus to the sea. He died some years ago, after my mother.

There are photographs of our first birthdays spent in

Italy. We are wearing crowns made out of grey cardboard. No one is there apart from my mother's cousin and maybe one or two friends of my brothers'. I have always thought that my mother was such an angel with her patients, taking care of them and never leaving them alone. But I look at the photographs and the letters I found, and I believe that it was more complicated than that. Back in her village, which she had been so desperate to escape from all her life, my mother felt more affinity with these people who, like her, didn't belong there.

But when all this will end we will be together 'forever', this period will be just 'a bad memory' and we will be able to be all 'normal' again.

I read this sentence again and again. The first thing I notice is my mother's use of inverted commas. She used them three times for *forever, a bad memory, normal.*

Normal is probably the easiest to explain. She didn't like the way she was supposed to act 'normal' compared to who was considered 'abnormal'. My mother didn't feel comfortable with those labels. She also knew that the normality she had created with my father, the normality she cherished, was not normal at the time. Mixed marriages were still rare in both of their cultures, and my father was the first foreigner in our whole county.

Bad memory: is she already detaching herself from that moment, as a way of isolating that bad memory from the rest of her life?

But it's *forever* that unsettles me the most. She seems scared that there is not a forever any more with my father, a happily ever after. From other letters, I can tell that she was feeling that the distance was destroying everything and that they would not have recovered from it.

La vita è così corta che questi giorni lontani, io e te, mi sembrano proprio buttati via.
Life is so short ...

*

To Ramallah

Amer was wearing the earring with the stone that looked like a diamond. He liked shiny things and wanted to impress his father with his new look. Amer had taken a while to get his ear pierced because everyone pestered him about whether he was sure, really sure he wanted his ear pierced like a girl. But he did want to. He thought he would look more like Baggio. That is why Amer grew his hair out too. It was not exactly long, though. It was rather a small ponytail, a bit longer than the rest. It was what Baggio had.

Baggio was Amer's favourite football player and he could talk about him for hours and hours: Baggio was Italy's hope for the World Cup.

Luckily that day Italy wasn't playing. So Amer and Marwan would not miss Baggio's great passes and goals. They were travelling by plane all alone to Tel Aviv airport for the three months of summer holidays. Anna had dropped them off at Rome airport and Rami was waiting for them at the other end. But on the plane it was just them! Amer was thinking about the look on his cousins' faces in Ramallah, and then his classmates' back in Italy when he would tell them about this trip. All alone on the plane!

*

When we got to Tel Aviv airport, they took us and brought us into a separate room, alone, but they didn't do anything to us.

They just checked our passports and asked questions.

I found my brother's diary in one of my mother's drawers. In every entry, my brother wrote the day but not the year. Thanks to the references to the World Cup and the music festival organised by my father, I know it is 1994. My brother was 12 years old.

He wrote in one of those notebooks with a brown paper cover and pages lined with blue ink. It reminds me of my first notebooks too. He wrote in cursive, like you were expected to do at school, with big letters. He must have been at the beginning of secondary school, but his calligraphy is still hesitant. I wonder how confident he felt, writing in Italian.

There is a video of him from around the same age, in a play at his summer school. In the video my brother speaks Italian with a strong Arab accent. How hard was it for him to make that sudden move from one country to another? What did it do to his sense of identity?

*

Amer was looking at his cousin's arm. George had tried to defend him at school and one of the older boys had bitten him. Now George's arm was all bandaged. George was Amer's favourite cousin, the first son of his older uncle, Milad. This is why he was named after their grandfather George. Amer thought that one day he would call his son Rami.

'Does it hurt?' asked Amer, pointing his finger towards George's arm, half tempted to touch it and half scared of doing so.

'No, it doesn't,' said George, straightening his back to make himself look taller.

Amer thought that he should have been the one to be

bitten, so that he could show the scar off at school. After all it was because of him that the fight had started.

It was their first day of summer school in Ramallah. Their fathers had sent them there to keep them entertained and they had come back with scratches and bites.

'It's not George's fault,' said Amer to his uncle. 'He was just helping me!'

'Helping you with what?'

'Those boys made fun of me. They said I look like a girl. That earrings and long hair are for girls, and they tried to pull my ponytail. I told them that they don't know anything. That this is like Baggio, but they don't even know Baggio!'

*

The village
It was not easy to get three weeks off in summer, but Anna had booked her annual leave months in advance. She knew that no one asked for that amount of time off, and that her colleagues would complain to the head nurse.

'Can you not take two weeks instead?' The head nurse had called her into his office just a couple of weeks before her departure.

'No, I can't. Have you any idea how much those flights cost? I haven't seen my boys in nearly two months and my husband in five. I need to spend time with them!'

'You know that no one asks for three weeks in summer.'

'No one has a family like mine!' Her voice came out sounding harsh.

Anna would not back down, not this time.

'Va bene, Anna. I understand. Take your three weeks and su che manca poco! And you will see your Arafat!'

Anna smiled at her little victory and at the nickname that

they had given Rami. For months they had called him that at the hospital. She should probably say something, ask everyone to make a little effort to remember her husband's name like they did with everyone else's.

But at the end of the day she didn't care, let them call him what they wanted as long as she could go for three weeks.

Ramallah, 14 August 1994
Today la mia mamma and my sister arrived, la mia mamma is more beautiful than I remembered.

CHAPTER ELEVEN

Qidreh I

Bethlehem, 1998

Helena was surprised she could remember her first ride on George's motorbike. How was it possible that after so many years, those moments, which had long since disappeared from her mind, were reappearing again, exactly when her body couldn't move anymore, and her bones were failing her?

Her eyes were the only things she could move without pain: she could move them to the side to check what was going on in her room, with all these people coming in and out – children, grandchildren, great-grandchildren too young to see this. But most of the time she would just search the white ceiling, looking for things she believed didn't exist anymore.

She looked at a specific point above her, where the sun coming in from the window on her left hit the ceiling and was brighter. In that brightness she saw another light, not in that room but on the sea. The blue, the reflection and the wind made her lower her eyes again. Through her lashes she could only see black silhouettes, interrupting the sunbeams. She felt unstable on the bike and, putting her hand below George's armpits and then around him, grabbed his torso tighter. Her head found space on his shoulder, her nose and lips only millimetres from his neck. While George drove that bike towards the Lebanese coast, his cologne mixed with the salty air. He looked like an actor with the collar of his shirt coming out from his brown jacket. It must have been their first time because she was still not sure if that intimacy – her breasts and belly squeezing against his back – was appropriate.

Voices – mama, mayye. They were interrupting her ride. She twitched her arm to send them away, but instead they took her hand and tried to make her drink, speaking to her in soft whispers – mama, mama ... shwayet mayye. The room was also full of voices the day she had to meet her future husband. Helena could not believe her father wanted her to marry a butcher. She went to a French school, played music, wrote poems, painted. A butcher, sixteen years older than her, why? For a good family name.

Helena expected a 30-year-old butcher to look old, like her father. His clothes covered in blood, his hands big and dirty, good for cutting chunks of meat, not to caress a girl. But when Helena laid her green eyes on George and saw his straight nose, the proud lines of his lips, his hair thick and black, elegantly dressed in his suit and with his long fingers, she had to tell her parents – trying not to betray her excitement – that if they really wanted her to marry that man, she would consider it.

The voices had stopped. Helena tried to open her eyes to see if she was alone. But opening her eyes was not easy. The light in the room was still too strong, like the shimmering sea. Like understanding George. That was never easy. George only ever used short sentences and never gave full explanations.

Their first night, while she was sitting on the edge of the bed, not sure what to do, George was sitting on the other side, silent, as if he too didn't know what to do.

That was not possible, thought Helena, so she started to undress. Maybe she was the one who needed to start.

'You are too young,' he stopped her. Then he lay down on his side of the bed and closed his eyes.

Why had he married her if she was too young?

She giggled at the memory, but what came out of her mouth must have sounded like something different, because people rushed into the room. That made her laugh again and another strange sound came out, like the starting splutter of a motorbike.

The first time George had told her about his bike, she didn't believe him. She couldn't imagine how his silence could get along with the rumble of the engine.

In their first months together, he had barely touched her and the times that he did, Helena didn't know if it was intentional or by accident.

It happened one day in the butchery, while he was tenderising the meat. She had accompanied him to see his shop and was observing him from behind, trying not to disturb him. The flesh, cut into big chunks, and the smell of blood made her nauseous and yet drew her closer to the counter. George turned around suddenly, as though he was scared his wife would get too close, and his fingers left beef blood on her cheek.

It happened on the balcony while she was hanging out the wet, white sheets and the wind wrapped them around her body. George came to untangle her and she closed her eyes while he peeled the layers of fabric off her.

And it happened in bed. After those first nights when George would lie stiff and distant and she would curl up on her side of the bed, their sleeping bodies started to become comfortable with each other. One day they woke up and found their limbs fully entwined.

Remembering that moment, Helena made an involuntary movement towards her right, the side where George used to be, but her body wasn't hers anymore. How old was she? Where was George?

'La, yamma, ihdi, don't move.'

On one of those mornings during the first year of their marriage, George told her he was going for a ride.

Helena didn't pay much attention; she still couldn't believe he had a motorbike. It was not a big one, it was actually quite sleek with the seat slightly lower than the fuel tank and the fuel tank looking like the body of a wasp. Helena wondered where George had bought it. Maybe from the British army.

But her husband didn't come back in time for dinner, nor when night fell. By nearly midnight Helena was still waiting, not knowing what else to do, when George opened the door.

'Wein kunet?'

'I went for a ride.'

'Toul linhar?'

'Aiwa! I told you.'

'You said you were going for a ride, u bas.'

'Na'am, this is a ride!'

'But you haven't even touched that thing before!'

'That is because I didn't want to leave you lahalek, alone, before, but now you are doing well.'

'lahali?! I am not doing well if I have no idea where my husband is.'

'Ana ... I went to Beirut.'

It was one of the longest conversations they had had, and Helena couldn't believe how many words this man was speaking. She was the one feeling speechless. Beirut? How far was Beirut by bike? And did he go alone? Did he visit someone? Helena felt for the first time a sting of jealousy. Was he not touching her because he was touching someone else? She wanted to ask, she wanted explanations, but 'Next time I want to come with you' was the only thing that came out of her mouth.

George nodded.

How many years had passed since then? Helena tried to count, but her mind kept mixing up the days and years.

Helena tried to grab the sheets on her bed, as if to grab at the passing time. Instead, the feeling of her husband's jacket came back to her. She remembered how she had squeezed him for fear of falling off his bike, and how for the first time she had recognised his body, feeling it under her fingers. For a second George had put his hand on hers – her fingers between his palm and his stomach – just a quick touch before putting it back on the handlebars.

They had left Bethlehem early in the morning and reached first Haifa and then Akka in under three hours. Approaching the town, Helena first saw the fortification on the sea – not as a reminder of wars and sieges but as a crown on the water. She could have walked for hours along the old stone streets and among the minarets and campanili, but George was impatient to show her the boats docked at the pier. The fishermen were gutting and selling the fish caught during the night before. The smell of seaweed, water and fish blood hit Helena's nostrils.

Back on the bike, driving along the coast, the air was full of salty water, and they could pretend they were on a boat, travelling even further away.

Three more hours and they were in Beirut. They sat in a restaurant near the port and looked at the boats and watched the big ships arriving. The architecture on the docks was so grandiose that someone seated at the table next to them was swearing that, wallah, Beirut was more beautiful than making love to a woman.

Helena blushed and wondered if that was true.

Back at home that night George touched her with purpose for the first time. Standing behind her, he unbuttoned her dress. He moved her hair, heavy from the salty air, and caressed her neck with the straight line of his nose and placed his lips on the soft dip at the base of her nape. He held her, his hands on her breast, then down her belly, and then just one more bend down, and the smell of seaweed, water and fish blood came back, eerie and familiar. Helena moaned ...

'Shu yamma?'

The voice of her oldest daughter interrupted them. Helena tried to shut it out.

She wanted to feel the weight of his chest, her hands on his back, her calves on his buttocks once again. She moaned again.

'Malek yamma?'

Her son's voice interrupted her thoughts once again. How could Helena tell them that she wasn't in pain?

After that first time, they would go to Beirut often, eating fish at the same restaurant near the port and making love at night. Then, in 1948, the world shrank. The Nakba took everything away from them. Nothing was theirs anymore. George closed himself back into his silence and he said he would never leave Bethlehem again. They were not free anymore, so what was the point of trying to go anywhere? For what? To see that the world they knew was gone?

Helena didn't like where her mind was taking her and opened her eyes. She could distinguish the shape of her five children around her bed. The sun was still shimmering above them all and Helena saw the sea – bahar Haifa, bahar Akka, bahar Beirut – one more time. The bed glided away, and so did the pain in her bones. She forgot her age and felt the motorbike moving underneath her. Her eyelids were lowered.

When she opened them again, the ceiling had disappeared.

People were sitting all around the house, on every free chair, on every armrest and or free space on the carpet. On the balcony, someone ventured to rest on the balustrade between the columns. Anna wanted to sit down too, but she couldn't. She stopped at the doorstep of the reception room with a tray of coffee in her hands, observing the men squeezed onto the sofas used for formal gatherings – the ones with white silk seats and the inlaid wooden armrest. The first time she had come to this house – twenty years ago? – she had sat there, close to the armrest. Yes, she had sat exactly there, Rami next to her, his sisters on the sofa next to theirs, and George and Helena on the armchairs. Now Rami's brother was in George's place, and Rami took the place where Helena had been.

Anna made an effort to smile and offer coffee to the people gathered in the living room. She tried to remember who all these men were. She knew some of them, but the house had been full for three days, people coming and going. She was sure she had never met many of them before.

Dozens of mouths smoked, chatted, sipped coffee, or ate bowls of qidreh. There were those who were remembering Helena with sweet words, those who pretended to, someone was talking about politics and Arafat's latest decisions, some had watery eyes, others patted each other's shoulders.

It was not the first funeral Anna had been to in Palestine, but each time she couldn't help but be amazed by the quantity of people, food, smoke and coffee. For three days family, relatives, friends, neighbours – but also friends of friends and neighbours of neighbours – would come, stay for hours, and be served the yellow rice and lamb. Anna had always felt overwhelmed. Why should you have all these people around you at the exact time when you want to be left alone? Because you actually don't want to be alone, part of her had learnt. In that way something of the person you have just lost is still there, in people's conversations, in their movements, while teeth are still chewing and lips are still sipping, present in the dozens of hands that keep touching and patting and in the warmth of bodies that fill the empty space.

Anna's life in that country, when they had just moved there from Italy, had started with a funeral: George's. That life was coming to a close once and for all with another. Helena had taken Anna under her wing back then, and it was only today – not when Anna had left seven years ago – that an era ended.

She tried to look at Rami through the clouds of cigarette smoke, but she couldn't see his face. She had not been able to see his face in days. His features had become like wax, no movement or expression detectable. The smoke cleared for a moment, between one drag and another. Anna saw Helena. Just for one moment sitting on the chair, in that crowded living room, filling the space with her presence, her features imprinted on the faces of all those people around. Then someone blew out his cigarette smoke and the image of Helena dissolved again, leaving the chair to Rami.

For days after my grandmother's death there was nothing to eat but this yellow rice with big pieces of lamb. My father kept telling me it was beef, that it has the same taste as burgers, the only meat I used to eat when I was nine. But it didn't taste like a burger at all.

'Why don't you look in the fridge?' my brother intervened.

QIDREH I

'You can have whatever you want, and no one will say anything!'

My brother's advice sounded clever. He always had these bright ideas that never occurred to me. He moved towards the fridge, opened it, the inside light bright on the white empty shelves.

'You see, there's nothing!' I protested.

'Nothing? There are a lot of drinks!'

He started to take out bottles of sodas and juices, and after taking a long glass from the cupboard, he mixed all together.

'This is called a cocktail!' he said before taking a big sip of the grey drink and giving out a satisfied *ahhhh* just in front of my nose.

'I want one too,' I said to my brother.

'Oh, but this one is my secret recipe. You have to make your one!'

And so he left, passing me a glass as a baton of complicity.

When I opened the fridge, I went for colours. Red cherry juice. I then added a gulp from one of the bottles my brother had used because it was already out and I wanted my drink to be fizzy.

'Aaaaaaah,' I gasped, after a sip, exactly like my brother did.

But it was missing something. If I wanted my cocktail to be the best, I had to add my own secret ingredient. I opened the fridge again and, out of the way, behind everything, there was, white, the carton of milk.

That was my final ingredient. I was sure no one had ever thought about it.

I poured it and saw the white of the milk reaching the bottom of the glass and coming back up like a grey cloud of plump grey worms. It smelled of cheese. Whoa!

What did I do? Whatever, I thought highly enough of it to be sure it required the attention of my brother.

I ran towards the dining room where he was sitting at the table with my cousins and our oldest brother.

'Look! I made the best cocktail ever! You should try it,' I whispered in his ear.

'Oh come on, non ora. Can't you see that we are playing?'

I looked at him and pulled his shirt. He let a snort out. Then he rolled his eyes and winked in the direction of my cousins.

I knew I was not one of them. They were four boys, all around fifteen, speaking all the same language, and remembering the same things. I was me. The only girl. The one who arrived when they thought it was just the four of them. Who didn't eat what they were eating, who didn't understand when they were talking.

My brother looked at the glass and started to laugh.

'What did you put in it?' he asked.

'I can't tell you. It's my secret recipe!'

That made him laugh even louder and he started to speak in Arabic to the other boys. I knew he was explaining what happened because he kept saying the word *cocktail* and laughing.

'So, are you going to try it?' I tried to interrupt them and get his attention back.

'Did *you* try it?'

I shook my head.

'You should try it first then!'

He passed the glass back to me.

I put my nose close to the liquid again, thinking that maybe the smell of cheese should not be the smell of a cocktail. But I love cheese, I thought, comparing it to another plate of yellow rice. I took a big gulp …

It was only pride that made me keep the cocktail in my mouth, trying to swallow it down. My eyes were burning not only for the taste of rotten milk.

I was focusing so much on keeping my lips closed that I could see the boys laughing only through the layers of tears getting thicker. In those cackles, I found the will to swallow everything.

I did it and they stopped, still and silent. I breathed once, puffing my chest. I won. For once. For one second, before the retching came and I had to run towards the bathroom, another burst of laughter following me.

*

Bethlehem, 2018

My oldest brother and I are walking from the Church of the Nativity back to my aunt's house. But instead of taking the main road – the one right in front of the church, the one for the tourists with all the souvenirs displayed on the walls, and the vendors calling out to you in the language they guess you may speak – we take a side road. The one the tourists don't go down.

The main road is the one I walk down every day. It takes twenty minutes to get from my aunt's house to my Arabic classes. I walk back and forth twice a day, five times a week if not more, and after a week the vendors still try to catch my attention, speaking in English, then in Spanish, then in Italian, until I answer back in Arabic. La, shukran. But all tourists learn those two words. *No, thank you.*

I don't look Palestinian. I don't talk like one, I don't walk like one, I don't dress like one, and apparently even when I stand still and don't say anything, there is still something that gives me away. I don't belong. I know I am not one of them.

I don't speak their language as they do. I don't understand them when they talk to me, I don't remember the same things, I haven't lived through the same history. I am always surrounded by people who talk for me, and I have a passport that at any moment can take me away from here.

'Yalla, look at this, what would you like?'

Every morning I keep walking. I ignore the vendors and, in this way, make the distance between us even wider.

When I am with my brother, it is different. He talks to them, answers them, they pat each other on the shoulder and laugh. I look at them and smile. Feeling embarrassed and guilty.

'Just talk to them,' my brother says. 'Tell them who you are, ask them how they are doing, you know all these words, don't you?' And he adds other words I might need. This is baladi, ahli, beiti – my country, my family, my house.

I know those words too and he is right that I could talk to people. Show them that I am from this balad, just like them. My brother starts talking to an old man in front of a shop of religious souvenirs, to show me how to do it. He tells the old man that our family is from here, the family house just around the corner.

'W inti?' The man asks looking at me.

'Ana kaman,' I answer. Me too.

The old man's shop is right in front of the building where I take my Arabic classes and I know he will be the man I am going to talk to for the rest of my time here. He already knows I am from here too. But one day he asks me what I do in the building for ajaneb, for foreigners, and I forget the Arabic words I need to explain to him that yes, I am Palestinian, my roots are here and I was born here, but my mother was not. I can say where I am from, more or less, and I can say what I am doing but I can't express myself deeply, bene bene, a fondo, mneeh mneeh. I can say that I am here to study Arabic, but I can't explain why, and I can survive in the streets, ask for help, say what I need, but I can't really tell people who I am.

I feel guilty because I can't find the words. Because I am here to study the language that the rest of my family knows naturally. Because I am an ajnabie. I can leave – anytime. I feel guilty because I am one of the few foreigners who come all the way along this road. Most of them come on the big coaches that bring them all the way to the front of the church and leave them there, warning them not to go any further than that, not to talk to the locals and not to buy from them, because they are dangerous. I feel guilty because I don't talk to them either, I don't buy from them either, and I ignore them in the same way. But how can I tell them that it is not out of fear?

My brother insists we go back home via one of the side streets. I never walk along it when I am alone, even if it is the shortest route. On that side street I will feel even more ajnabie and I don't want to.

The street is dirty. The white tiles are the same as on the main road, but the white is barely visible here. Boxes of vegetables take up half of the road, with the leaves and rotten fruit discarded on the ground. Skinny men in T-shirts negotiate prices with heavy women wearing their thobe with embroideries as red as the tomatoes they are selling. Children are running around everywhere: some venture into the corner shops full of sweets and crisps to ask the price and run out again. If they don't have enough coins, they try to convince their friends to do a whip-round.

My brother goes into one of those shops too. He has recognised the crisps he used to buy when he was a child. While we are in there, a little girl enters. A bright pink T-shirt, two chubby legs sticking out of yellow shorts. She asks the price of the same kind of crisps my brother is buying.

'Talat shawakel,' the owner says.

She opens her palm, full of small coins, a hair pin, a plastic toy, and sticky with sweets she must have eaten. She counts, but she doesn't have enough and so she leaves the packet of crisps on the counter and runs out. My brother takes it and, before the girl reaches the door, he stops her.

'Stanni!' he says. 'Hada ilek.'

And throws the pack of crisps towards her. She catches it, smiles and keeps running.

When we are back in the street, my brother switches his attention to something else. From a dark doorway the strong smell of meat broth fills the street, stronger than all the other smells around.

We go closer and put our heads across the threshold. Inside it's dark and hot. The only thing we can see is a flame and the dark figure of a man working below ground level. I would never have entered, but my brother is inside before I can even think about it.

'Ahlan, keefak? Shu bt'amal? Shu btutbokh?' my brother asks.

It is a communal oven, where people bring things to be cooked or come to buy food for special occasions. The wood oven is in a sort of hole in the ground. The man is bustling down there, swallowed up by the heat. He is wearing a white sleeveless singlet, his skin blackened by the coals and smoke, shiny with sweat. A dirty towel hangs from his belt, which he uses to dry his sweat, to clean the top of his working table and to take out big black copper pots from the fire. This man is so small and skinny that the pots cover half of his body when he brings them out from the oven to the worktable.

He places the pots on his table with a thud, and opens

the lid. A cloud of that strong smell of broth spreads thicker in the room.

My brother and I move closer to see what he has just taken out. When I see it, I have no doubt. The yellow rice, the smell taking me back to that afternoon of sour milk cocktails and scorn.

'Hadi qidreh,' says the man from his hole.

He makes a spoon shape with his right hand and takes a mouthful of broth and rice. He sucks it all in. He tastes it and curls up his lips. He doesn't seem happy. He shakes the pot, vigorously, and with the same hand reaches out for the bowl of salt, and adds some. Then turmeric – a handful splashed in, with a halo of yellow powder. He grabs two, three more pieces of lamb from another pot and tosses them in as well. He mixes everything with his hand, all the way to his elbow, and then takes out another spoonful with his hand, tastes it and nods. He puts back the lid, lifts the pot again and with the same effort drags it back to the oven. As he faces the fire his body is lit up by the blaze of the flames. He stands there for a moment that seems long enough to melt him, but when he turns around, he is just shinier. He takes the towel from his belt, dries his hands, his forehead, and quickly the table, before tucking it back into his belt.

My brother takes photographs and asks questions. He even takes a selfie with the man, who for the first time reveals his white teeth for the picture.

He starts talking more openly with my brother.

'We have lots of funerals these days,' he says, 'shughul ktir.' He waves his hand, showing the queue of pots waiting to go in the oven. 'Before, people just brought their rice pots ready to go in, but now they place their order, pay and leave, and I am here to do all by myself.'

'Can I taste it?' asks my brother.

CROSSING

The man nods and goes to fetch one of the pots from the fire, stumbling on his way back. He opens the lid, releasing clouds of fragrant, yellow rice – afternoon of cocktails, my grandmother's funeral. The man scoops the broth up with his hand and tastes it. He takes another handful and waves with his head for my brother to move closer. My brother goes and stretches his hand as a cup towards the hole with the confidence of someone who works in a kitchen too. He comes back with a small pyramid of yellow rice and a paddle of broth in his palm. Before it burns him, he slurps it in and closes his eyes with a sigh. Was he remembering my grandmother? Or all the people who came to pay their respects at her funeral? Or was it something hazier?

'It's a strange job that he does, isn't it?' I ask my brother when we get outside again. The summer heat outside feels cooler and the sun brighter.

'What do you mean?'

I think about the fact that this man is a cross between a cook and a mortician. People come to him not just for food, but for funerals. When someone shows up at the threshold of this dark place, it's often because someone has just died. Yet what he does is enabling life to go on. Keeping the bodies of the people left behind functioning, hydrated, rested, fed.

I think about this and regret not having tried the qidreh from the hand of that man. Suddenly the yellow rice starts to have a meaning for me, deeper than the memory of my grandmother's funeral that it awakens. How warming it must be to take a spoon of hot broth, in a moment when your mind is wiped out, and life feels heavy.

*

Ventoruccia farmhouse, 1999

I have two memories of my great-grandmother, my mother's granny. In the first, she has her apron around her waist and is wearing a headscarf. She was around ninety years old and was starting to bend over due to the hump on her back, but I still remember her as the biggest woman in the family. She used to wear dark glasses – not sunglasses, just brown lenses. Every time we went to visit her in the old farmhouse she would keep going back and forth, from the kitchen to the pantry, from the pantry to the henhouse, from the henhouse to the pergola.

Certain smells and flavours bring up my memories of her: the taste of tomato sauce, dark red, with a layer of bright green oil on top, the pieces of white baccalà moving up and down while simmering. She used to cut a piece of bread for me and, leaning the loaf on her belly, she would slice it with the blade facing her body. The bread was always hard, two or three days old.

'Don't worry,' she would say, 'put it in the sauce.'

My hands would smell of the sauce and fish for days.

I also remember the sweet and yet pungent smell of uva fragola. She would make me eat the grapes straight from the vine with bread: small purple beads, warm from the sun, exploding under my teeth with a quick pop.

My hands would have red stains on them for days.

But that memory of her in the fields, in her farmhouse, is distant, faded and not entirely connected with me. Towering, hard, wild, her hands would scratch my cheeks every time she wanted to caress me. That woman belonged to something I couldn't understand: a life so long, a time so past that I could not even begin to imagine and of which I was more or less scared.

The second memory I have of her is the more familiar one,

the one that connects her to my childhood. It was after she had a stroke and had been found unconscious in the henhouse. Unable to live alone anymore, she was forced to leave the farmhouse and move in with her daughter (my granny), her son-in-law (my grandfather) and her sister (my great-grand-aunt), who she still hated enormously.

As a child, I went to my granny's every day, spending entire afternoons there when my mother was working her shifts at the hospital. I used to sit at the dining table with my homework in front of me, the fire lit.

Sitting there in the brown armchair, folded in two, barely able to speak, my great-grandmother wasn't scary anymore. She also had a new pair of glasses, with light lenses, and I could see her eyes clearly: there was nothing inside them.

My granny had bought a trolley for her so that she could take small walks back and forth in the hallway.

'Nonna!' I would cheer her on. She would smile because this is what my mum used to call her. Her eyes came back for one second and then they would disappear again.

During the summer I spent even more hours in that house, playing in the garden, or trying to find something to occupy me around the house.

One day my granny gave me an old notebook for drawing and scribbling. I had played with it a bit that morning, pretending to be a teacher, but it didn't entertain me enough. It was different now that I was a police officer: that was my tickets book, and my great-grandmother a restless driver to fine.

I sat straight in the armchair and every time my great-grandmother came closer, I stopped her.

'Where are you going?' I would ask.

'There!' she would mumble, trying to point her rumpled finger towards the end of the hallway.

'Why are you going so fast?'
'Ehm!' she would shrug.
'This is not a good excuse. I will have to fine you!'
I would write a price on one of the pages of the notebook and give it to her.

She would take it, smile and keep walking. At the end of the hallway, she would turn back, wheels squeaking all the way back to me, and hand me the ticket. I would accept it as money and wait for another round to issue another fine.

That Christmas I received a hard plastic dog, covered with brown fluff, and a button to make it bark. I knew immediately that it was going to be my police dog.

The next time I went to my granny's, I brought the plastic dog with me. I had it in my backpack, hidden, waiting for my great-grandmother to start walking with her trolley to show her the new asset.

When she finally took off, I fined her twice as usual and when she went for a third round, I took out the dog and made it bark.

My great-grandmother came faster towards me. I proceeded with my usual questions, wrote her ticket and handed it to her. She stretched her arm to take it, but instead she reached out for the plastic dog.

'Not the dog, the ticket, the ticket!' I told her.

But she didn't listen.

'Nonna the ticket, the ticket!'

'Take this!' I said again, trying to put the ticket in her hands and take back the dog.

But she didn't let go, her strength suddenly back, her eyes sharp.

One afternoon I came back from school and my great-grandmother was not there anymore. That's it. In my memory there is nothing else. No funeral, no people going back and forth from the house, no qidreh. In Italy funerals are a fast affair. One dies and is buried, everything in a matter of a couple of days. Then things move on.

She died when she was nearly one century old. I was not even ten years old.

CHAPTER TWELVE

Qidreh II

Palestine, 1999–2000

The road unfolded through the hills of rocky dunes. In summer, the refraction of the sun over the white of the rocks would dazzle the eye. But the winter sun is gentler: it leans over the surfaces, making shapes neater and colours more solid. It seems possible to see every rock on the hill. The skies are always light blue, the clouds suspended cotton wool. Even our car felt as if it was not touching the dark tarmac.

It was my first time in Palestine for Christmas. That winter I got a sense of belonging there. For the first time my brothers let me sleep in their bedroom, in our house in Ramallah. We would spend the nights listening to Celine Dion and Ricky Martin's new songs on my brother's new CD player and headphones.

During that Christmas trip I wrote a journal as my school homework. I expected to find my memories confirmed in those pages, yet none of the things I remember now are written down there. Maybe they weren't important to me when I was only ten, or I couldn't understand them, or they were too hard for me to write down. Yet these are the memories that have stayed in my mind.

As I scroll through this journal, I see, as for the first time, the things that were instead important to that girl – eating outside, receiving gifts, doing sleepovers with new friends, being allowed to open (but not drink) a bottle of champagne for New Year and to dance with the rest of my family until 1 a.m.

It was the edge of the new millennium, and excitement was all around us. It was in the people celebrating, the glittering velvet dresses, my brother's new life at university, the songs we listened to, the happiness of my parents, the unusual heat of that December and the unusual snow of January, and in that freedom of movement.

That day in the car I started to belong to the landscape, to see it as part of my identity. Before then my memories of Palestine are fleeting. A corner shop selling strange crisps. A shawarma sandwich in one hand and a green bottle of soda in the other. A tall slide with a Mickey Mouse head at the top. The dark green of trees and bushes that I can't recognise. Dust on my sandals. Boxes of little chicks huddled together sold by an old lady in the crowded streets of a market. The taste of meat and cucumber at sunset. Being squeezed into a shared taxi, music on the radio. A lemon tree in the garden.

But what I saw from the car window that Christmas is what stands clear: the beginning of something, not just fragments.

Then the car stopped. For a moment we were dazed. No one expected a checkpoint. Not today. The soldier looked out of place, with the oversized chinstrap of his helmet sliding up over his mouth. His only sense of purpose seemed to come from his assault gun dangling from his left shoulder and leaning on his side from knee to chest.

The soldier tapped the sweat under his helmet with his right hand and with the same hand signalled to us to lower our windows.

'Where are you going?' he asked, as if just out of curiosity.
'To Bethlehem,' my father answered.
'Give me your documents.'
My mother bent towards my father and passed the documents to the soldier. He looked at the back seats, at us, before reading them.
'Ah! You are Italian ... Italian Italian?'
'Sì!' my mother said.
'Spaghetti, spaghetti,' he started to say. 'Mi piacciono gli spaghetti. Mmm!'
He was trying to show us how much he loved spaghetti, moving his right hand in the air, his eyes lighting up.
'Are you hungry?' I remember my mum asking, but I don't remember in which language.
'Yes,' he said, while his left hand pushed back the assault gun, which kept getting in his way. 'I have been here all morning, but no one has come through. You are the first!' He looked into my mother's eyes, smiled and gave her back the documents. We closed the windows and moved on.
'He was just a boy,' said my mother, when the soldier was no more than a speck in our rear window.

Everyone had hope. Many even believed that it was the beginning of a new era. It was not just the excitement of the new millennium, or the big celebrations, the renovated towns and squares, the tourists, even the Pope's visit. It was more about what *wasn't* happening: no checkpoints, no clashes or soldiers rushing in at the slightest movement. Nearly eight years after the end of the intifada, it seemed that something had finally changed – look we can go everywhere, we are free!

My diary: *Today 2nd of January, I woke up really early at my friend's house and I went immediately downstairs where my friend's parents were talking over the phone with my father who was explaining that he would pick me up at 4pm.*

Right on that page I was lying, and I was lying out of regret. In fact, in that phone call my father had asked me if I wanted to go to Jerusalem with the rest of my family that morning. We had never been there all together, and my parents were trying to convince me to go. But I said no. My new friend had toys and dolls, and even though the two of us could barely communicate, it was more fun playing with her than going anywhere else.

When they came at 4 p.m. to pick me up, it was clear they had had a great time together – my brothers couldn't stop saying how much they had done and seen. My regret started then. So that night, writing my diary, I censored myself. I didn't want to let my teacher, who would read my diary, know that I had missed out on something. Years later the regret became even greater: what I had actually missed out on, and none of us could have imagined it then, was the only chance I would get to visit Jerusalem with my father. After the second intifada, my father, as a holder of a West Bank ID, would not be permitted to enter Jerusalem ever again.

Time plays tricks on us. Here and there it jumps back and forth, does somersaults.

That New Year, Anna was sure that time was playing a trick on them all. Anna, Rami and the children joined the people in the main square to watch the midnight show. Lights were turning all around, illuminating the acrobats with colours. Everyone had their faces pointed up, waiting for the next feat of the acrobatics, holding their breath to see if the feet of the tightrope-walker would land on the point from which they had leapt. Anna worried that this display of lights and tricks would distract them. Would they even be able to see the rope with these flashes of light?

'What are you thinking about?' asked Rami, taking his eyes away from the acrobats and looking at Anna's profile.

'Do you think this is going to last?' asked Anna.

Rami was not sure what she was referring to.

'What do you mean?' he asked, not wanting to say the wrong thing.

'This sense of peace. The soldiers who only ask about spaghetti. Being all together. The sun, the warmth, the euphoria.'

'It depends,' he said.

'Yes, I know, but it doesn't feel real.'

'But it may be, it may be possible that it's going to last.'

Anna smiled and looked back at the tightrope-walkers. They were balancing a big white-and-red pole. The wind and the height made it oscillate to the right, and then to the left, and the little figures dressed in their shiny suits couldn't go either backwards or forwards.

Another blow of wind and the acrobat lost his balance, falling onto the big safety net underneath.

The village, 2001

Memories play tricks on people too. People forget entire years of their lives, closing off painful memories, obsessing over events of their past. In Palestine, sometimes this is the only way people can cope with what has happened and is still happening to them. An entire people, generation after generation, trying to come to terms with the past. Tragedies become milestones in the trail on which the community holds together. Everyone swears to remember exactly what happened that day in 1948, or in 1967, in 1982, in 1987 and so on.

But memories do play tricks. They change. They adapt. They are influenced by the aftermath, by other people's memories, by the media, by emotional responses and finally by the lenses of history and hindsight.

Memories make *us* as much as we make our memories.

So I know that I need to be careful with the memories of that September afternoon when, at 3 p.m., my favourite TV show was interrupted for a special edition of the news.

The short theme tune announcing the news was out of place. Why was the news on now? I wanted to watch cartoons, so I took the remote control and changed channel to look for something else. I clicked the number three, but there was another journalist sitting seriously at his desk. I clicked number one, another journalist. Annoyed, I was about to switch off and go back to my homework. Then the plane hit the tower.

As always when something big happened, my mother took the phone and called my father. On the other end of the line no one picked up. On TV the images of smoke, fire and people covered in dust kept coming, the journalists fumbling for words.

In the small world I was living in, it seemed there was nothing beyond my own life as an eleven-year-old. I was born under occupation, I had seen checkpoints and soldiers, I had been stopped and searched at airports, a conflict in Kosovo had unfolded, heavily televised, just some years before, I had participated in the big celebrations of the new millennium. Nothing, though, felt like it could really affect my life. Instead, this time, when, among the images of New York burning, the journalists pointed their fingers and speculated on who did it, the walls of our house vanished and we, in the middle, became visible to everyone.

We kept trying to call my father, who was supposed to go to the airport that day to fly to Italy. The journalists kept saying that the Palestinians were involved in all this and repeated the word terrorists.

'Why is Babbo not answering? Did we really do this?' I remember asking my mother.

*

'Where were you that day?' I ask my father.

'I was at Amman airport. My flight was on the twelfth, but you know how things work. They can stop you at the border. So I had to be there in advance.'

'And where did you see the news?'

'In the hotel.'

'What do you remember of that day?'

'People's response to it. So different between the East and the West. The shock on one side and people celebrating on the other. I felt so ashamed when I saw the streets of Ramallah with that bunch of boys cheering. It was just that, a bunch of boys, but it was the biggest news. It was not just us, it was the whole Arab world, and that made me understand how easy it is to influence us. Everything turned into alliances and sides. I felt so impotent. While I was looking at those images I knew that my destiny was not mine anymore. It was in the hands of world politics.'

*

Breaking news. The short jingle on the television froze everything in the house again. Someone had claimed responsibility for the attack. A man appeared on the screen, white turban, olive skin, a long black beard. The TV said that this was what terrorists looked like, how Arabs look like, but I hadn't seen many Arabs like that. My father had never worn anything on his head. He had always shaved as soon as I told him that his hairs were poking my cheeks. He had a moustache though. Did that count? He also had the same olive skin as the man, so yeah, maybe they looked a bit similar. I was looking at the screen and then at my father's photograph on the coffee table, trying to assess whether I looked like that too.

'Go back home, filthy terrorist!'

Tommaso was pushing me back down the stairs. My classroom was on the first floor and Tommaso had placed himself right at the top of the staircase. He was not going to let me pass.

I had a crush on him. Tommaso was the oldest boy and the bully of my school. It must have been that bad-boy attitude, but it was also something about his green eyes and the fact that he looked so much older than the rest of us. I liked him, but there was no chance of Tommaso liking me back now. That September I became just an Arab. The only Arab at school, if not the only Arab my schoolmates had ever met. My family and I were for them the closest thing to that white-turbaned, long-bearded, olive-skinned man on TV. I don't remember what had triggered Tommaso that afternoon on the stairs, but that was not the only time and he was not the only one. That year, *go home* spread around the school.

Even my friend Martina once told me 'go home'. I admit I deserved it. During sports, straight after our lunch break, I had revealed to her the name of my very best friend's secret crush. We were in the gym, on the ground floor of the school, the black linoleum smelling of shoe rubber and sweat. The space was so big that many classes practised their sports there at the same time. It was the best time to look at boys and girls, to make ourselves noticeable, to show how good we were at football so we would be picked by the boys, and to gossip – who liked that new girl, who *she* liked, did Marco tell you something, did you hear what happened between Samuele and Linda? I was sitting with some other girls on the side of the court. We had our backs to the wall, facing the window, and the autumn afternoon light warmed our naked legs.

'So who does Elisabetta like?' Martina asked.

I liked Martina. She always smiled and her small, slightly pointed teeth made her look mischievous, but in a good way, someone to have great fun with. Her eyes were always brightened by something clever she had thought of, or a joke she was about to tell.

'I don't know,' I answered, shrugging.

'Don't be silly. Of course you know.' She pushed her shoulder against mine.

'No I don't!' Of course I did. Elisabetta and I were always together.

'Come on, I am not going to tell anyone. I just want to know so I can help her!'

'I can't tell you, really. She made me promise!' My tone had already changed.

'I'm sure she'll tell me herself soon anyway.'

'Okay, I'm going to tell you, but don't tell anyone else!'

I am not sure I told her that secret because I actually trusted her. I think I did it because, in my head, it was something bold to do. I enjoyed having a secret that someone else wanted.

'Samuele,' I said, leaning towards her ear. Our shoulders pressed against each other.

'Aaaaahhh!' she said, her eyes shinier. She covered her mouth with her hands and started to laugh.

'Shush! Don't do that!'

But she laughed, a big unstoppable laugh, her head back, mouth open.

'Don't worry, I'm not going to tell anyone!'

After school, in the courtyard, Elisabetta came to me, a frown on her face.

'How could you do that? It was our secret! I trusted you. I can't tell you anything anymore. I don't want to be your best friend anymore.'

Martina was right behind her, arms crossed, a look of judgement, her little teeth pointed like a cat's.

I could have said many things to defend myself – that I trusted Martina, that I was sorry for revealing the secret, that Martina could actually help her and introduce her to Samuele's group of friends.

'I didn't tell her! She is lying!' I said instead.

'What do you mean I am lying?' Martina came forward. A small crowd formed around.

'Yes, what do you mean she is lying? You were the only one who knew, and now she knows too!'

'I don't know. She might have spied on you, or she might have guessed.'

'And why should she say that it was you then?'

'Because she's jealous. And she wants to be your best friend!'

'You're a liar, you're a liar!' Martina started to shout ...

'No. You are a liar. You're just jealous!'

Elisabetta stood in the middle, not knowing who to believe.

'You're a liar like all people like you! You terrorists! You foreigners! Go home!'

Martina was right. I was the liar, quite a bad one, but I

couldn't understand how she went from being angry at me because I was a liar to being angry at me because I was a foreigner. Was I? A terrorist? A foreigner? I didn't feel exactly like one. My home, the one where I had lived for most of my life, was, after all, a ten-minute walk from that courtyard.

CHAPTER THIRTEEN
Pasta in Palestine II

Ramallah, 2000–02

Rami opened one of the bags of dried pasta. There was a strong smell of dehydrated vegetables. He moistened the point of his index finger with his tongue and then touched the greenish powder, which stuck to his skin. He looked at how it got darker before putting his finger into his mouth. It was not a familiar taste, not the one he had hoped for, and his desire to eat dissipated. No water could transform that into a normal dinner. *Normal.* Anna hated that word and he had never understood why. Normal was good. Normal meant that everything could carry on as usual. As normal. A normal day. A normal dinner. Not the sounds of tanks, or that dry pasta which smelled of foil and dust.

He had thought about staying in Italy, stop this back and forth, but once again he felt that he needed to be in Palestine. He probably felt it even more than before, now that the illusion of the Oslo Accords was completely shattered and the occupation army had fully re-entered the West Bank and Gaza again.

Rami put the bag of pasta on the table, left the kitchen and walked through the hall to the living room. He went to the window and moved the curtains with the tips of his fingers, just enough to peep out: it should be spring, the sun out there somewhere. The sky should be blue, not that grey yellow. The trees in the garden were almost rusty with the colour of heavy dusk.

The tanks were still there, looming on the brow of the hill like storm clouds. Between them and Rami's house there was empty wasteland. He used to like that empty space and the open view. Now the tanks were occupying all the sightline and threatening to come down the slope to take over the whole side of the hill.

A tank lazily turned its metal turret. Rami let the curtain fall down and pulled away from the window. Had they seen him?

With the curtains closed, everything was darker, greyer. Rami went to the phone and dialled Anna's number once more, but the lines were still down. He kept walking back and forth between the rooms, thinking about doing the laundry, trying to find something to do. He checked the phone again, adjusted the rug and then went back to the dry pasta.

He might as well eat. Rami opened the cupboard and took out a small pot. He then checked on the pasta package how much water was needed to make that stuff edible and filled the pot without measuring it. No point in putting much effort into something that would not satisfy him anyway. He switched on the gas ring that, as usual, took time to ignite, releasing a strong smell of gas. Rami wondered if that could attract the attention of the soldiers and tried again, and again with the lighter, the knob clicking and clicking. Some sparks, and then slowly, one by one, the circle of little flames. How stupid he was, thinking the smell could reach all the way up the hill to the soldiers. A fart could linger for longer. Memories from his night in prison came back to him unexpectedly, the jokes in the cells to release the tension.

The tension had been the same then, the same fear of what might happen.

The water in the pot was stagnant. No sign of warming up. Rami stared at it, waiting for something to happen. When finally a bubble interrupted his contemplation, he emptied the bag in one splash into the water. Whisk with a spoon, said the cooking instruction. He opened the drawer and the flashing green of Sabrin's plastic baby spoon brightened the room like lightning. Rami pretended to ignore it and took out a normal spoon. Yes, a normal spoon. Metallic, grey. The bag didn't give any other instruction except to wait.

Rami walked to the phone and checked it again. No line. The cordless handset in his left hand, the normal spoon in his right.

When he came back to the hob, the water had become a dense brown soup. Rami looked at the name on the bag. *Pasta alle verdure.* Such a normal dinner. But it was not normal.

He turned off the fire, moved the pot to another hob, and opened the cupboard above the sink to take out a plate. Sabrin's baby bottle was there, green too. And Anna's favourite plates, and the boys' breakfast cups, and the sugar jar that they had bought together.

Rami took out a black plate and poured the overcooked pasta onto it. It was nothing like the dinner he wanted. His imagination moved everything from the cupboard to the table. Anna's plates, the boys' cups, Sabrin's bottle. The table was set. Then his mind started to add smells – the starches of the pasta, onions in the pan, the acid rennet of the parmesan. Then sounds – the sizzling of the tomato sauces, forks against plates, his children laughing.

The kitchen was full again, he could see, yes he could see ... Marwan playing with Sabrin, Amer sneaking around, Anna tasting the pasta. He got closer to her. She was wearing her blue dressing gown, tight around her waist, yes he could see it. He looked over her shoulder to see what she was cooking and inhaled her perfume. She turned. Did she notice that he was there too? Anna went through him towards the table.

'Amer, sit down!' she told the boy, but he made some strange face, as normal, and she smiled. Rami smiled too. A normal dinner.

How to prepare a normal dinner.
Open the bag of instant pasta
Pour it in boiled water
Set the table for your family
Remember their voices to cover the sound of silence
Eat with them even if they are not there

The strong, loud whistle of a low-flying plane made his brain vibrate and he found himself alone again. He went into the living room. The tanks started to move: they had been there, still, for so long that Rami didn't expect they could move away so fast, their cannons aligned like good schoolboys. The hiss of another plane passed above, and then another.

The phone rang.

Rami ran towards it.

'Hello?'

'Oh mio dio! We've been trying to call you for hours!' Anna's voice reached him.

'The line was not working.'

'Che succede? They are saying on the news that they are entering the town.'

'Sì, they are already here, with tanks and planes.'

'Oh mio dio! What are they going to do?'

'Non lo so. We never know!'

Rami took the cordless phone and moved to the kitchen.

'Are you having dinner?' he asked.
'No, not yet, why?'
'Just asking. Are you wearing your blue dressing gown?'
'No, my red one. Perché?'
'Nothing. I had a sort of dream,' said Rami, going towards the toilet.
'Which dream?'
'A dinner all together,' he answered, sitting on the toilet.
Another plane.
'Are you okay?'
'Yes, I just miss …'

*

The village

We had been trying to call my father for the whole afternoon, but we couldn't get through. That was normal in those days. Our afternoons were full of fruitless calls, calls answered in unknown languages, the familiar sound of a phone ringing, then scratching and broken voices. Sometimes there was just silence. My mother hung up the receiver every time with the same indecipherable expression. Then she would go to the toilet and close the door behind her. When she came out, the smell of cigarette mixed with the sting of the cold air from the window.

That afternoon we were interrupted by the sound of breaking news on the television. The presenter was sitting up straight in his chair and explained that a new military operation had just started in the Middle East. The images on the screen showed a winter sky over my father's house with clouds low to the ground, like a misplaced fog. The camera made the light look pale, a patina of yellow over the grey, the colour of approaching storms. We could recognise the street that led uphill to the main road of the town: the camera operator must be standing on a roof nearby.

My mother took the phone again and focused her eyes on the numbers. I could hear the short beeps of the keys. Then the phone ringing at the other end of the line.

'Hello?'

'Oh mio dio! We've been trying to call you for hours!'

From the sofa, I ran towards my mother and Amer rushed in from his bedroom. The cat chased our legs, thinking it was a game. My mother sat down at the table and my brother and I squeezed up against her from both sides, trying to put our ear to the receiver so we could hear our father's voice. *How are you, what is happening, can't you go somewhere safer?* We shouted the questions into the phone and urged my mother to report the answers.

The moment seemed to unfold in three parallel dimensions.

One. The monotonous reportage from the TV. The journalist described what they called operation 'Defensive Shield' and how, after almost two years into the second intifada, the army, under their new elected leader Sharon, entered and re-occupied the West Bank with the biggest military operation in the territory since 1967. It was intended to punish and prevent further terrorists attacks, they said, with statistics on death tolls and military personnel armaments deployed moving across at the bottom of the screen. Our neighbourhood in Ramallah was shown from above, with its white-stone houses and the gardens with lemon trees.

Two. The bundle of bodies there at the table in our living room in Italy. With our ears glued to the phone, we kept an eye on the TV, to associate what my father was saying with what the TV was showing. My mother pushed us away to hear my father's voice instead of ours, but we grabbed her red dressing gown and stayed there. The cat was jumping around thinking we were all playing.

Three. My father and his reality, alone at home. Where was he standing? What was he doing? He said he was in the bathroom, with the big bath beneath the window, the washing machine next to the toilet, the mirror over the sink. What was he seeing? Was he scared? How was the light in the house? Like that heavy yellow on TV? And the sounds? Which sounds could he hear? From the phone, the scratching of the line, my father's sentences echoed over a background of different noises – planes, whistles, voices, the journalist's reportage.

'Are you okay?' my mother asked.

'Yes, I just miss …'

Boom. A clear, precise, unmistakable sound. First from the TV, then from the phone, the delayed signal giving us some more seconds with my father's voice. The screen was filled with fire and smoke, the sky red. The line went dead. Silence.

'Babbo, Babbino, amore, Babbo, amore, Babbino!' we all shouted at the phone, calling him all the names we had for him.

'Babbino, Babbo!' No answer.

I started to cry. I couldn't see the TV, or my mother, or my brother, and my father had disappeared. We saw it live, that was our street. We heard it. He was there on the phone, and then he was not. I remember lifting the cat and holding her tight, but she just chewed my hair and kept playing. I fell in a heap on the floor, drying my eyes and nose on her fur.

'Babbino, Babbino, Babbino!'

My mother touched my arm and lifted me up, hugging me. Her red dressing gown soft against my cheek.

'It's okay. Sit down here, on the chair. Keep stroking the cat. We are going to call him again.'

She took the phone again and called. No line. Again. No line. Again. No line. Again. No line.

*

'My memories are all muddled together,' says my father. 'I remember when those two soldiers from the occupation army had wandered near Ramallah and were later killed by a group of people who stormed the local police station where they were in custody. It was horrifying. It was just the beginning of the second intifada but so many Palestinians had already been killed and people wanted to take things in their own hand. After what happened at the station, people were so scared, running, rushing out from work, away from the streets. I walked back home fast. Then the occupation forces came in and with three missiles took down the police station and the radio.'

'Are you sure? I think the bombing came later, in 2002.'

During the second intifada, attacks like those were so common that my father's memories and my memories are all jumbled up. I thought the second uprising started after 9/11. But no, it started before. The tension has been built for years from the frustration of the Oslo Accords and then the Camp David summit in July 2000, which further hindered any real self-determination for a Palestinian statehood. The last straw was the televised walk of Sharon in the Al-Aqsa mosque compound in September 2000 when he came in escorted by more than a thousand soldiers. Seven Palestinians were killed in the clashes that followed and I remember seeing all of this on TV.

'But, so what happened that time we called you and there was that explosion?'

'They came in, with tanks and soldiers, and the curfew. It

was like the first intifada, but worse. We didn't know what to expect. They bombed the radio station at the end of the street, to cut off any communication from there.'

'I remember you were in the toilet.'

'Yes, thank God I was there! That bomb scared the shit out of me!'

*

The village, 2002–05

Anna looked at Rami, but Rami was not there. He was trying to stay longer in Italy: after the last bombing, so close to their house in Ramallah, he wanted to find a way to spend more time with Anna and the children. But his mind never stopped going back over to Palestine.

That was it, wasn't it? What her friend Luisa had warned her about was actually happening.

'Sharif is not himself anymore,' Luisa had told her over the phone, crying.

'What do you mean?' Anna had asked.

'He wants us to do things we have never done before. He doesn't want the boys to eat prosciutto, or drink wine. We are in Florence for Christ's sake! And he even told me I should think about wearing a veil. Is he crazy, did he go mad? We have been together for more than twenty years. Twenty years! He has never said stuff like this.'

Anna had tried to calm Luisa, to reassure her, he may be shocked by everything that is happening, the second intifada, the constant dehumanisation, the islamophobia. Give him time. But while she was speaking, the light of that winter afternoon felt to her like a sort of cold indifference, an omen of loneliness.

Now, lying on the sofa in their living room, Anna was

watching Rami, who didn't take his eyes off the computer screen, not for a second, and she felt that same loneliness.

They were the women who didn't marry Italian guys. What did they expect? The proverb said it: Mogli e buoi dei paesi tuoi. Anna had always wondered what it really meant. What made something from your own country better than something from abroad? Even when she had been alone in a foreign land, pregnant, under the never-ending occupation, it had been difficult, but she had never doubted she had made the right choice. There should be a proverb for that as well, for that excitement, for that sense of expansiveness of becoming part of another world.

So what was it now that, for the first time, made her believe that maybe all those grumpy old proverbs could actually be true? Rami hadn't asked them to stop eating prosciutto or drinking wine. He hadn't asked her or their teenage daughter to wear the veil. There was nothing further away from Rami than those religious rules and habits. Yet, like Sharif, he too was not himself anymore.

It seemed like nothing Anna or the children were doing was interesting enough for him. No matter how much they struggled to please him, there was always someone or something back home who could do it better, or faster, or more. If the children made any mistakes, then they were typical *Italian* mistakes: the children would have not made such mistakes if they had grown up in Palestine. But they were not 'children' anymore. Marwan was living more than an hour away in Pisa for his university studies, and Amer was never at home either, his life all parties and casual jobs. And even that, the fact of their not being children anymore – who are those men, they were children, where did they go, his children – even growing up, getting older, not needing him anymore, even that must have been something related to being half-Italian. Because he would have never let them go.

Anna kept observing Rami, looking at the shape of his cheeks while smiling, his hands typing, his neck stiff when he was nervous, the way he sat, or crossed his legs, or shaved his beard. She couldn't detect any change, yet everything seemed slightly different. She wanted to be able to point to something, to show him something clear – look see it's different, you were not like this before. But she couldn't put her finger on anything in particular. In contrast, no matter what she was doing, Rami would find a flaw: you eat too fast, too noisily, you switch the light on too often, you should stop smoking, you should be stricter with Amer. He was quicker than her at that game, and by the time she had found something to criticise too, it was too late, he had said it first. He had already won. Damn it.

Rami had also started to enclose himself in long silences. The first time it happened was when Sabrin had broken the blue handmade ashtray, a gift from Helena. She had made one of her uncontrolled movements, so common with her body growing into adolescence. The ashtray fell and splinters of ceramic scattered everywhere. Rami had looked at the blue pieces on the floor, but didn't react. He didn't say anything. He left the room silently, and went to the balcony to stare at the horizon. Sabrin tried to get his attention by telling him that she could make another one, but he could only manage a forced smile. His silence had lasted the whole afternoon, but by dinnertime it had gone.

With time, however, his silences had become more frequent and lasted for longer, as though George's inability to express himself had taken longer to reach his youngest child, but now had him in its full grip. Rami couldn't let go of anything. Amer disobeying: silence. Sabrin raising her voice: silence. The occupation army putting the Church of the Nativity under siege: silence. Anna making him notice his mistakes: silence. An interrupted phone call from his brother: silence. Amer getting bad marks at school: silence. Marwan not coming home to visit: silence. Missile strikes: silence. Sabrin watching too much TV: silence. Anna smoking: silence. Tanks running over people: silence. Amer crashing another car: silence. The apartheid wall tearing apart his land: silence.

Rami got the news from TV, the phone, the computer, and these pieces of information became a lump absorbed with everything happening in his life. With the children's problems, the money problems, their marriage's problems. There was no way out of that loop. Their problems were not significant enough to be compared with those of his people back home, yet they could not disappear, both made smaller and bigger by the comparison. Anna felt that her greatest fault, the children's greatest fault, Luisa's greatest fault, was not being there too, not being them too.

*

'I was watching the news, trying to work from Italy, calling my sisters and brother, and nieces and nephews as much as I could. But it was not enough. Because I was here, safe and happy, and they were there fearing for their lives. I was divided between wanting to be with you and wanting to do something to stop all of that. I just felt so guilty.'

*

It was not a good period with Rami, but he softened a bit and hugged Anna as she cried. Her father had just died at sixty-five with a lung disease he got from all those years working in the mines. She didn't even know why she was crying so much for that father of hers. They had never had a good relationship, had they? They had barely talked in years, and Anna had never felt part of the family. But today she cried for all the stubbornness, the arrogance, the *donna*, the cold, the cheating – all that had died along with her father.

Anna found Attilio's old cologne. She smelt it and felt the way she had felt when Attilio used to put it on before going out on a Saturday night. How elegant he looked, how fascinating, and cheeky, and cheesy, and malicious, and a cheater. Anna had wanted to run away from him and from her mother who let him get away with it, let him treat her like that.

Anna had never wanted to be the wife of a man like her father. Rami could not be more different, and yet, ironically, he was becoming more and more distant and almost unreachable, like Attilio had been. He might even be cheating on her, for all she knew. They didn't talk anymore, there was a barrier between them like a wall: Anna didn't trust him and he didn't trust her. He said that she didn't understand how he felt. There wasn't much left but the children. So Anna cried. For her father and for herself. Maybe people were right, she shouldn't have married a foreigner.

Vittoria insisted on putting the cologne on her husband's dead body for the funeral. Ironic, isn't it?

It was hard to light the cigarette in the wind, the skin on her fingers cracking from the cold. Anna would have preferred to smoke inside, like they used to. Clouds of smoke in the living room, the furniture smelling of nicotine. Or at least in the bathroom, with the window open, like they had done when Marwan couldn't stand their bad habit anymore.

Later Rami had started to take his children's complaints seriously: they kept asking about his cough and his yellow fingers.

And so they agreed, let's stop. And Rami did it, stopped completely in one day. One day he was smoking two packets a day, the next day zero. Anna took her time, half as many cigarettes as usual at first, and then just five a day, and then three. Then the intifada started again and she went back to five, maybe as many as ten. Only at work, away from the children. Back to three a day for a couple of months, and then Rami's silences had started – a packet a day. Rami had become intolerant of her smoking and so she had to hide it. Hide the activity, hide the smell, hide her breath.

The warmth of the cigarette between her lips made Anna feel the cold more intensely. Shit. This was her eighth cigarette today, a bad period. She wondered what Rami would have said if he had caught them.

'We should stop smoking!' she said.

'I don't give a shit!' That man's voice was still surprising her. 'I don't give a shit if he finds us. I don't want to hide it. *You* do.'

'Calm down!'

'No, I don't want to, I hate him, why is he like that?' His voice broke a bit, and Anna could recognise the boy she used to know.

'Calm down. He's your father, and you shouldn't talk about him like that.'

'And you shouldn't smoke with me, but you do!'

Anna didn't know what to say. She was tempted to tell Amer that she was only doing it for him. To make him feel okay, realise that he was not alone, that he could rely on her. But it was not true, not entirely. Yes, smoking with him and showing him that it wasn't exciting or cool was better than shouting at him to stop. But that was just an excuse, something to make her feel less guilty.

She was smoking because she needed to. She needed to do something raffish, something nonsensical. She felt like she had when she was a teenager herself, not going back home, eating butter-and-anchovy sandwiches and smoking, yes, smoking like back then. Those first puffs, how free she had felt, how grown up. She used to smoke to rebel against her family, her school, her village. Who was she rebelling against now? Rami? Really?

'We need to try to understand him. It is not easy for him, with everything going on.'

'Non me ne frega un cazzo. We are here and he is here too. Why can't he just enjoy being here, with us?!'

Good question, one Anna had asked herself in one of the many arguments she and Rami were having.

'Are we not enough for you?' she had asked Rami.

He hadn't answered. What was that supposed to mean? Anna felt guilty for having asked something like that, asking him to choose. But no, she was right. He had to pull himself together. She had also lived away from her own country: was his situation so much different? Could he not just start over, as she had done for him?

Anna took another drag, the cigarette smoke mixing with her cold breath. Were they still in love?

'Why don't you break up with him? You fight all the time. He behaves like a dickhead. He doesn't want to stay here clearly, so just file for divorce!'

She smiled, remembering when, as a young child, Sabrin had made up a pregnancy just to shut down any rumours of divorce. But they had been in love back then: it was hard, the distance, the loneliness, the prejudice, but they had stuck together. Now, despite living together again, they were worlds apart and couldn't understand each other. For the first time they couldn't understand each other. Even when they had met and couldn't speak the same language, even then they could understand each other. Yes, even during those first walks along the river, holding hands and singing, even then with the language mistakes, with the 'I'll-see-you-last-week.'

'Are you crying?' asked Amer.

Could Anna lie to him? Could she tell him it was just the wind in her eyes?

CHAPTER FOURTEEN

Carbonara

The village, 2005

When Anna broke the first egg, cracking the shell against the edge of the plate, a similar sound – the dry sound of something irremediably broken – echoed inside her. She put a hand on her stomach: was it coming from there? She touched her belly. It was a bit bloated, even if her children would say that she was just chubby. Did she really need to lose weight?

She broke another egg, same sound.

How many are we going to be for dinner?

Just four, Marwan is not coming.

So six eggs will probably do, whisked well, adding a bit of milk, a lot of cheese.

The taste of milk on her tongue mixed with the smell of egg yolk. She felt sick. It must have been a stomach bug: the hospital was full of it those days. She didn't want to get ill just before the Christmas holidays. She went to the tap and drank some water. It was okay.

She opened the package of diced pancetta, turned on the gas ring, placed a big pan on top of it and threw the pancetta in, without oil. In another pot, the water for the pasta was already boiling.

'Dinner will be ready in five minutes. Can you please set the table?'

'Sabrin, Amer, help your mother with the table!' Rami's voice reached the children in their rooms. No one moved, hoping that the other would get up and do it first.

'Why do we always need to tell you twice! Come on!'

'Uff. Why is it always me? I'm studying,' Sabrin said.

'It's time to eat, not to study, yalla!'

In the pan, the pancetta was sizzling and Amer kept stealing the bigger pieces, burning his fingers.

'Amer, stop! Mamma, why are you always letting him do whatever he wants?'

Sabrin was never happy these days. She could turn everything into a fight.

Anna didn't say anything because she liked it. She liked all of it. The children teasing each other, the noise, the rituals of dinner time. Amer had calmed down. Rami had settled in Italy almost for two full years now and even enjoyed being at home all the time now that the second intifada seemed to have passed its worst peak. Sabrin had turned sixteen and was starting to assert herself – in such an annoying way, but with determination.

'Mamma, why do you need to use so many eggs? It's going to be so heavy!'

Her daughter always had something to say in her know-it-all voice. Sometimes Anna would have liked to throw everything in the sink and shout: cook for yourself then! But she never did.

'Why don't you prepare dinner?' was the closest she came.

It wasn't the wasted food that irritated her, it was the obstinacy she could sense in Sabrin's voice. The same obstinacy she herself felt, Teresina's obstinacy.

'Next time I will!' Sabrin always wanted to have the last word.

Maybe the irritation was behind another wave of pain in Anna's stomach.

'Why don't you just set the table?' she snapped, manoeuvring the pot of hot water and spaghetti towards the sink.

'I'm doing it already! Why don't you tell Amer instead?'

Sabrin kept going back and forth with the plates and knives and forks, getting in the way on purpose. Anna came back with the pot of the drained pasta and Sabrin stopped right in front of the cooker, where the pancetta was about to burn. Her daughter looked at her defiantly but then moved, as if she had changed her mind.

The spaghetti touched the oily pan, joining the hiss of the pancetta. Anna quickly moved the strands of pasta so that they could absorb the flavours and the shine of the fat. She reached for the egg-cheese mixture on her left and poured it over the spaghetti. The smell of egg got stronger and Anna had to turn her head. She couldn't take it. She turned off the gas and stirred the mass of pasta. Sabrin would have certainly complained about how gluey it looked.

'È pronto, let's eat.'

It wasn't until she sat down that the pain became stronger.

'Do we have any cheese?' asked Sabrin.

'No, I put the last bit in the mixture.'

'Lo vedi! I told you there were too many eggs. It tastes too strong.'

'Why don't you leave your mother alone?' intervened Rami.

Anna was relieved not to have to deal with her daughter, because it was true: she could taste the eggs too. She didn't feel like eating and hesitated to put the first fork of spaghetti in her mouth.

'Am I right? You see ... I told you it was too strong!' Sabrin was looking at her.

Shut up, she wanted to say, *shut up*, but nothing came out. The smell of egg, her daughter's eyes, the chair suddenly becoming smaller, the table bigger, the walls closing in on her. Anna put a hand to her lips, stood up, assessing the dimensions of where she was, and ran to the toilet.

*

I often think back to that night. Images flash through my mind. My mother's hunched body in the white light of the bathroom. My father and my brother helping her towards the bed. My mother rolling in bed in pain, incapable of speaking, and yet trying to convince us – with quick movements of her hands, like we were flies – to go away, back to the table, finish that damn carbonara. I remember the ambulance coming, two people dressed in blue in my parents' bedroom. They were saying she was too yellow: it must be the pancreas. Nothing to worry about, but we will take her with us just to check.

Then, in my memories, there is a gap. I don't remember how my mother left the house, my father following her, what my brother and I did afterwards, whether we finished the carbonara or threw everything away. I do remember which movie was on TV. I remember the exact date, 7 December. Out of everything that has affected my family: the years of war and occupation, the distance between us, the curfews, the misunderstanding and language mistakes, the travel back and forth between countries, the struggle of being part of one culture or the other, *go home, foreigner*, the eggs in the courtyard, the chicken breasts, the graffiti on the wall, the abortions, the lies, the bombs and instant pasta, the onions, the fake pregnancy, cigarettes, the pieces of meat hanging in the butchery, the bread with grapes, the butter that was not butter, the silences, the rides on the motorbike, the music playing in the car, the homesickness, the baby bottle, the sugar jar, the friends' secrets, the fights over dinner – out of all that, it was that day, that day only, that hit us the hardest.

*

That was when Anna thought about writing a book about her life. She looked back at everything, with the clarity of knowing that nothing was going to last, and she thought that, well, her life had value after all. There were things to say about it.

Yes, it was in that moment, with needles and liquids entering her body, lacking a piece of pancreas and the whole spleen, that Anna grasped something about all those years. She didn't know what exactly, it was more a feeling that she had won, that she had reached a place where she didn't need to justify her choices anymore. Was it just an impression, or had her longing for lontananza, that familiar need for something, somewhere, just eased a bit? Was that lontananza somewhere no one could follow her? Anna remembered the stories of the well in the old farmhouse of her childhood and, for the first time, she understood what the well meant. She could see it now: the well was the final comfort, when you are not scared of death anymore.

Anna lifted up her shirt: the surgery hadn't left any visible scar. She was among the first lucky ones in Italy to undergo robotic surgery for cancer removal. She had just three little holes where the robot's arms had entered her, reached the pancreas, made an incision on the affected part, sucked it up and burnt the tissue. It had been easy.

Now was harder. She could see it in the nurses' faces.

Was that pity? She had been on their side so many times: asking a patient to extend their arm, touching the soft skin of the forearm to look for the right vein, pressing the purple bump of the vein to check if it was strong enough, tying the band around the arm, preparing the needle, piercing the skin after a small resistance of the tissue, feeling relief when the blood came out.

Her colleagues had to do these things to her every day as part of her treatment. They would take her blood first and then inject her with chemotherapy drugs. Her veins were becoming frailer – a strange feeling, a vein becoming frailer, it is like feeling your blood flowing. It was one of her colleagues who suggested that they should try a direct venous access. Why not? Anna agreed to it and now she had these tubes coming out of her chest so that she could be directly connected with any machine pumping fluids into or taking fluids out of her body. She lifted her collar and saw the tubes between her breasts, rising and falling with each breath. It was as if she had been plugged in to charge, like a robot herself, though she had never felt more alive.

'Tutto bene? Why are you smiling?' Rami had just entered the room.

'Guarda. I look like a robot!' But Rami didn't smile. He tried to look elsewhere, discreetly, thinking she wouldn't notice.

'It's okay, you don't need to like it!' Anna reassured him. 'The doctor said my blood tests are okay, so I can keep on with the chemo.' She had tried to change the topic, but was not sure she had changed to a better one.

'That's good,' said Rami. 'That means that everything's under control!'

Anna smiled again, but this time she tried to hide it and looked inside her shirt again, the pink skin, the blue and red of the wires. *Under control.* Rami was trying to keep everything under control. Being rational. Being unaffected. We can fight this. She knew he was scared from the way he talked and the way he turned his face away from her tubes and wires. From the way they had decided to keep their children out of this. Minimise, nothing to worry about. However, she couldn't tell what kind of fear was affecting him. He was able to deal with the vomit, the blood, the saliva, the loss of weight and hair, the sleepless nights, the wasted days in hospital rooms. He just did it, without thinking about it, no doubt, no hesitation. So what was he really scared of?

'Do you want something to eat or read?' he asked.

'No, I'm fine.'

'Okay.' He sat down and took out his phone.

It was easier with technology, to be together. When Rami bought their first computer, Marwan and Amer had been so excited. They were the first ones in their village to have a computer at home. And when Rami had bought a photocopier and a scanner, Sabrin's teachers had asked to use it before the school had been able to buy either. And the first time they had installed the internet at home, not even the village library had it. Anna could still remember the mechanical sound of the computer screen turning on, and the intermittent beeps of the modem connecting to the internet. For years, that had been the sound of Rami's presence. It was the sound that made it possible for Rami to connect with his country and to work and made it possible for her and the children to see him when he had left again for Palestine.

In her hospital room Anna heard those same sounds, but this time it was her being connected, like a computer. Anna imagined how people around her would react – the nurses, the doctors, the other patients, Rami himself – if after Rami had dialled the number on his phone, Anna started to ring, her body vibrating. A call direct to her insides: the perfect epitome of how their love had been for the past fifteen years.

It was the first time Anna clearly saw the unfolding of her life, how she had been a pioneer, in a way. She had left Italy and married a foreigner when most people in her village hadn't even seen one before; she had started her life abroad, had become the foreigner herself, learnt to cook, speak another language, had lived through occupation, wars and shootings. And then she had left, come back to Italy again, a mother alone, when being alone with children was still unacceptable. She had learnt how to have a long-distance relationship before it was even a thing; she had watched the news on satellite TV because that was the only way to know what was happening in her far-away adopted country: on the roof the big satellite dish stood out, like a big label on her forehead. She was the one who looked for new and unusual ingredients at the local supermarket, dreaming of a place where jibne beda could be found next to the anchovies and butter, the prosciutto next to labaneh. And then all that technology had come into their lives, making their worlds closer, more accessible. Now people could see that they had always been connected.

Here it was, the truth. She had always been connected, in different ways of course, but she had always been the one connected to a broader reality – look at these cables going in and out of me.

Procida, 2006

In August that year we went on holiday to the island of Procida. My parents' friends hosted us in their house on the cliffs, with its big terrace facing the Mediterranean, flooded with light.

CARBONARA

In the mornings we would have breakfast out on the terrace and then my mother and I would lie down on the deckchairs, her with one of her books, me with a newspaper. That was the summer, before I turned seventeen, when I became interested in politics. The world suddenly got bigger. Italy had won the football World Cup and the government in power was gaining credibility and trust from the rest of Europe. I felt proud because we were sending aid to facilitate the ceasefire of the 2006 Lebanon war. Yes, we, because that made me feel Italian. I thought I was understanding things: I could talk politics with my parents' friends and I knew where I stood.

My mother kept teasing me. How could I be so serious, so boring and so know-it-all at my age? I would get so mad at her. What did she know? She was just a nurse. But I would go back to her, looking for her, every time something inside me felt inexplicable, tangled up. And she could untangle it.

So it happened one night in Procida. I got restless. There was a festival, an end-of-summer party. People had started to get their gardens ready and prepare their banquets and the streets, days before. From our sunchairs on the terrace, we could hear the voices of the men and women setting up stalls and stages or taking cooked food and fresh ingredients back and forth between houses. Those sounds reached us through the summer air. We could imagine what and who was producing them, and that imagination, merged with the smells coming from the kitchens, the reverberation of the sea, and the sweat under my arms and knees, put in me a fever, an anxiety to be part of it.

My father's friend came back from the market carrying two white plastic bags. She put them on the table and took out red round tomatoes, a dripping packet – the chalky liquid and pungent odour of mozzarella – and the shimmering tails of four fish wrapped in paper. The sun hit their scales and for a second I could swear I saw them moving. The scent of deep water in my nostrils added to my agitation.

'Are we going to the party tonight?' I asked my mother.

'Of course we are,' she answered with a smirk, reading my thoughts. 'There is going to be a parade, and the coronation of the Queen of the End of Summer, and music, and dances ...'

She wanted to continue, but I had already looked away. My eyes were back on my newspaper, reading the same line over and over, thinking about the hands of some boy touching my skin in the moonlight. I wanted to be the Queen of the End of Summer, the most beautiful girl on the island. I wanted to be someone who had lived summer to the full. The truth was that I had never been happy with my summers, which I usually spent mostly alone, preferring to read books in the quiet of my room rather than with my mates from school.

I remember exactly what I wore that night for the festival: a black tank top, white shorts, and heels. I also put on red lipstick. The streets had been lit up with little paper lanterns strung up between the houses. There were red and white flowers, some real, some made of paper, decorating every single surface, and two enormous speakers had been erected at the end of the main street, right before the final bend, before the cliffs. People had opened up their gardens, offering food and drinks, wearing their best clothes. The girls in the running to be crowned the Queen of the End of Summer were all wearing long skirts, their dark hair held up in plaits and chignons. They were walking along the streets, entering the houses, wishing everyone good luck for the autumn. I strolled around with my parents and their friends, the crowd growing bigger, people dancing, the sweat mixing with the smell of fish and wine. I was trying to lock eyes with someone, anyone. The moon was full, and I was trying to convince myself that I didn't want to be part of all these celebrations. I was aching.

'Why don't you come to our house party? We have our own DJ and music there.'

Our neighbours were inviting all of us, but my parents and their friends knew it was directed at me.

'Come on, go!' they insisted.

I walked there, entering the garden of their villa with its white balustrades and bad replicas of Greek statues. Boys and girls my age were already dancing to the songs of that summer. I looked around and felt terribly alone. The bass vibrated inside my ribcage and seemed to amplify the shouting and laughing. I closed my eyes, trying to move my body to the rhythm of the music, dying to be like those boys and girls and yet dreading the touch, the sweaty hands, of someone I didn't know.

'Are you okay?' said her voice.

'Mamma!' I was relieved. 'Let's go!'

'No, let's dance!'

We started to dance. She danced her clumsy, out-of-rhythm 1980s moves. I was trying to be sexy but my mum just grabbed my hands and started to jump, up and down. Boom, the fireworks started, the moon covered in smoke, up and down, boom, sweat, music, the familiar hands of my mother holding mine, the glimmering black of the sea, up and down, 'jump, jump!' my mother shouts. The garden with its statues disappears, so does the anxiety I felt. I only remember my mum dancing with me.

She always had her way of making things lighter, so that me and my brothers cherished even the moments that were full of pain, understanding them as a natural part of life, and could feel proud of our struggles. One of her favourite ways of doing that was to drive us through the hills around our village in

Tuscany, preferably at sunset. She would drive slowly, taking her time round each bend. She would put her favourite music by Lucio Battisti on the CD player, and then she would wait. With *Sì Viaggiare* as our soundtrack, sometimes we talked, let our sadness out – break-ups, bad marks, fights between us, bullying at school, discriminations and injustices, fears for our future, fears of losing our father, of losing her – and share it with her so we could understand it more. Sometimes we would just stay quiet and let her, the road and the music soothe us.

'They found another one,' said my mother at breakfast, a few days before my Maturità, the final school exams, two years after our holiday in Procida.

Perfect timing, I thought, but I said 'Where?'

'Liver, probably colon too.'

I remember writing in my diary something like 'another flower', but when I look at the pages from those days, I can't find anything like that. I wonder if I am remembering another time, a different cancer. Those pages are full of dramatic self-reflections. I read them and feel stupid: I always used to write abstract images, referring to reality only through symbols and metaphors, and now I have no idea what I meant. On one page I wrote: 'my mother cried today and I couldn't do anything but hug her, then I asked why are you crying even though I knew the answer, and she didn't answer even though I knew what she was thinking'. I don't remember my mother crying. In all those years I have just one memory of her crying and it was from later.

Of that liver-cancer summer, the memories I have of my mother are of her lying on the sofa, her light nightgown barely covering her. She was sweating from the heat and the chemotherapy. I close my eyes and I can see the soft flesh of her arm lifted behind her head, the skin always porcelain white. I can also see her legs, naked, bent. If I stay in that moment for a bit longer I can hear her snoring, and see the curtains shutting out the sun, a brown light in the room, the TV on.

We spent that summer just me and my mother – my father was in Palestine for a couple of months and my brothers were by now living their own lives away from the village. On Mondays and Tuesdays we would go to the hospital for chemotherapy, then come back home and shut ourselves in. Some days after the chemo we would go out for fresh air, when the light and the heat were not too strong. Then a new week would start with another round of chemo.

I tried to keep busy and distracted myself by thinking about the university life waiting for me in September. I found accommodation, prepared to move and dreamt with my friend about all the new things we would do and people we would meet, but in my diary I kept writing: *I am not ready*. My mother might have sensed my hesitation because that summer she decided she needed to teach me how to flirt. We were sitting on the sofa, watching TV, and I was fidgeting, zapping between the channels, my skin sticky from the humidity.

'You are bored,' she said. 'Come on, let's go out!'

I didn't want to go out because it was too hot for her, but she insisted. We walked to the park, and after a few steps we had to stop so my mother could rest. We bought something to drink at a nearby cafe and sat down at the only free table, under the pine trees. In the shade we could feel the breeze, and my mother inhaled it and dried the sweat on her upper lip with the back of her hand. Children were playing and groups of friends were gathered, chatting and smoking.

'Do you like that guy?' she asked me after a couple of minutes, using her nose to direct my gaze.

'I don't know, why?'
'He is a good-looking guy.'
'Yes, I guess!'
'So why don't you go and talk to him!'
'Oh come on! I can't do that!'
'Of course you can!'
'He is with his friends. He doesn't care. He hasn't even looked once in this direction.'
'That is because you didn't look in his. Look at me.'

My mother started to gaze at him. A proper, long gaze, and then she moved her eyes away suddenly, only to then look at him again. He started to look back. He did. Looking startled at first.

'Come on, Mamma, stop! He'll get upset. You're twice his age!'

'Just wait!'

Then that guy's eyes changed. Curiosity, then interest, then proper flirting.

'You see ... if you want something, don't wait for it! And that doesn't apply just to boys. You can get whatever you want!' she said and abruptly stopped looking at that boy to turn to face me. As if released from a spell, the boy stopped looking too, a bit confused.

In my diary, at the end of that summer, I wrote about Luca. I met him at the beach and looked into his blue eyes the way my mother had taught me to.

New Year's Eve 2008, 10 p.m.
The last thing Anna saw, her eyelids heavy from the anaesthesia and blinded by the lights above her head, were the closing doors of the operating theatre. It was the night of New Year's Eve. When they had told her that her surgery

was planned for that day, she had thought it was such a waste of the night. Not just for her, for whom that New Year might be the last, but also for all the doctors and nurses who were preparing to operate on her, in shifts, for sixteen hours, starting at 10 p.m. the night of New Year's Eve. Could they not all wait? Let's go and celebrate!

No, they couldn't wait. It was already too late: those lumps in her liver and colon were bigger than expected. They clung to the organs and the bends of the intestine. Anna felt sorry for all those people who were there for her, some of them young, with small children. She thought about all the times she had had to work a shift at Christmas, or New Year, or even on a birthday. It was not worth it. Let's all go home.

'This is a twelve to sixteen-hour surgery, with two teams taking turns,' the doctor had said. 'I am sorry but this time the scar is going to be big, from here to here.' He drew an imaginary line from his pubic area all the way to his chest, with a small roundabout encircling his navel.

He had described the surgery in detail. Maybe under anaesthesia, Anna's mind could still imagine what they were doing to her. She could see them opening her body following the same line the doctor had drawn, her skin and muscles and ribcage opening up, the organs pulsing. They detached the main vessels entering and exiting the liver, blocking the blood flux with big tweezers. They turned the liver, cut off the tumour, and put the organ back before unblocking the blood. Then they focused on the colon, a wriggling, purplish serpent. They removed the whole part where the cancer lay, put back together the two stumps and cleaned the tissue around them in case the cancer had affected the lymph nodes. Finally they brought closer the two edges of her body, like sliding doors, and someone was left behind to zip her up.

10.30 p.m. On the train

The door between the two carriages was broken and kept sliding open and closed. It was ominous. It was as though the old year didn't want to leave and was trying to break through the threshold between past and present.

Sabrin tried to distract herself by looking out of the window, but it was late and the darkness reflected her face. For a second the eyes looking back at her were Anna's. Her mother must be in the operating theatre by then. Sabrin felt guilty. Why was she here, on that train? Rami had forced her to go, to leave the hospital and try to enjoy the New Year's Eve with her friends. That pressure to be happy, do something cool and unique, on this specific night, felt so out of place. A familiar feeling took over – the same one she had had when she was just a little girl, going to school in a grey car, 'Heal the World' playing on the radio, fearing she might never see her father again. It was the same desire for the journey to never end, to stay on that train forever, time suspended, no one entering, no one exiting, until she felt ready to stop and step out.

Boom. The door slammed shut as the train braked.

12 a.m. The party

'Why do you have that long face? No one died! It's New Year! Let's party!'

A curly-haired girl was trying to pull Sabrin onto the dance floor, but she didn't want to be there with those people.

Her phone rang: her father's call saved the overenthusiastic girl from Sabrin's anger.

'Happy New Year, bibina my love!' Rami was trying to be cheerful, but Sabrin could hear the effort he was making not to cry.

'Babbo, are you okay? How is Mamma?'

'They took her in about three hours ago. I brought a cake for the nurses! They have closed the ward, so I am in the corridor.'

'Babbo why don't you go home? It will take the whole night. They'll call you if anything happens. Go home, rest.'

'Oh no, I am fine. She is here, I am here … what if she comes out early and doesn't see me here?'

Someone tugged at Sabrin from behind and she dropped the phone. She tried to call her father back, but the lines were too busy. The sweat of the people was suffocating. Such a wasted night. Did New Year's Eve need to be such a big event? Couldn't people understand that they were celebrating the passing of time, a step further towards everyone's death?

She felt sorry for all those people around her, all their high hopes for the evening, the money spent on dinners, clothes, make-up and hairdos, that pressure to have fun. It was not worth it.

'Where are you going?' the girl with the curly hair asked as Sabrin was leaving.

'It's none of your fucking business!'

Sabrin took her puffer jacket from the hanger, put it on and zipped it up before opening the door to leave.

*

When I arrived at the hospital next morning, my mother was in intensive care. My father told me not to worry, it was normal after surgery. Are you sure you want to see her?

Mamma was lying in the bed, unconscious. Wires, cables and catheters were going in and out of her body. Her mouth was forced open by a transparent tube. More tubes in her nostrils were pumping oxygen to her lungs. The suction of liquids, the bubbling of air, the beeps of the screen made my mother look like a failed experiment. The bandage wrapped around her torso, from her pubic area to her chest, was dyed with the bright brown of the iodopovidone that looked like blood, but not human blood. My mother was a broken robot, an unfixable one.

I felt like I was about to faint. I might have heard the voice of a nurse instructing someone to take me out of the room.

I don't remember anything else, but in my diary I wrote that I was given a bed to lie on in the room next to my mother's, and that when I came back to my senses I started to cry.

*

Pisa, university accommodation

The light in the bathroom was green, or maybe it was the tiles. Sabrin sat down in the empty bathtub – an old bathtub with white varnish that was peeling away, the surfaces so thin that by lying down and putting an ear to the bottom of it she could hear voices in the flat downstairs. She crunched her legs up towards her chest, her breasts pressed against her knees. From the open window in front of her, she could hear the sounds of summer: people chatting, the voice of a TV presenter coming from an open window, the audience applauding his old jokes, someone clearing a table, cutlery scratching against plates, a train arriving at the nearby station, pigeons cooing.

'Can we close the window before a pigeon comes in and takes a bath with us?' asked Anna. 'Look at this, this windowsill is covered in pigeon shit!'

Anna brought a chair in from the kitchen and placed it next to the bathtub, by Sabrin's head. She turned on the tap and adjusted the water to a warm, but not too hot, temperature. Making a cup out of her hands, Anna started to move the water from the flow to her daughter's head and hair.

'Is it warm enough?' asked Anna, oblivious of the July heat.

'Mmm, yes, it's warm enough.'

Rivulets of water ran down Sabrin's face, heavy and warm. She reclined her head, eyes shut. Behind her eyelids she was looking at the pages of her textbook for her big Italian literature exam. She had prepared for this exam for months and was mentally reviewing all the main points, concepts, names and dates. It was the last exam of the year before the summer break, and the majority of the students had already left campus and gone back home, to the sea. Sabrin and a few others had remained until the end of July, when the town was almost deserted. Even her flatmates, one by one, had left, and she had been alone for a few days, possessed by the fear of failing, the desire for salt and sand, and the echoes of solitude.

Anna had called that morning. 'They cancelled my chemo for today. I am coming there so we can eat pizza and watch TV. No studying, just relaxing, before your pretty head explodes!'

Instead of answering, Sabrin had started to cry down the phone.

'Are you okay?' Anna had asked.

'Yes, Mamma, I'm just happy you are coming!'

How could she tell Anna that she had missed her, and that for all those months after her big surgery she had been afraid of touching her, of breaking her? That she was afraid of calling her – was Anna real? Or talking about her pain – could Anna take any more? Or asking for help – were those chemo treatments ever going to end?

Anna poured shampoo onto Sabrin's head and started to massage it into her black hair.

'Tomorrow I have my last exam before graduation and look at me … being washed by my mum like when I was three.'

'Oh yes, but it's a great pleasure, isn't it, to be spoiled, to be a daughter for a bit longer?'

CHAPTER FIFTEEN

Sahlab

Towards Ramallah 2012

I spent twelve years imagining Ramallah through a collage of memories, images on TV, phone calls, struggling for it not to become a fantasy or two-dimensional, a town of only bombs and tanks. Twelve years and I was finally here, just a few miles away from my hometown, yet never so far away. I had been at the Tel Aviv airport security for over three hours and was starting to think that things were not going to go well. Maybe they would put me on the first flight back to Italy. I still didn't have my passport back, and my mother was already humming the revolutionary songs of her twenties.

My mother and I were not the only ones in that waiting room.

Sitting in the seats in front of us was a family: mother, father and three children. One asleep, one eating a chocolate bar and smashing it all over the room and the third asking again and again when they could go home.

A young woman was crying in a corner. She was already here when I arrived, and from the dark circles and the mascara streaks under her eyes it looked like she had been there for quite a long time. The soldiers kept taking her out of the room and bringing her back in. They called her name, took her to one of their offices and brought her back after five minutes. Then they called her name again, took her back out to the same room and then brought her back after five minutes. A sort of ritual.

Two women arrived wearing black shoes, black trousers and black shirts. I thought they had come to call the crying woman again, but instead they called my name. I stood up and so did my mother, but one of them was there to keep her from following me.

'Va bene, Mamma. It's okay, I can manage,' I said, before being taken to a different room.

That was my second interrogation that day, but the woman dressed in black started asking me exactly the same questions, in the same order as her colleague had done before. What's your name? What's the name of your father? Of your mother? How old are you? Why are you here? How long do you plan to stay here? What is your address? Your email? Your phone number? The man in this photograph came two years ago: is he your brother? Is the man in this photo your uncle? Where were you born?

'In Ramallah.'

I tried to answer using exactly the same words as before, adapting myself to their rituals, ready to go back and forth between that small room and the waiting room with the coffee machine.

I was tired. I had already been interrogated four times and had been there for so long that I started to fear the worst. The more time passed, the more I looked like the child asking again and again to go home, without getting an answer.

'Come on! We are nearly there.' My mother soothed me.

She couldn't have known, but as long as she was there by

my side, I was eager to believe her. I put my head on her lap and looked at the clock on the wall.

Would I see Ramallah again? The orange light at sunset, the round flat khubez, the sofas my father had built, the kitchen balcony, the roses in the garden, the lemon tree. Or was everything bound to remain a childhood memory?

I was nearly asleep when I heard a new voice calling my name.

Tall, blond, deep blue eyes, the shape of his arms visible under the tight white shirt.

'Follow me, Miss,' he said.

So I followed him. Of course I did.

'Please, sit down.' He told me in his velvet voice, smiling at me, his eyes shining.

I obeyed and he started asking exactly the same list of questions. I answered like an automaton: I only vacillated when he asked for my phone number, tempted to ask for his back.

'Where were you born?' he finally asked, as though I could change my answer just for him.

'In Ramallah.'

*

Ramallah, 2012

When at last Sabrin and Anna opened the door of the house in Ramallah, the smell of mould overwhelmed them.

Everything was exactly the same. Everything in the same place, but with mould, dust and time. Their house.

At that moment Anna didn't even know if she could call that place her house. She hadn't stepped inside it for twelve years. And before then, how long had she spent there? Maybe a couple of months each year? She needed to go back twenty years – twenty – if she wanted to remember a time when the house had really been hers. She stood still in the entrance hall, her luggage at her feet. She didn't know if she wanted to move from there, explore, touch things again. For Sabrin it was different. She was already opening up all rooms, looking at everything: the black chairs around the glass table, the Japanese paper window between the hall and the living room, the broken glass in the door on the left.

She wanted to follow Sabrin, to stop her, leave everything as it was, but the only thing Anna could do was stand there in the middle of the hall. She could feel the movements of her small children running from the veranda to the kitchen, her nephews chasing them. She could see Rami's brown arms playing the oud or bringing a cigarette to his lips. She could even hear the laughter, the cutlery, the music, the language slowly becoming hers.

The smell of the mould brought her back to the present moment. This house was not hers. Not anymore. The last time she had felt at home here, Anna had still been a young woman in her thirties: she had still been her whole self, maybe a bit wounded, but intact. Now parts of her were missing, parts that didn't make it, that couldn't come back to that country she used to love.

Sabrin kept exploring the house, heading to the veranda.

'Please don't go there yet!'

Anna wanted her daughter to give her some time.

'Why? The veranda is my favourite room! Come on, come with me.'

Sabrin simply couldn't understand how her mother felt. For her this flat, after all, had never been a home. It had only ever been a holiday playground, nothing but happy memories: camping in the living room, Rami making a fort for her with the sofa cushions and blankets, picnics on the carpet, playing on the veranda with all her gifts from her aunts, listening to music with her brothers their last time here, in Christmas 1999 ...

'Mamma, look what I found! The little white and green airplane. Oh, the doors still work! I want to take this back to Italy.'

... and then games and tiffs with her brothers. Or the times they used to pick lemons from the tree in front of the kitchen, or transform the kitchen terrace into a swimming pool during the hottest days of July.

For Anna it was different. This was a home that she had never expected to leave. Her first home in her new chosen country. A house that helped her to not feel homesick. The living room was where she used to host friends, musicians, writers, all avid smokers, who took over the space with sounds, words and smoke. The kitchen was where she had learnt how to prepare Palestinian dishes. She was the one who had filled the terrace with water – one step down from the kitchen window, she just needed to cover the drainage hole with an old T-shirt to make a homemade pool.

'Wait, we have already passed through here,' said Anna to Firas. 'Yes, look, that's the same man under the same tree!'

'Are you sure?' asked Firas.

'Of course I am. Why don't you pull the car to the side and ask him where we should go?'

Firas was trying to drive Anna and Sabrin to Sebastia, a village less than a couple of hours away from Ramallah, famous for its Roman theatre ruins. A young colleague of Rami's, Firas had been entrusted to drive and show them around the country. His country was supposed to be theirs too, they were supposed to already know it, but things had changed so much since the last time they had been here.

'These damns roads!' cursed Firas, turning the map over

and over. 'You see: we should have been here already!' His finger pointed at the centre of the map.

'Well, we are clearly not, so please ask that man!'

Sabrin, sitting in the back of the car, was not sure if Anna and Firas were arguing. They were speaking so fast in Arabic and after a few attempts to get their attention, she gave up and started looking out the window.

The April air was hot. It could well be the summer. Sabrin opened the window slightly, now that Firas had stopped the car and turned off the air conditioning. The sound was feeble, but Sabrin could recognise a cicada singing, so close that it might have been just under that tree. She opened the window completely and put her hand out. The late morning sun was hitting the tarmac hard.

'What time is it? Were we not supposed to arrive early to avoid the midday heat?'

'Non ti ci mettere anche te!' snapped Anna. But she was not angry.

Sabrin had realised in the last few days that her mum liked to fully embrace the role of the Arab matriarch. It was amusing, so Sabrin played along and shut up.

'Tayeb, I am going to ask that man under the tree,' said Firas, giving up.

'Marhaba, can you tell me the way to Sebastia?' asked Firas.

The man lifted his head and raised his eyebrows, letting out a sound that was like a shy kiss or the chirping of a cicada. After a few more seconds, as though he had completely woken up, the man started to gesture with his right hand and put together some quick words, none of which made sense to Sabrin.

'Shukran,' said Firas and switched the engine on again, and with it the air conditioning and the car stereo.

Firas had chosen some old songs to play and was completely taken by surprise when Anna started to sing along.

'Eh, how do you know these songs, Um Marwan? When did you learn them?'

'Ahi Firas, you weren't born when I first sang these songs!' answered the old matriarch. And they started singing together, rocking in their seats and exchanging looks when they got all the words right or when the best part of the song played.

Sabrin, sitting behind them, looked at their backs rocking from one side to the other. She knew those songs too, Anna and Rami had taught them to her, but she didn't want to intrude by getting the refrain wrong or pronouncing something incorrectly. There was something about her mother singing those songs that Sabrin didn't want to interrupt, something about her mother that she had rarely seen and yet recognised. Maybe the love for those things you keep close to your heart for years.

'Shit!' Firas snapped.

'What?'

'That man and that tree again.'

'But did you follow his directions?'

'He didn't give any. He doesn't know where it is. I just kept going where I thought it was.'

'Firas ...' said Anna with that matriarch's voice.

'Yalla, I am going to drive back. We can ask someone else!'

Firas drove on a few metres and then turned the car round, going back where he had come from.

'Marhaba, can you tell me the way to Sebastia?' Firas asked an old woman who was walking along the road. She was wearing an embroidered thobe, her hair covered with a white veil, a basket balanced on the top of her head and a big black plastic bag in each hand.

She shrugged, without pausing or letting go of her bags.
'No, she doesn't know.'
'Yes, I got that,' said Anna with a smirk. 'Give me your map!'
Anna took the map from Firas's hands and looked intently at the point that they were supposed to reach.
'Why don't we try to take this turn,' she eventually concluded.

So Firas switched the engine on again, air and music coming back on at the same time. He followed Anna's instructions, between one line of lyrics and the other, singing and directions fusing together, until the car stopped in front of a high grey wall. Anna and Firas both wound down their window and stuck their heads out at the same time, one to the right and one to the left, while Sabrin was still trying to lower her back-seat window.

It was not the first time Anna and Sabrin had seen the wall cutting through Palestine, isolating and dividing towns, destroying fields and lands. It was hard to avoid when it enclosed you. The occupation forces had started to build it during the second intifada with the excuse of safety and, even if the International Court of Justice declared it illegal under international law, they had kept building it since. An apartheid wall, 700 kilometres long, 8 metres high. It was in Qalandyia, at the checkpoint on the road to Jerusalem. It was in Bethlehem, circling the town like a crown of thorns. It ran along the tops of the hills, darkening the skyline. It cut through schools and villages: big blocks of concrete, one next to the other, with a hole at the top where the crane had lifted them and then planted them down. It was not an unusual sight, but there, right in front of the car, it was as if they were able to take it in for the first time because no matter which direction they looked in, it never ended.

'What the fuck?' said Firas. 'Oh sorry Anna, I didn't mean to …'

'What the fuck!' repeated Anna before Firas could apologise for his language.

'We were not supposed to reach the wall. We were not supposed to come close to it at all!' Firas kept repeating while furiously spinning the wheel to turn the car around.

'Wait, wait. There is another car there. Maybe they know!'

'I don't want to stay here one more second. We are too close to the wall! And you never know what may happen if they see that my car does not have a yellow plate.'

'Oh come on! We are completely lost. Better take a chance and ask that car for directions. What can happen that's worse than this?'

'Tayeb,' said Firas, moving closer to the other car.

'Marhaba, can you tell me the way to Sebastia?'

'Na'am.' The man looked sure enough and asked for the map from Firas to show him where to go.

'I've got it!' Firas closed the window and switched on the radio again.

They started to sing, this time paying less attention to the words and more to the road. Sometimes they stopped altogether, and Sabrin didn't know if it was because they had forgotten the lyrics or because they had been distracted by a turn on the right, a crossroads, or another uncomprehensible road sign.

'Why aren't there signs in Arabic?' asked Anna.

Firas didn't answer but switched off the radio.

'Why, in all the hours that we have been going back and forth, haven't we seen a single sign in Arabic?'

'Um Marwan, it's normal now.'

'Normal! I hate that word! I preferred it when there weren't any signs at all then.'

They fell silent for a while and the roads became dustier and dustier until they became unpaved.

'Are you sure we took the right one? This doesn't seem right. This road is strange, it's too quiet. And what are those numbers on those stones? Please, Firas, turn back.'

Firas drove slower and slower, looking at the numbers along the road.

'What do you think they mean?' he asked. 'Maybe they are miles?'

'I am not sure. But I am not convinced. It looks like an army road. It'd be better if we drive back before ...'

A siren, first soft and then louder and louder, interrupted the conversation. Two army jeeps arrived from behind. One stopped at the back, the other overtook them, boxing them in. Four occupation soldiers with heavy boots hopped off the jeep in front and started to shout in an incomprehensible language. Three of them pointed their assault rifle at Firas, Anna and Sabrin, whose hands were already up.

It was at that moment that Anna began to laugh.

Sabrin was shocked. It was the first time a weapon had been pointed at her face. It made you sweat even with the air conditioning on. It sucked all rational thought from your brain.

'Why did you laugh, Mamma?' Sabrin asked as the soldiers walked back to their jeeps.

'Why didn't you show your legs, instead?' She came back. 'It would have been much faster than showing your passport!'

Firas was shaking from head to toe. After all, he was the only one without a European passport or beautiful legs to distract the soldiers.

'If you hadn't been here with your Italian passports, I don't know what would have happened to me,' he confessed while driving behind the jeeps that escorted them back on the main road …

'People got killed for much less than driving on a military trail.'

They were driving back along the dust of the road in the evening quietness, the music on again. Firas and Anna singing the words of Darwish, the poem about the pointlessness of a passport when the valleys, the trees, the rivers of your land can recognise you.

Compared to the journey that morning – getting lost and almost assaulted by the occupation soldiers, and painfully finding their way to Sebastia – the checkpoints along the way back home seemed like a feeble obstacle.

Firas, though, breathed a sigh of relief when they passed the first one without being stopped for too long. And he started holding his breath when they approached the second one. From the change in Firas's breathing, Sabrin could tell when they were close to a checkpoint, even before seeing it.

Near the last one, Firas's breath was less heavy. After all they were nearly there, they had nearly done it.

'Your documents,' the soldier said as they pulled up next to him.

Firas handed him the permit which allowed him to drive along those roads. Anna and Sabrin passed him their passports.

'Ah, Italians, what are you doing here?' asked the soldier in a different, kinder tone.

'We were visiting the villages,' Sabrin answered from the back-seat.

The soldier half-smiled, not entirely convinced.

'Souvenir shopping,' Anna corrected with her make-do English and the soldier gave them their documents back.

The sun had nearly disappeared, but the movement around and across the checkpoint kept on. Shepherds were bringing back their sheep for the night. Children were playing football along the road, while old men sat cross-legged, wrapped in their smoke, and stalls were selling green leaves and apricots. As they drove on, Sabrin looked back at the checkpoint they had just passed: a man was lying down on the tarmac, his hands on the ground, assault guns pointed at his head, a big bag by his side. No nice legs. Not the right passport.

'Mamma, can we take these with us?'

Sabrin was going back and forth between rooms, trying to collect all the things she liked and fit them into the only suitcase she had. Anna ignored her.

The detachment Anna felt from the objects in her old house was the same detachment she had started to feel from the entire town, the entire country. Ramallah was no longer Ramallah. It was just a town with an unmanageable urban sprawl, which was changing everything she remembered.

This house, once at the edge of the town, a step closer to the countryside than the city, surrounded by fields and hills, was now overshadowed by huge buildings around it, the new residential area, a shopping mall, a lemon tree covered in sick lemons.

'Mamma,' Sabrin insisted, not getting any answers.

Palestine was no longer Palestine. People in the streets didn't say sabaḥ il-kheir anymore, they were all rushing somewhere. They didn't keep chickens in their gardens, but ate KFC. After the second intifada there wasn't any strength left. Everything looked like a business venture. Fedayeen had become entrepreneurs: it was easier to make money than a revolution.

'Mamma, what do you think?' Sabrin kept trying to get Anna's attention.

Anna didn't know which had come first: feeling detached from the house or from the entire country, but at some point her home and Ramallah had become the same thing – a hostile lump in which she could no longer find her place. Her chosen place. They refused to recognise each other.

'I will never come back,' she answered.

*

I read from my journal of that trip. I noted down my mother's words: 'Nothing is as I left it. Nothing as I remember. It looks like they have all given up.'

*

To the village

The phone call came while I was waiting for my train. August. I had just spent a day in a tourist spot on the sea and was trying to go back home. There was a big crowd of people waiting for the same train. The smell of sweat, salt and sea lingered over the platform. The blue line of the sea was still visible from the small station platform. People spoke in French, German, English, eating gelato Italiano. I took my phone out of my bag. My shoulders were sunburnt so I struggled to reach it without hurting my skin with the strap.

When I saw the screen, the green icon of a phone quivering on the black background and the name of my brother at the top, something inside me started to burn stronger than my skin.

'What's up?'

'Dove sei?'

'I am waiting for the train?'
'Are you alone?'
'Why?'
My brother hesitated.
'Come on, dimmelo?'
'Something arrived in the post today. Mum's CAT scan results. She was not at home, so I took them and opened them.'
'E?' I insisted, the air harder to breathe, the crowd multiplying.
'I don't know, but it doesn't look good. It is full of white spots.'

I ended the call. Vaffanculo, cazzo, cazzo, I wanted to yell. I looked around me, all those people and children on holiday, with their ice creams and sunscreens: it seemed impossible that they were still all there, all doing what they were doing as if that call never happened.

The train arrived and everyone on the platform seemed to be sucked through the sliding doors. I couldn't move, looking down at the yellow line on the ground. Women wearing shorts with burnt legs rushed on, pushing their children and balancing their gelatos. I could see people's toes squeezing out uncomfortably from their sandals, red from the heat. I wanted to shout and stop them all. Can you please all stop? I need to think. Think about small white spots, like the ones twinkling on the waves at midday. The ones you were swimming in. But nothing stopped. The train conductor blew his whistle, waved his red card, and some more tourists squeezed on. The loud beep of the doors resonated before the mechanical slam. And I was left alone on the platform in sudden silence – the noise of the chatting, the children's games, my brother's words, all still echoing in my ears.

'Guarda, isn't it beautiful? It looks like a night sky full of stars!'

'Can you please stop, Mamma!'

My mother was trying to convince me that the thick plastic sheet on which the image of her inner body was printed in black and white was nothing to worry about. That all those metastases, those white little spots, were just like stars.

'Ma come è possibile?' I kept on. 'In May you told me that the doctors hadn't found anything, that after three years you were clear and out of danger. You said that to me. You did. How long ago is that? Two months? How is it possible?'

'They don't know,' said my mother. 'But it can happen, like an explosion of stars.' She mimicked an explosion with her palms open.

'Mamma! Can you please talk to me seriously?'

'What do you want me to tell you?'

'Non lo so. What is going to happen?'

'As always, they will try chemo and see if it works.'

'And if it doesn't?'

'We'll cross that bridge when we come to it. But you know me, I am a warrior. I am going to fight this one too!' Her voice dropped a bit.

*

Mamma,

After weaving all these scenes together, maybe the book you wanted to write, I am still not sure who you are.

A few months after that conversation about night skies and stars – when you were joking, proud of being a warrior – you too had to let go of your mask.

We had a video call. It was me now who lived in another country, studying in Paris, me who followed your *desiderio di* lontananza. The quality of the video was not good. The images were moving, breaking, yet your bald head – only white fur left – was so clear to me. I kept asking you to repeat yourself. You did and your voice broke again, and again. It took me some time to understand that it was not just the video which was breaking up.

'I am going to die,' you said to me and fell silent.

You turned your face away from the screen for one second, as if you had said that final sentence to yourself. You turned back again and faced me, looked at me, no hesitation, no trembling of the video, no trembling in you, and you started to cry soundlessly, tear after tear.

'Don't be stupid!' I told you. 'Why are you saying that?'

'Because it is the truth. There is nothing else they can do.'

I didn't accept it.

'If you are like this, if you are so negative, then it's going to happen. You have to be positive. You have to fight this!'

You never talked about it again, Mamma. At that moment you took off that mask and, maybe for the first time, revealed yourself to me, your reality, who you really were beyond a wife, a mother, a nurse. At that moment I forced your mask back on.

'Of course,' you said. 'Of course I am going to fight this!'

Fighting what, Mamma? There was nothing to fight against. It was not a battlefield. I am sorry I forced you to fight more instead of allowing you to lean on me, to rest on me.

In the weeks following that call, you stopped eating. For a while you had only eaten sahlab, a dense Palestinian drink made with milk and orchid bulb powder. You used to say sahlab was easier to swallow and that you felt the warmth coming to you. In those final months, Babbo couldn't find anything like it in Italy so I would send boxes of it every time I found it in the Arab shops of Paris. I wondered then why your final comfort food was Palestinian rather than Italian. I can see now how stupid that sounds. Yet at the end you wouldn't even drink that.

Then you stopped talking. I would stay connected for hours through that screen: Babbo would put the computer right in front of you, on the sofa. Every time I asked you questions, or tried to have a conversation, you would just shake your head and look away. Your eyes were somewhere faraway. I would spend hours looking at you while you were looking elsewhere and I could learn nothing more, not even something irrelevant, about you.

And now I am trying to look for you here in these long pages. Anna is my way to find you, to cross time and space all the way to you. Can you feel me? After all, you are not just gone and me here, left behind, but we are in the crossing – in Anna – in what you made me and what I made you.

EPILOGUE

Tel Aviv Airport, 2013

What's your name? What's the name of your father? Of your mother? How old are you? Why are you here? How long have you stayed here? What is your address? Your email? Your phone number? Did you pack your bags yourself? Did you receive any gifts? Did you buy something that was already wrapped? The officials at the airport asked, again and again, the usual rigamarole of questions. I am leaving. Leaving, leaving, leaving. Arriving and leaving never end in this airport.

'Please follow me,' says a woman in black, who takes me to the middle of the departure hall. There is a circular counter with big suitcases open on top of it. There are bags and luggage scattered all around, on the floor too, where their owners are trying to put everything back as it was before the officials carried out their security checks.

When it's my turn, the woman opens my carry-on luggage and ransacks it. I always joke about putting my dirty underwear right at the top – so that they have to touch it and smell it if they want to keep looking at my stuff – but I never do. She takes out my laptop, turning it upside down, looking carefully at the battery and the screen, before carrying it away. I try to see where she goes, but she disappears behind a door. When she comes back, she does the same thing with some of my other belongings and gifts – the olive soap, the blue ceramics, the za'atar – and finally asks me to hand over my phone and passport. I obey.

'Please follow me,' she says again.

She leads me into a side room. It's just white walls, but there is a line of dark camera screens on the right, and a curtain on the left. The woman moves the curtain and waves her hand to say, you first. I step in. It's a changing room, with no mirror, but with hangers on the wall.

'Take off your shoes and trousers,' she says, leaving my passport and phone on the chair.

'But my suitcase is still …'

'Don't worry. We will take care of it. Take off your shoes and trousers.'

I do as I am told. My jeans are really tight, and it takes an effort to pull them off. The task throws me off balance and I lean towards the woman. She opens the curtain and steps outside.

'Take your shirt off too,' she says from behind it.

I do what she says and put the shirt on the hanger as the woman comes back in. She wears medical white gloves.

She starts with my feet and asks me to take my socks off too. I do it. She keeps going, touching my ankles, my calves, my knees – around the bones and behind, where the skin is softer and thinner and you can see the veins – and she goes up to my thighs. Her head is close to my breast, while she moves up my body. I keep looking up, my chin in the air, to make sure I don't look at her, to prevent her hair from touching my face, and maybe because I feel ashamed of my hairy legs.

She touches the elastic band of my knickers and then proceeds. She touches my back, the deeper groove along

EPILOGUE

the vertebrae, and I wonder if she would touch me differently if she were not wearing medical gloves. She then inspects my bra. She slides her fingers inside the cups to check if they are filled with something, moves along the wings and reaches the hook, then moves back along the wings to handle the underwire.

She nods, takes my clothes, and leaves.

I quickly look at my phone that she has left on the chair. It's 3 p.m., two hours until my flight and I haven't gone through the check-in yet. I hear footsteps and put the phone back down. The woman in black comes back with a colleague, a blonde girl wearing a blue shirt. The new girl starts touching my bra too, while the other touches my hair and asks me to bow my head. She pushes her fingers through my locks and moves my head with them. The blonde girl stops touching my bra and grabs my passport and looks through it. She looks at her colleague and with a movement of her head tells her to leave.

What's your name? What's the name of your father? Of your mother? How old are you? Why are you here? How long have you stayed here? What is your address? Your email? Your phone number? Did you pack your bags yourself? Did you receive any gifts? Did you buy something that was already wrapped?

I answer.

'Okay,' she says. She takes my phone and passport, and leaves.

She comes back with a plastic bag, which she passes to me through the curtain.

'Put your underwear here,' she says.

'What?'

'Your underwear.'

'Why?'

'Security.'

I take my knickers off, her arm still hanging through the curtain. I put them in the bag. The new weight makes her arm tilt a bit. I take my bra off, her arm still there, and put it in the plastic bag too.

'Done?' she asks.

'Mmm. Can I have my phone please?'

The bag disappears through the gap.

'No'

'Why?'

'Security.'

I don't want to sit on the chair – the metal against my butt cheeks and my pubic hair. I imagine how many other people might have sat down there, their scrotums and vulvas pressing against the same surface.

I stay still, standing. I look at my toes, move them a bit as if they are not mine. I can see them getting paler. It's January after all. A cold one. There was snow when I arrived three weeks ago. White covering everything. It was the first time I had seen the country like this. In silence, as though everyone had left. It was soothing.

As I stand here, images of my mother come to me in waves. It's the first Christmas without her. I don't even know why I wanted to come here. I hoped for meaning, I guess. But when the snow melted, cold was the only thing left.

I feel the cold of the floor, the air surrounding my body, my thighs, and nipples. I hear voices beyond the curtain. I wrap myself with the fabric and look outside: the blonde woman is talking on the phone.

'Excuse me.' I try to get her attention. 'What is going on? My flight leaves soon.'

'No worries,' she says and disappears again.

EPILOGUE

I stay wrapped in the curtain a bit longer, but then images of other bodies being wrapped in the same cloth make me flinch backwards. I put my hand around my breast, suddenly aware of being naked, but I don't know how to cover my genitals properly, so I go back to standing still, fully exposed, my hands hanging by my side.

The cold comes in waves too: sometimes it is the cold of this winter, sometimes it is the cold grip of grief, sometimes it is the cold fear of last moments. I can still feel my mother's nightgown surrounding me: I was in her arms beneath the duvet – half-asleep, half pretending to be asleep. It was the month before she died. Send her to bed, said my father. Leave her while it lasts, my mother answered and squeezed me in the warmth of her body. I could hear her heart beating against my cheek and knew she was still alive.

A gust of cold, I shiver. I came all the way here to escape a house without her, and now here I am alone. Waiting. Waiting without knowing why. I wait for my clothes, my passport, I wait for someone to tell me what to do. I wait for things to get better. And I wait for her.

Waiting becomes unbearable and I realise the full extent of my situation. I am alone and naked, only a curtain to hide me. I have no phone or passport. I have no name. They could leave me here for hours and forget me, pretend I was never here.

I hear a noise behind the curtain. I wrap myself again in the hanging cloth to spy outside. It's a man.

'Excuse me. Excuse me,' I wave at him with my naked arm. He looks at me and then keeps walking, ignoring me.

I unwrap myself. My navel suddenly looks bigger, a big black hole, and I am finally defeated. I sit down on that abused chair. The metal touches my flesh and I contract my muscles, trying to make my hands into a cushion below my butt. Another wave of cold and I see my mother's body.

Naked. Laid down on the metal mortuary table. The doctor had slipped her wedding ring into my father's hand. They had to pull it off before the grip of her hand forced them to cut it. The doctor shook his head, she didn't make it. They had covered her with a white sheet, like in the movies, while we waited for the morticians to come and clean her, dress her, adjust her in the coffin, before the body became too rigid to do it.

My hands are still under my body. I remove them and try to feel the metal as my mother did. But she didn't feel anything by then. I lifted the sheet and my mother's naked body was all there. The scar running from her pubic hair to the middle of her breast was there too, and I could see clearly where the two hems didn't fit back together properly. Her skin had already changed colour and had patches of yellow and purple. My fingers and my toes have similar patches here in the cold. I touch my face to be sure I can still feel my hands. My mother's face had no expression, except for a strange line her thin lips had formed sagging down with gravity. It made her look sad or maybe disgusted. I put my lips in the same position, pulling the sides down with my fingers, but the muscles of my face are still alive and my lips snap back up.

Her hands were resting along her sides, and they looked so normal, as though she would move them again any moment.

I can see her hands around the wheel as she drives me to the countryside – it's one of those days when everything aches – music on, no need to talk, let the pulsing in the mind calm down, the lontananza will call less strongly. Cry if you need to cry. I can drive the whole afternoon. The hills around loosen their shapes. You just stay here, recline your seat, close your eyes. See, it's better.

*

Now

It is always too late when you realise you haven't asked the right questions, or that you haven't asked questions at all. Now that I want to absorb all my mother's life, and ask her all the questions that I need, it's too late. But why did this curiosity never strike me before, in the twenty and more years when she was able to answer me? I am more or less the age she was when the first intifada started. I am in a foreign country as she was, and my future here is not secure, as her own wasn't in Palestine.

Our situation is not comparable (I have no children, I am not in the middle of the fight, I have stability if not security) and yet I see unfolding before my eyes the genocide of my people with a level of violence and dehumanisation we have never seen before. Yet I am witnessing the dissolution of the pillars of democracy within Western institutions and the cracking down on freedom of speech, right of assembly, and international human rights. Yet I believe for the first time in a global, resilient movement calling for justice and freedom for my people and for all oppressed people. And I wonder how my mother would have lived through these days. I ask myself whether her years in Palestine taught her something valuable that I could lean on now.

This morning, I found a picture of me and my mother in Jerusalem. Our last trip to Palestine together in May 2012. No picture can explain what I feel better than this one: when I see it, I have to deal with a double loss. A few weeks after the picture was taken my mother discovered that she had only a few months to live and died a year after, in May 2013. The pain, suffering and powerlessness I experienced those months belong to the same range of emotions I am feeling now as I watch what is happening in Gaza and in the West Bank.

There are three reasons for this.

The first one is that the experience of loss and the process of grieving do not work in an organised, compartmentalised manner. When I experience grief for something, that grief opens all the boxes of all the griefs I have been living through. This brings me to the second reason. The grief for Palestine and the grief for my mother have always been linked. And that's weird because my mother was my Italian side. Yet there was something in her choice of marrying a Palestinian man, living in Palestine during the best years of her youth, learning Arabic, cooking Palestinian food, singing the revolutionary songs, committing herself and her family to the hope of freedom that have always made me see her as the true spirit of Palestinian liberation.

Third reason, the one I feel in my whole body: in this moment where I have lost friends and connections because 'I am too political', because I should not be 'so passionate', 'so aggressive' and I'm just in a lot of pain, the first thing I would instinctually do, even after more than ten years, is call her. I still remember her phone number by heart. If I silence my mind for a second, I can still hear her voice. She would be able to help me from afar and hold me through the distance and with all her aggressive, political, passionate love she would tell me: don't worry about this, I am here ... you focus on the fight.

When I tell my father I want to write a book about Mamma and Palestine he does not ask questions. He does not ask why, he simply nods. He knows why. So I do not give him the explanation I had prepared. I ask him if he can help me instead.

'How much of the copyright are you going to give me?' he asks with his cheeky smile.

EPILOGUE

This becomes a running joke between us. A sentence he repeats every time I call him with a question about Mamma, or about Palestine, or about him, or Italy – about how these four strands in my story keep intertwining, over and over like a braid.

We travel together to Ramallah, Bethlehem, Birzeit, where he walks me through the places of his childhood, of his youth, and of his years here with my mother; where he introduces me to the people who can tell me more about our family and Palestine; and where he opens up with me the memories that he had stored away for a long time.

I learn to listen to him, really listen, beyond him as my father and right into who he is as a man. When that happens, when I listen deeply and let him bring me where he needs to go – where we need to go – we always encounter patches of silence. He takes a deep breath, his eyes focus away from me and into something, maybe someone, else. I cannot help but feel that in those moments, through me, he grasps certain things for the first time. And I do too, through him.

One of the best times this happens, we are in Florence. During one of my visits to Italy I ask him to come to Florence and walk me through the streets where everything started.

It is a sunny day of April, in the way that only April can be sunny: warm and fresh at the same time, the light bright but not blinding, the air smelling of grass even in the middle of traffic. We leave the car in a car park he remembers from years ago which, surprisingly, is still there, and we start to walk towards the historical centre of the town.

'Everything happened in a few square metres,' he starts. 'You will see, we will criss-cross the same streets again and again.'

Our first stop is the restaurant where he used to work while studying at the Accademia delle Belle Arti. The restaurant is still there, but it is a different restaurant now, doing mainly pizza for tourists and lunches for office workers.

'They haven't changed much,' he says, looking at the bar counter. 'That's the kitchen; I can almost see the big sink where I used to wash dishes.' He stretches a little over the counter to point at a door at the back.

'Can I help you?' A waiter comes, his tone friendly but his eyes inquisitive.

'He used to work here in the 70s,' I intervene.

The waiter does not seem as impressed as I am about this situation. My father says thank you and goes for the exit door.

We continue our walk. Right at the end of the street there is the square where my father and my mother performed one of their first dabke shows. There is a market now and we buy some fresh fruit to eat while we keep walking. My father wants to go to Via dei Servi to show me the first place where they lived together. As I get close, I can smell already the sweetness of Robiglio. I remember coming here with my mother during one of our day trips. But my father shares with me much earlier memories and while I look at the shop window with all the pastries, colourful wraps and golden boxes of chocolate, I see my mother in the reflection, just behind me, in her mid-forties, sharing her Florence with me, and behind that version of her I can see her twenty-year-old self, getting the key ready to enter their flat. I see her wearing a brown flowery dress, her hair in a short bob. She may have looked exactly like that, or my imagination may have made that dress up for her. It does not matter. In any case she is here with me, with us.

My father and I spend the whole day walking, talking, remembering. He brings me to more places: Palazzo Vecchio where they got married, the hospital where my brother was born, my mother's favourite alleys, his favourite corner, the

EPILOGUE

balustrade of Ponte Vecchio where they met with friends to play the guitar or the oud and sing the songs from their lands. We also walk in front of the Accademia delle Belle Arti where, many years ago, he realised that beauty is the answer.

'Let's go in,' I say, putting a hand on his arm to encourage him to enter.

He hesitates a bit, he almost does not want to disturb the past. But then he glimpses colours and shapes and lights in the internal courtyard just visible through the columns of the entrance and he can't resist. He goes in and I follow. We find ourselves in the middle of the school's exhibition, art and students everywhere. And my father lights up. He walks, mesmerised, among the art pieces and comments to me about how he likes one, how he would change the format of that other one, how he had a similar idea once.

I lose track of his words, and the specifics of people around us … I lose track of time and I can see my father's curls grown back like a wild bush on his head, his moustache full and a bit unkept, all the rage in the late seventies, his blue shirt becomes a white cotton T-shirt revealing his lean young arms, his eyes are less tired but also more hungry, and now someone calls him. It's my mother and we both turn to look at her. For a moment I am back there, in their Florence, with them, or maybe it's them who are with me, all the versions of them, stored within my body here with me.

'Bibina, are you okay?' my father calls me back.

'Can I ask you a question?'

'Of course.'

'Do you ever miss Mamma?'

As always with one of my questions, he falls silent to think.

We move from the sunny courtyard to the shade of the side arcades. I would like to prompt him again, but I have learnt to wait.

'No,' he eventually says. I am a bit taken aback so *I* fall silent now, waiting for more.

'We have gone through so much together. So many good and bad moments, Italy, Palestine, health, sickness, strength, weakness, deep connection, misunderstanding, love, yes, but above everything, joy. Mamma had a way of going through the pleasures, but also pains, of life with a sort of playful fondness. And when I am happy, or sad, or worried and a bit lost, that obstinate joy is what I remember and all that I feel.'

He's right. Obstinate joy. What my mother had and gave. What Palestine has and gives. In the children of Gaza using the rubble of their homes as a slide in a playground. In the defiant smiles of the Palestinian women arrested to protect their olives trees. In the sweetness of the grandfathers kissing their granddaughters goodbye. In the music played, the art painted, the poetry written until our last breath. The obstinate joy of those who – even under continuous bombing, centuries of oppression, brutality and genocide – remember and feel that beauty endures and justice will come.

For every question I ask my father, for every answer he gives me, I catch a glimpse of my mother smiling at us. There, with us. In the way our father–daughter love grows, my mother's love keeps going.

In the way I go through her letters, talk to my brothers, learn more about my uncle and aunts, walk the streets of Florence, find my way through the hills of Birzeit, map my way through time and space, I learn the biggest of my mother's lessons. That even when we lose something or everything, no matter if at the bottom of pain or at the peak of joy, in days where everything seems possible and in days where it looks like there is no more hope, the way we love cannot be taken away from us. And how we use that love is our revolutionary act.

NAMING THE OPPRESSOR

IN THIS BOOK I never mention the name of the oppressor. This is because when I was writing the book I wanted the space into which I wrote myself and my family to be a safe one. Removing the name of the oppressor helped me reclaim our existence as something not defined by something else. At the same time, I am perfectly aware of the importance of naming, and of not letting any possibility of unaccountability available to what and who is trying to erase my people. As they refuse to say Palestinians and only refer to us as Arabs, or terrorists, or human animals, as if they could take away from us the connection to our land, so I refer to Israel only as an oppressor and coloniser, to take away from it any other mythology around what they are doing in Palestine.

There you go: every time in the book I refer to the oppressor, the oppression, the coloniser, the occupation, the occupying army, the occupying government, I always and only refer to Israel. Make no mistake.

GLOSSARY OF SOME OF THE WORDS, EXPRESSIONS AND SENTENCES USED IN THE BOOK

'48 areas: the areas of historical Palestine which became official Israel after the 1948 Nakba; Palestinians who managed to stay in those areas are called '48 Palestinians
Allora (Italian): so
Ana biddi mayye (Arabic): I want water
Arghileh (Arabic): water pipe used to smoke scented tobacco
Battikh (Arabic): watermelon
Chi vuole un caffè? (Italian): who wants coffee?
Dabke (Arabic): traditional Palestinian group dance
Desiderio di lontananza (Italian): a desire (or sort of restlessness) to be anywhere but where you are. A yearning for change.
Ecco (Italian): there you go. Exactly.
Fedayeen (Arabic): Palestinian freedom fighters
Il-harb il-'alamyye it-tanye (Arabic): World War II
Ka'ek (Arabic): traditional Palestinian almost sweet bread covered in sesame seeds
Khod (Arabic): take (this)
La (Arabic): no
Labaneh (Arabic): thick white yogurt similar to Greek yogurt.

Mish mushkile (Arabic): no problem
Na'am (Arabic): yes
Noi siamo sole da sempre (Italian): we have always been left alone
Ovvia giù (Tuscan dialect): come on!
Puttane (Italian): whores, bitches
Quindi (Italian): so
Ricordati (Italian): remember!
Ruz u loz (Arabic): typical Palestinian dish made with spiced rice with minced meat and almonds, often eaten with fresh salads and yogurt
Saber: prickly pear, symbol of Palestinian steadfastness
Sambousek (Arabic): typical Palestinian pastry, and common in other Arab countries, made of a thin dough, typically shaped like a half-moon, filled with a variety of ingredients and then either baked or fried
Sfiha (Arabic): a typical Palestinian dish, a sort of flat bread covered in minced beef or lamb
Shayef (Arabic): filler word, similar to 'you see'
Shu sar? (Arabic): what happened?
Shukran (Arabic): thank you
Trippa alla Fiorentina (Italian): a traditional dish from Florence made with tripe (the stomach lining of a cow) in a stew with onions and other vegetables
Yalla (Arabic): come on!
Y'ani (Arabic): used often as a filler word. It can means anything from *I mean* to *more or less*
Zaghrouta (Arabic): a traditional, high-pitched ululation often performed by women to express joy, celebration, excitement or incitement

ACKNOWLEDGEMENTS

THIS BOOK IS VERY PERSONAL, yet at the same time it's a shared effort, and so I want to thank all those people who over the years have made this book possible in one way or another.

I would like to thank Richard Kerridge, who recognised the seeds of this book in some clumsy short pieces back in 2015 and encouraged me to take my writing seriously. I also want to thank Professor Ilan Pappé, whose advice was precious in honing aspects of this book.

I would like to thank the team at Footnote Press, especially my editor Leonie, who helped me see my book when I could not see it anymore. And thanks to my agent Laura for the patience she had with my rookie panics.

Then my thanks go to the community of PhD students with whom I have shared the beginning of this writing journey and to my colleagues and friends both at Bath Spa University and Cardiff Met University, especially Elen Caldecott, Kristien Potgieter, Kate North, Ben Fergusson and Lucy Windridge-Floris.

So many friends have held my hand and offered sofas to write, countless cups of coffee and tea (or glasses of wine when needed), but also precious feedback and encouragement.

Cami, you made me feel so safe and allowed my writing to become vulnerable; Mira, you are the first one who read the whole book and I still have the pages that you filled with little hearts to tell me you loved my words; Alyssa, you taught me how to give myself space when I most needed it and that a little treat goes a long way; Zosia, without your fire I would have given up so many times or made compromises I would have regretted – thank you for keeping me blazing.

Cinzia, I see you. You showed me that life is beautiful because, like books, it has chapters.

Bibi ti dirò grazie anche a te, ma guarda!

I want to thank all my family in Palestine, especially my cousin Nicola, my uncle ('ammo) Aisa and my aunt (tata) Norma: you helped me reconnect with Palestine and I am so grateful for it.

To my brothers, I hope you can see a bit of Mamma in these pages.

And at the end I want to thank the two people without whom I would simply not be who I am:

My father (abui) Taisir: this book is yours as much as it is mine. You gave me everything that allowed me to be here. You taught me how to never be one thing, how to refuse labels, and always reinvent myself. You showed me that being Palestinian means believing in the beauty you can make despite everything. I love you Babbino mio.

And my husband: Sergio, in these years and months, during the ongoing genocide in Palestine, when I was tired, defeated, scared and lost, you sat next to me making sure I had nothing else to do but focus on my work, making sure I took that grief and sense of injustice and transformed it into words people could listen to. You always tell me how powerful my words are ... what you do not see is how much these words are powered by our love.

ACKNOWLEDGEMENTS

*Mamma, all this time I was looking for you,
and you were right here.*